CRUEL
HARVEST

Lance Clarke

Manor Cottage
Books

Lance Clarke

This novel entirely a work of fiction. The names and characters and incidents portrayed in it are the work of the author's imagination. Any resemblance to actual persons, living or dead, events or localities is entirely coincidental.

Copyright©Lance Clarke 2021

Lance Clarke asserts the moral right to be identified as the author of this work.

The catalogue record for this book is available for the British Library.

ISBN: 9798564424226
Cover design and typesetting: Lance Clarke
Cover image: Shutterstock

All rights reserved. No part of this publication may be reproduced, stored in or introduced into a retrieval system, or transmitted, in any form, or by any means (electronic, mechanical, photocopying, recording, e-book or otherwise) without the prior written permission of the author. Any person who does any unauthorised act in relation to this publication may be liable to criminal prosecution and civil claims for damages. Purchase of this book in e-book format entitles you to store the original and one backup for your own personal use; it may not be resold, lent or given away to other people and it may only be purchased from the publisher or an authorised agent.

This book is sold subject to the condition that it shall not, by way of trade or otherwise, be lent, resold, hired out, or otherwise circulated without the author's prior consent in any form of binding or cover other than that in which it is published and without a similar condition including this condition being imposed on the subsequent purchaser.

Acknowledgements

To Judith Leask of Just Right Editing and my muse, Diane who faces my demons when I don't like making changes. Also, my brother-in-law Alan Campbell who thinks I keep forgetting his excellent grammar checking.

Author's Note

When I read many years ago, Alistair Cooke's body had been exhumed in an FBI investigation of a funeral director's practices and that his thigh bones had been replaced with plastic tubing, I was perplexed: why? He was my favourite journalist, known for his, 'Letter from America.' Then it was revealed that many of the other bodies had had various parts removed illegally before burial.

My research took me from missing persons all over the world, to events in China, even allegations against Albanian mercenaries fighting in the Balkans. More macabre are the prices paid for human tissue, especially those of aborted babies. It is big business.

The long and short of it is: *if you knew how much your body was worth, you would not walk alone at night!*

Lance Clarke 2021

Other books by Lance Clarke

30 Days
Balkan Tears
Not of Sound Mind
Horizons I
Horizons II

Cruel Harvest

Prologue

Katrina woke up frightened and confused, and slowly looked around. She lay on a simple iron-framed bed in a room that barely resembled a hospital ward, with rough walls painted light green against which stood a number of stainless-steel cabinets with glass beakers and instruments on top. There were no flowers in vases, or books and magazines on the table. It had all the intimacy of a public washroom.

She gripped the white sheets between her teeth and tried to ignore the excruciating pain she felt from the operation scar in her left side; but failed. The stitches stung and made her skin itch as they caught on the threads of the sheets and she was sure that the scar was bleeding.

The feeling that something was not quite right clung to her. She turned to look at the bed next to her.

"Hey, Romano, how is it?"

He looked up and forced a smile. "How do I look?"

"You look great. Better than me."

"You lie, my little friend, but thank you. My God, was it all worth it?" He winced, then wiped his shaking hand against his sweaty brow sat up resting on one arm.

"It was for me, Romano," she said, shrinking back into the covers, her voice becoming strained and resentful as her past loomed in front of her. "I'm not getting any younger and who wants to pay for sex with an old woman?" She paused, adding, "yes, I was a prostitute. I saw this as a way to freedom – sell a kidney – pay off my pimp and get a new life. Does that shock you?"

She looked across at him and saw that he had a puzzled and yet reassuring look in his eyes.

His arm stretched across to her – it was a comforting gesture she rarely experienced. "I'm not at all shocked, Katrina. We all have to make a living somehow in this hollow economy. I sold my kidney too, for a miserly four hundred US dollars, nevertheless a tidy sum in when there's no money around at all. Times have been bad for my family after I lost my job over two years ago. I was ground down by money worries and so very desperate. So, you see, we all have stories to tell my lovely little friend."

He winced again and half-smiled. "At least we are not like Lenno," he said, gesturing to the bed on his right. "He told me he was out on the town drinking his way from bar to bar and woke up the next day to find himself here, minus a kidney. How about that? At least we had agreements," adding uncertainly, "didn't we?"

Katrina nodded and gave him a nervous, thumbs-up. "Yes, Romano, agreements, that's right, agreements."

They had only met twenty-four hours earlier and yet were totally at ease with each other; their shared experience bonding them together. She sighed and leaned back against her pillows. Talking to Romano gave her some comfort and soothed her anxiety, nevertheless, a tangible air of uncertainty remained. The pain in her side was difficult to ignore and it hurt whenever she moved. She pressed her hand gently against the wound to relieve the discomfort and soreness.

Suddenly the locks rattled and the doors burst open. Two swarthy young male doctors strode in followed by three nurses. Without any decency or privacy, the nurses began stripping the patients for bathing and examination.

"So how are you today?" Katrina said brightly, hoping for some response.

She was totally ignored. The tallest of the two doctors gave her an injection, without speaking or looking at her and the pain began to ease, although the scar still stung. Curiously, after prodding her stomach in several places, he began to mark her torso, using a felt pen to draw red and green lines around the stomach, chest and back.

"What are you doing?" she demanded, waving her arms wildly about, but the doctor carried on without explanation, as though she did not exist as a patient, rather, an object. She became scared and reacted to the invasion of her privacy.

"Get off me, you bastard!" she shouted.

Curling up into a ball only brought more force to bear as the nurses straightened her arms against her sides. The doctor continued to draw coloured lines on her body despite her protests. When he finished, Katrina was left confused and violated. Anger burned in her chest and tears of frustration filled her eyes.

Romano and Lenno were also treated to this macabre process, but were too exhausted to protest.

When they finished, the doctors left as quickly as they had arrived. The nurses noiselessly covered the patients in clean white sheets, left a mug of warm tea and they too started to leave. As they reached the door, one nurse switched out the fluorescent lights, stopped and half-turned. She tried to smile at the patients, a clumsy half-smile.

Drying her watery eyes Katrina turned her head towards the kindly nurse. "Oh, nurse. Listen, this is very upsetting, I need to ask you....," but before she could say anything else the other two nurses grabbed their colleague and hurriedly ushered her out into the corridor, slamming the doors hastily shut behind them.

Katrina put her hands to her face and turned to the now sleeping Romano, "What the hell is going on?"

There was no response.

She was angry. A healthier, fitter Katrina would have taken them on - all of them. As she sat up unsteadily the bed sheet slipped from her breasts, but she made no attempt to cover up. She was drowsy, miserable, in a lot of discomfort, and needed some water. What was this damned place? She expected a hospital environment but this was nothing like it.

Only a dull blue security light now lit the room and it took a while for her eyes to adjust. She regarded the sleeping bodies of her fellow patients and said wearily, "At any other time, boys, I would charge you handsomely for a peek, but tonight I simply don't care."

With that flat attempt at humour, she stepped naked from the bed and walked unsteadily towards a steel cabinet by the door on which there were glasses and a water jug. She was woozy and as she filled a glass, water spilled onto the cabinet, dripping to the floor.

As she raised a glass to her lips, she heard the nurses talking. She placed her ear close to the door and although the voices were fading slowly down the corridor could hear what they were saying. Two of the nurses were chastising one of their colleagues. Katrina presumed it was the one who had smiled at her.

"Are you stupid or soft in the head. Our bonuses are dependent on keeping those in there healthy, not befriended or entertained," said one nurse testily.

A quieter voice added, "Look, Sonia, be realistic, some live and some die, but on the other hand some people actually live because of all this and there's money in it too. So, that's not so bad - that's life! Now shut up because you are part of it all now."

Katrina nearly dropped the glass. She looked down at her body, and the ink lines above her pubic hair, stomach and rib cage. It all became clear and her stomach churned as she fought back the bitter bile. She looked helplessly at her sleeping companions.

The voices and clicking of heels on the tiled floor sounded far away now and she grasped the round door handle to steady herself. To her surprise, and joy, it opened. Locking the door had been forgotten in the fuss in dealing with the nurse with a conscience. Her heart beat hard against her chest.

She pushed the door open a few inches and looked carefully into the corridor. There was no one there, so she stepped out. It was empty, silent and frighteningly dim, and one of the few fluorescent tubes was flashing intermittently. Her feet felt the coldness of the tiled floor. Despite her nakedness, she knew she had to find a way out.

As her eyes grew accustomed to the light, she saw a large desk farther down the corridor, behind which sat a scruffy uniformed security guard. She silently moved forward a few more paces trying to control her shivering. Thankfully, the guard was facing away from the corridor, watching a small television that blared popular music. He seemed well settled, idly smoking and tapping his fingers on the arm of his chair, singing along to an old Abba song. She stealthily crept even further along the corridor.

Katrina bit her top lip. *Give me just one chance, oh Lord, please, help me*, she pleaded to an unseen God. Then something caught her eye. Between the guard and where she was standing was the dim outline of a door, slightly ajar. A small silver shaft of moonlight illuminated the edge of the floor.

The guard stood up – fearful, she froze.

To her relief, he merely stretched his arms above his head, shook his spine and settled down again to watch the television. As she turned to go back and get something to cover herself, sounds of laughing and the clicking of heels came from around the corner at the end of the corridor.

She was fearful and felt trapped.

Looking urgently both ways she put her hands to her head and realised that there was no other option open to her but to flee, there and then, naked or not. Moving soundlessly to the exit door as fast as she could dare, she saw to her relief, a laundry basket one metre to the side of it. She dived into it with both hands and grabbed the first garment she felt. It was a grubby white gown. As she put it on, her face tightened and she looked back at the ward whispered softly, "Sorry, Romano, I must go.*"*

Katrina squeezed quietly through the door and into what looked like a courtyard. Small stones dug into her bare feet as she hobbled over the paving and out of the main gate. She would have readily swapped the gown for a strong pair of shoes, nakedness or not.

Judging by the starlit sky it was late in the evening and she was thankful that there was a good chance she could limp away from the building unseen.

"Argh," she muttered and pressed her hand to the wound on her left side. Hurt or not, she could not stop now. As she reached the road, she heard raucous female laughter from the building behind her. She balled her fists.

"Don't look at the door, bitches, just walk past it, walk on, keep laughing," she said through gritted teeth.

The dark streets were deserted, but to be safe she moved from doorway to doorway, sticking to the shadows wherever possible. The air was damp and she was sweating. This was no place for a half-naked girl to be at this time of night. Occasionally, she saw groups of young men, the worse for drink, and had to hide to let them pass. They laughed and joked, and she would have given anything to have joined them; but not now, not like this.

After only ten minutes, Katrina staggered and had to hold onto a railing to stop herself from collapsing. Her head was fuzzy and she was finding it difficult to think clearly. Just as she put her hands to her face, she heard a rattling car exhaust. A taxi turned the corner and drove slowly down the street towards her.

She had to take a chance.

Stumbling into the middle of the road, she waved the taxi down, her gown flapping open in the breeze. It slowed and then stopped two metres in front of her, its lights illuminating her like a puppet on a stage. The driver was content to leer at her through his open window.

This was her only chance of survival. Katrina had to choose the best possible sanctuary, but would avoid the police, who all knew her very well, as they did all the prostitutes in Sofia. Like many others in the city, she did not trust them - for all she knew, she would end up back at the clinic.

Breathing deeply, she drew the gown tightly around her, held her head up high and said in a very English accent, "Please, take me to the British Embassy."

The driver got out of the taxi slowly, put his hands in his pockets and leaned against the open door. He smirked as he sucked in smoke from a cigarette in his mouth and casually blew it towards her.

1

Jane Kavanagh lay comfortably in her cool silk sheets and yawned as she heard the front door close softly. It had been a much needed, but all too brief weekend of mutual enjoyment, without the unwanted complications of a relationship. Now it was back to work.

One hour later, she completed a session of demanding morning stretches. The previous week's karate training had taken its toll of her muscles and she ached. She decided not to work so hard next time, but knew that would not be easy. Fitness and self-defence saved her life on a number of occasions and she never forgot that. She got up from the exercise mat and looked in her full-length mirror. Her titian hair shone in the light from the window of the studio flat. Despite being streaked with sweat from her body she looked good. Only a three-inch knife scar on her left shoulder, courtesy of a Chechen gangster, spoiled an otherwise smooth skin.

Jane walked wearily to the shower room, but stopped by a large mirror and wiped off a small smudge, returning it to its perfect state.

The hot water relaxed her muscles, but not her mood. Putting her head back she loudly exclaimed, "Dear Providence, give me a clue, or two...please! So much information but so bloody little evidence!"

After a light breakfast she sat at her desk by the window and gazed at the spectacular view of Tower Bridge. It was drizzling with rain and the streets were alive with miserable umbrellas that fought for space. She often watched people going about their business and wondered what their lives were like; how they loved, how they laughed and how they relaxed.

How to relax - now there's a thing!

Something caught her eye. It was a scraggy old pigeon with a broken beak wobbling ungainly along a roofline, slowly – too slowly. Behind was a tabby cat, crouching low, eyes fixed on its prey, allowing a few seconds between each careful placement of its paws as it closed the gap.

Jane winced instinctively looking back to the bustle of people in the street below. It was a familiar technique: if it hurts and you cannot prevent it, turn away, ignore it, think of something else. She used it often – too often.

Her flat was furnished in a minimalist style, dove grey walls were lit with modern lighting. The only concession to wall ornaments was a collection of photographs and military diplomas that were arranged above her writing desk; identity claims that held her together. A single photograph of her parents walking along the seashore was allowed to join the memorabilia. It sat slightly crooked on the lower edge of the collection.

She switched on the coffee machine and fumbled irritably with the coffee pods, eventually snapping the lid closed. The phone rang.

"Hello, Jane K," she said formally.

"Hi. It's Andrew. I thought I'd give you a quick call."

"Go on. I hope you've got something good, my head is bursting with frustration, Andrew, I really need some direction of travel on this case."

"Well, I think I can help you there. You know that we've been staking out a dodgy clinic just outside Bucharest, well, we struck lucky. I know it's taken months but it pays off. Anyway, a regular visitor is a privately registered white van, pretty posh with air conditioning vents and so on. We decided to follow it back to the UK. It's collection and delivery point is the Maria Cresswell Hospice in Norfolk."

Jane's mind raced. When cases stall for too long, patience grows thin and funding dries up. The pipeline is swollen with investigations ready for an outing. A friend had given her a tip-off that pressure would soon be placed on her project to come up with results.

"Andrew, that's brilliant. I'll tell the boss. I suspect you've been driving all night, so away home now, to Abby and the boys."

"Yeah, I'm a bit tired, but I thought I would give you this news first. I'm glad to have made your day. Bye for now."

The coffee machine finished its jets of steam and she sipped the scalding black rich roast from an old, cracked Royal Logistics Corps mug; a friendly object from her past. She clasped it in both hands. Time to think. It's one thing confirming a link, but quite another to gain prime evidence.

As she replenished her coffee, she looked up and saw the broken-beaked pigeon land on her windowsill – they looked at each other fleetingly. As it flew off, Jane smiled with relief.

Gathering her resolve, she reached for her phone and dialled. A cultured, deep voice with a rumble to it that suggested a larynx coated with tar and nicotine, answered, "Hancox."

"Hello, Mike, it's Jane."

"I can see your number on my phone, dear heart, get on with it."

Jane looked at the ceiling. "I have some news."

"About time," he said abruptly, "people in the top drawer are beginning to get anxious. In fact," he paused awkwardly, "I was about to call you myself."

"That doesn't sound good," Jane said with trepidation.

"Look, Jane, I respect your values. I avoid giving you political work and let you have a pretty free rein on projects. Your interest in your fellow man is commendable, but in this case, without results, I am experiencing severe pressure_" Jane started to speak but he hushed her and continued, "_Organisation Sapphire is my baby. I nurtured it, breast-fed it for God's sake and it bloody well works."

He was almost out of breath but gathered speed.

"You know the form, Europol and Interpol can only work in countries when they are invited in, so Sapphire does it for them. Our paymasters are pretty high up the food chain and, Jane, they're beginning to lose interest."

Jane's heart raced - this must not slip. Hancox paused again, but before any thoughts of cessation could loom large in the silence, she cut in.

"Boss, hang on a minute. I know Sapphire's mission objectives well enough. You mustn't give up on this case. The more we dig, the more suffering we uncover. Give me a chance. It's dreadful, cruel and needs sorting - quickly. I know you're under a lot of stress, but we're on to a really good lead, I promise you, this is very hot. We've been staking out a clinic in Romania. It appears that they have a frequent visitor, a white van that travels regularly from a hospice in Norfolk to Bucharest. I want to go to Norfolk and get the local police to help me with my enquiries. We mustn't let this go. You're so good at challenging the powers that be. What say?"

Hancox was silent.

Jane pressed him. "Is that a yes?"

Hancox huffed. "Yes, yes, bloody yes! You minx, you knew I'd bend! You must understand though, it had better be good, your persuasion doesn't alter the pressure. I can only hold them off for a while longer."

Jane muttered her thanks. She was aware of the pressure but happy at the reprieve.

After a strange pause, he changed to a more avuncular tone. "Jane, I don't want to spoil your party, but your Bulgarian witness, Katrina, her mother's dead. Her throat was cut and her body dumped in the countryside just outside Sofia. We broke the news to Katrina this morning and put a guard on her London flat. She's devastated, but I'll tell you what, she's got guts. She's even more motivated to make her situation known to every national forum she can."

Jane felt bad, very bad. Intelligence work often meant helping, but sometimes using victims. Although it never sat easily, the importance of mission focus was hardwired into her; but it still hurt. She knew deep down she would never get used to it.

"For form's sake I'll send a note to Katrina, if that's all right with you," she said shakily.

"Yes of course. As for your Norfolk jaunt, go ahead. I'll tip off my contacts in the Home Office in case the local police get precious. Good luck, my girl, and don't let me down."

Jane put the phone down and finished her now cold coffee. She bridled at his use of the phrase, 'my girl', but strangely it was rather like a family term. That was what it was like in MI6, a family; sometimes dysfunctional, sometimes warmly supportive, but a family nevertheless. She muttered, "Might just call you Daddy some time!"

Plans had to be made and a strategy formed. She reflected on her self-reliance and confidence. Her days of being the token woman in a military unit were long gone; she now had operational street-cred and time served. The real Jane was locked in the dells and hollows of her mind. The frenetic world she inhabited kept her on higher ground.

Papers in bulky brown files on her desk demanded her attention, so she skim-read them, highlighting and making notes in the margins. It was six months into this toe-curling frustrating investigation. The surveillance of the delivery van was the fillip she needed.

Jane had high hopes that her trip to Norfolk in a few days' time could yield positive results, otherwise reassignment beckoned.

Now she wanted to solve this case not just for its own sake, but for Katrina.

Fate smiles generously on some men, dealing them a hand of cards glowing with good fortune, leading them effortlessly to a happy life. Other men are less lucky. For Dr Jack Beamish, life's events wore down his soul. Unhappiness cleaved to him, dulling his spirit, logic deserted and judgement became redundant. Tears streamed down his face, so fast the salty water fell from his chin and soaked the collar of his shirt.

At first, he believed that a golf partner had taken pity on his financial situation and that the money had been no more than an extended loan from a rich guy. Then came the soft sell: *People died all the time – fact. They often died, wasting at least fifty per cent of their organs that could be used to save lives – fact. Relatives became far too emotional over donor cards and suchlike – fact. Something can be done – fact.*

From there it had been a short trip to hell as he nibbled at the bait and was slowly reeled into 'the project'. It dealt efficiently with the simple facts of life and death, harnessing the inevitability of the latter for the greater good of the former. It was the harnessing bit that he was starting to question. Well then, if he were to go to hell in a handcart then at least his bank account, left in trust to his wife, would ease her burden.

Despite a pulsating headache, Beamish finished writing a short note and carefully put it into a clear polythene envelope, tucking it into his inside jacket pocket. He held his hands up in front of him and watched as they shook with the realisation of what he was about to do. His practice office was in a mess, but he had neither the mental state, nor the will to tidy it up. In fact, he had lost the will to do anything for some weeks. But then it wasn't going to be his responsibility anymore, so why should he care?

It was long past midnight and he hoped that Cromer Pier would be deserted on this late spring night. He liked the Norfolk coast because it held happy memories for him and Angela. Those wonderful days of sunshine walks, toes in the sea and cockles and mussels. How he yearned for the sound of her uninhibited, gay laughter – to hear it just one more time. He shuffled outside and opened the boot of his Ford Escort, now a classic car, but in pristine condition - it was the only thing he took any interest in these days. As he threw a long rope inside the boot, he scratched his hand. He just stared at it for a few moments looking at the trickle of blood, then he laughed - he knew that this would soon stop.

He squeezed into the driving seat and keyed the ignition. His old friend seemed to want to give him an extra chance and the engine spluttered and died twice, but he persisted and it eventually burst reluctantly into life.

The drive took on an almost surreal characteristic. His state of mind was so scrambled that street lamps appeared bigger than they were and stars moved erratically in the sky. He cried endlessly, for the love of his wife, for his stupidity, for being put into an impossible position and for people's lives that he had ruined. He knew what he had to do to bring it all to an end. His head throbbed ceaselessly.

He parked his car fifty yards from the pier, alongside rubbish bins with neatly tied plastic bags and folded cardboard piled to one side. After gathering up the rope, he nervously felt in his jacket pocket for a half bottle of single malt whisky. He was grateful he had not forgotten it - he would need courage. Hunching his shoulders, he made his way along the deserted street, moving from one orange street lamp to another, their glow casting his shadow, making it appear gargantuan. The pier was empty, not even a romantic couple cuddling in the seating booths that ran down the middle.

He was glad of the solitude and walked alongside the pier rail feeling the sea breeze on his face. A five-foot high maintenance fence had been erected just short of the end of the pier where he knew there was the longest drop. Undeterred, Beamish climbed the wire mesh and it shook crazily, rattling noisily as he heaved himself over the top, eventually falling heavily onto the wooden boards. Despite the exertion and partially winding himself, he got up and plodded wearily to the end of the structure, his steady footsteps thumping against the boards, like a bass drum, echoing in the quietness of the night.

Watching the lights of boats at sea and listening to the tinkling of yacht halyards twanging against masts some way off calmed him a little, but didn't dim his purpose. He had a big wedge in his heart where his conscience had slammed into it. Nothing would change his mind now - absolutely nothing. He slowly unscrewed the top of the whisky bottle and took a generous mouthful, screwing his face up as he swallowed. It tore at his throat, but tasted good. He took another slug and this time his mouth reacted more easily to the liquid.

Unsteadily, he tied the rope to the safety rail on the end of the pier, making extra turns to ensure that it wouldn't fail. He didn't have clue as to how to tie a noose, so he wrapped the bottom of the rope around his neck a few times and again tied several knots. He gingerly climbed over the rail, hesitated, then laughed, finding it funny that he was being so careful to avoid falling - something he was about to do deliberately.

The effect of the whisky and his state of mind made his head swirl and tears flowed again, so that he could hardly see what he was doing. An overwhelming sense of guilt, failure and sadness made his chest heave and he sobbed. He took a deep breath and let out a long hopeless agonized moan.

Detective Superintendent Ted Sanderson, of the Cromer Police, purposefully strode down the garden path to the wrought iron front gate and cursed as he always did when he saw it swinging in the breeze. A broken latch stood stubbornly upright, rusted into a permanent mocking salute. His car was wet with dew, and it splashed lightly on his collar when he opened the door. He brushed the drops of water from his neat fitting blue suit and eased his six-foot frame in the driver's seat. It was important to drive off slowly without waking his neighbours, many of whom were quick to complain about his unsocial hours.

The A140 from his home in Horsham Saint Faith to the quaint seaside town of Cromer on the east coast was quiet and although not anywhere near tourist time, the early morning farm and industrial traffic annoyed him. Almost everything did these days. The journey would take about a half an hour, but despite his anxiety to get to the incident scene and so take his mind off his personal situation, he really wasn't that bothered. The car was his safe haven, that place where one-way conversations can be acted out in the full certainty that no one will overhear, lines prepared and memorized for future use, excuses invented, or endless questions postulated to a non-hearing God. These days his neural pathways were clogged with competing self-constructed frustrations that dragged at him.

As he accelerated along the highway a car unwisely pulled out in front of him without properly checking. Ted cursed loudly and pressed his horn, then touched the button that activated blue lights set inside the main beam.

He pulled alongside the car, an elderly Ford, driven by an equally elderly gentlemen and lowered the passenger window. "That was bloody bad driving, sir. Watch you step in future. Understand?"

The driver looked cowed and acknowledged the instruction with a wave.

Ted continued his journey – angry with the driver, angry with life, angry with the world, just bloody angry...

His thoughts roamed from one irritation to another; he knew he was irascible and cynical these days. His wife Alison had always kept his feet on the ground and in her lucid and alert moments she was more than a match for Ted, her socialist views blasting his corporate attitudes to smithereens. She had always been better than Ted at taking a reasoned view of situations – but not now.

It was a relief to Ted not to have to endure breakfast with Alison. He felt bad thinking that way, but it was true nonetheless. The 6 a.m. call from the station had been welcome – it excused him from making excuses. He had not slept having listened to her sobs on and off throughout the night. Two years of emotional exhaustion sapped his strength. He was as attentive as any partner could be in the circumstances, but at times it wore perilously thin. It was difficult to find a way out of the circle of sadness.

Ted's fingers dug into the steering wheel and his heart thumped with the stress of his home life that spilled over and inevitably affected his work. It was a nightmare, in which he was trapped between the love for his wife gripped with severe depression, and a police force daily paralysed by the dull hand of politics, form filling and a mountain of rules.

And now some silly sod decided to commit suicide.

Ted drove over the crest of the last large hill to the coastline and looked down on the quaint seaside town of Cromer, with its neat gardens and tree-lined roads. It was the maiden aunt of seaside towns, not as gritty as her bigger west-coast cousins, nor as noisy and frenetic as its east-coast neighbours. It was a town where people came and went, but drama had never visited.

Today was the exception. Residents awoke to the sight of police cars in the pier road and screens erected on the sands below the pier itself. The gulls were the only spectators that got a good view of the incident, as they screeched and wheeled in the air above the screens, having feasted briefly on bloody flesh earlier in the morning. A group of local people, bored by a long, wet spring, milled around looking for a scintilla of excitement. Bad news travels fast.

Ted lifted the blue and white police cordon in front of the pier and strode to the end of the pier barely acknowledging the police constables or scene of crime officers.

It was worse than he imagined.

A rope dangled from a handrail at the end of the structure and swayed gently in the morning breeze. The severed head of a man, grotesquely contorted, was attached by several turns of the rope. Below, surrounded now by a white screen, sitting upright in the soft muddy sand was the man's torso, with shards of ripped skin, bone and flesh where the head should be. It was a macabre sight unfortunately made comic by a large advertising hoarding on the side of the pavilion immediately above the corpse. It cried out, *Come and see the Funniest Man in the World,* the age-old exhortation to attract punters to be entertained by a usually long-forgotten comedian, but now heralded something quite unfunny. This would inevitably provide black humour for of the coppers back at the station.

"He obviously hadn't read Albert Pierrepoint," said a voice behind him. It was Detective Inspector Mike Daniels. Mike worked for Ted and knew his personal situation.

"Albert who?"

"Pierrepoint, Albert Pierrepoint. Lovely man by all accounts. He was the last official hangman in the UK. He wrote a very interesting book. In it he describes how he perfected his task of hanging condemned criminals with great speed and dignity. He felt that if people had to be executed then it should be done as humanely as possible. He hanged the Nazis at the Nuremburg Trials. Anyway, the point is that he would assess the weight of the person and calculate the drop needed to carry out the sentence without mishap."

Mike glanced over the rail and waved his hand dismissively at the bloody, headless torso below, adding, "Mr 'Porko' down there didn't factor in his enormous bulk and the drop required – hence the, er, separation."

Ted was in no mood for humour or flippancy. Nodding to Mike he snapped, "Name?"

"Doctor Jack Beamish, local general practitioner in North Walsham. He helpfully kept all his documents, including photo id, in his coat."

Ted exhaled. "Why this?"

"There is a note. It rambles quite a bit. Trouble is, you never know with these types why they are so troubled and whether what they say is rubbish or the truth. We need to go to his home and office and see what we can find. I can't help feeling that there's something strange about it."

Ted smiled wryly. Mike was a very sound policeman, boring, lacking in personality and innovation, and a bit scruffy, but very sound. He had an uncanny quality of reading between the lines when considering evidence and would probably have made a better superintendent than him. It was a low thought and he wondered if depression was catching.

"Okay, Mike, you know the drill, let's follow the book. I'll leave you and SOCO to it. I need to go back home for something, but I'll see you at the GP's practice at about midday. And just in case you forgot, tides have a habit of coming in as well as going out."

Mike gave a perfunctory wave and no indication that he knew why Ted needed to go home.

Ted arrived home to find the table laid for breakfast, but the cereals and toast were barely touched and the coffee was cold. Alison was still in her nightclothes. Her face was ashen and expressionless, her blue eyes bloodshot and watery. A thin smile tried to crack the mould that disguised her hopelessness. She sat back wearily and brushed her hands through her short dark hair. Even now, she was still attractive.

"How is it?"

He touched her arm gently and she pulled away from him irritably. He hated that. To offer tenderness and have it rejected always hurt, but he persisted.

"Come on now, I'm on your side, remember? Have you taken your pills?"

Alison forlornly stared at the ceiling, eyes welling with tears. "Pills, pills, bloody pills." She took a deep breath and glared at him, "How would you like it, eh? Your whole life controlled by bloody pills."

"Yeah, it's tough but..."

Alison stood up quickly and knocked the milk jug which, despite its sturdiness, tipped over and spilled its contents on the table.

"Tough? What do you bloody know about tough? You, with your successful career and everything going for you. Mr Successful. Young constables, looking up to you. Some of them female and pretty too, I bet. Any of them come on to you, darling?" Her smile was twisted, angry and menacing. "Any of them want to bed you?"

He was now beyond hurt. In the beginning, he had felt wretched and her words ripped into his chest like a red-hot corkscrew. Now there was nothing, nothing except that disciplined loyalty that comes of not knowing what the hell to do except stay the course and pray for a miracle. All he knew was that he would be there for her until it got sorted and he would never let her down. His love was being stretched further than he ever thought possible, but guilt clung to him - he was okay and she was not.

Ted took Alison in his arms, feeling her limp shape that did not even want to acknowledge him. In the car he felt bitter and angry, but at home and with her, he held onto love. He encouraged her to take her pills and she slowly went up to bed. The milk had spilled all over the table and was now sticky – it took an age to clear up and he reflected on their need for a housekeeper or cleaner. In temper, more at the world around him and his situation than anything else, he threw the cloth violently into the sink and without rinsing it and walked out of the kitchen, his pulse racing and his throat tightening.

Ted Sanderson met DI Mike Daniels and DS Nicola Bradbury at Dr Beamish's practice in North Walsham, nine miles from Cromer.

"Mike, sorry, but this task doesn't need three people, you go back to the station and get to grips with the forensics and medical reports. All hell will break lose and I really want to stay away from the office a little longer."

Mike nodded in agreement and left. Early checks revealed no next of kin other than his wife who was in a nursing home and too ill to take anything in or give access to their house, so these matters would need careful handling.

The small medical centre, located in a modern white building on the edge of town looked bright against the clear blue sky. The waiting room was full of patients and the reception staff looked harassed. Ted looked around and wondered what it must be like for Alison to have to endure regular visits to her GP.

"Can I help you?" said a middle-aged lady, looking sternly over the top of her reading spectacles, every bit the archetypal 1950s doctor's receptionist: crisp and starched in a white blouse and dark grey skirt, clearly the centre of this small universe.

"Can we talk somewhere private, please, with you and the other doctor in the practice?" he said, showing his warrant card. Several people looked up and craned forward to listen.

"Well, I suppose you had better come inside," said the receptionist tilting her head backwards, feigning irritation, "but we are rather pushed today. Dr Beamish hasn't turned up. I don't know, I really don't."

She stood up, moved papers this way and that on her desk, finally putting them back in the centre where they had been in the first place and ushered Ted and DS Bradbury to a side room.

The room was used as a quiet area for staff and patients, sparsely furnished with several comfortable unit chairs and two coffee tables on which paper cups waited to be emptied. She tut-tutted and hurriedly moved them to the wastebasket, flapping a tea towel over the surface. A cheap seaside print hung at an angle on the magnolia painted wall. Ted took a deep breath and thought that this was the last place he would want to have a serious chat about having his leg off.

Five minutes later, a doctor entered and introduced herself as Dr Patricia Lenahan. She was young, petite and blonde. Her stethoscope looked almost too heavy for her. Ted would swap her for the aged witchdoctor in his Norwich practice any day.

"I'm sorry to keep you waiting, but I was just finishing with a patient. I couldn't stop mid-consultation. What's this about?"

"No problem, we could've waited," he said, and realised that he was smiling broadly. A pretty woman was talking warmly to him. This was disarming in his current mood. He quickly pulled himself together, dismissing unprofessional errant thoughts, and frowned to counter his doe-eyed introduction.

"I'm Detective Superintendent Ted Sanderson and this is Detective Sergeant Nicola Bradbury, Dr Lenahan, and..." he turned to the receptionist.

"Oh, I'm Elaine Harmer," she said folding her arms across her chest, anticipating bad news.

"Well, I'm sorry to tell you that Dr Beamish is dead," he said gravely.

They gasped and both sat down at the same time.

"How on earth did he die? Was it a car accident?" spluttered Elaine Harmer.

"This is going to be difficult for you both to take in I'm sure, so please brace yourselves. It would appear that he took his own life by hanging himself off Cromer pier."

The receptionist put her hand to her mouth. By contrast, Dr Lenahan merely seemed ill at ease.

"As part of our investigation into his death, we need access to his office and papers," he said, "it's purely routine, we will of course respect confidentiality. But it's important that the office is, for the moment at least, immediately closed to everyone, and I mean everyone. I'm sure that you understand. We need to rule out suspicious circumstances. I assure you it won't take long."

Dr Lenahan leaned back and carelessly crossed her legs and Ted noticed how shiny her tights were. He reluctantly looked away.

"Yes, of course," she said, looking straight at him. "If we need anything then we can always ask you, I'm sure. Most of our records are computerised anyway. Do we know the circumstances?"

"No, not yet. We have to sift through details of his personal life for possible stresses. It's too early to tell."

Drying her tears, the receptionist led them to Dr Beamish's office. Ted followed her with Dr Lenahan. When the door was opened, Elaine Harmer gasped.

"My God, what a mess. He was normally so tidy," she said, then her face screwed up and she rushed past them back to the main office holding a tissue to her eyes.

Ted left DS Bradbury to get on with her work and waited a few minutes before looking at doctor Lenahan. "I may be wrong, but you didn't look so surprised that he had committed suicide. Why is that?"

Dr Lenahan was small by most standards and Ted towered over her. She looked up at him and despite her status and character, resembled a child addressing a parent about something deeply embarrassing.

"Yes, you're right, but please don't think I'm heartless. It's just that he was acting a bit strangely. And, well," she hesitated, "we argued. He was a bit vague at times and his administration has been erratic – frankly, sometimes it was hopeless. He is a lovely man, well, was. I was upset when he accused me of thinking that he was inefficient and uncaring. I asked myself if I had been a bit bitchy or heavy in my criticism. I was just concerned about his record keeping, that's all. I think the stress of his wife's illness, she has Alzheimer's you know, has been getting the better of him. Anyway, we made up and I thought nothing more of it."

"Alzheimer's? That goes some way to understanding his state of mind, I suppose."

Ted wanted to know more, but now was not the time. Besides, the thought of interviewing Dr Patricia Lenahan again, just the two of them, guiltily pleased him. She agreed to could come to the station at a later date, then left. Ted made some notes.

Nicola was only half-listening to the exchange. She was tightly focussed on the work at hand. The prospects of using this case to establish her new position back at the station excited her. She was already thinking about how to delegate tasks to her constables, display her ability to control them and work strictly to procedures. This was her big chance and she would make sure her bosses noticed her.

She boxed as much of Beamish's paperwork as she could, together with sundry other items, to take back to the station for review. The office door resisted being locked at first, but surrendered when she pulled it hard into the architrave. She tagged the key and secured blue and white 'police' tape across the frame to bar unauthorised entry.

The reception staff looked irked when she approached the main desk and she tried to disarm them with a smile.

"It's only a temporary measure, "she explained, "I'll come back tomorrow with the key. We just need to put together some facts and try and work out the cause of his action. I'm sure you must all be feeling very shocked."

They nodded, but said nothing.

Meanwhile, Ted spent a few minutes with Mrs Harmer, who in the best interests of her trade, managed to talk freely about Dr Beamish's situation at the practice.

"His wife has had Alzheimer's disease for over five years. It must have been a great strain on him. She was an outgoing and lovely person, and everyone liked her. He never let it affect his work though and was often in the office until very late at night, arranging special attention for some of his patients. To my knowledge he has no other family. He was a saint, you know, a real saint of a man." Ted thanked her and walked back to the main entrance.

Nicola joined him at the door. "Time to go. Sign here, guv," she said, proffering a list of items removed from Beamish's office.

Ted was deep in thought and hardly looked at what he was signing for.

As they walked across the car park, she nudged him.

"Don't look now but they're watching us all way. It's either shock or they think we did him in!"

Despite Nicola's humour, Ted remained moody and regarded the situation with careless detachment – his mind was still at home. As they drove away, he idly wondered how Dr Lenahan and the staff would react to the gory outcome of Dr Beamish's suicide.

That detailed information was best left until later.

2

Doctor Johannes Ziggefelde looked into a mirror next to his office door and regarded his fading looks, impatiently removing a loose strand of grey hair from his shiny forehead. His eyes narrowed behind rimless spectacles and he irritably straightened the collar of his neatly starched white shirt. He was not a people person, at least not in the sense of grieving relatives. He was a surgeon and that's what he was paid for. Work in the Maria Cresswell Hospice was lucrative and measurably better than his previous position in a Rumanian hospital with poor pay, poor equipment and poor prospects. He reasoned that given that situation, he could at least knuckle down and do what was expected of him without question. He slipped on a beige sports jacket, sat down and dialled reception.

Jim and Mavis Grant sat motionless in front of his desk and he regarded them with fraudulent sympathy. Mavis fiddled ceaselessly with her wedding ring and Jim clasped and unclasped his hands repeatedly, his gaze fixed straight ahead. Ziggefelde let the news sink in, pulling his knuckles so that they clicked.

"I don't understand, he was all right yesterday. I know he came here to die, doctor, but we thought it would be a gradual process. What the hell happened?" wailed Jim, holding his shaking palms open. "Why, why...?"

Mavis hugged him and he looked at her helplessly, as only a father and husband can in such circumstances; impotent, yet desperately trying to stay in control.

Ziggefelde leaned forward and with practiced empathy took her left hand softly in his.

"Mrs Grant. You must understand, his body has taken so much strain. He had a relapse last night and we thought it would be all right, we expected him to rally as he had done a number of times. He didn't and sadly died of a massive heart failure. I am so very sorry."

Jim's face contorted and he broke down. In circumstances like this, although expected, grief arrives like a steam train and knocks the wind out of a person, rendering them helpless. Mavis's strength took over and she cradled his head in her arms as he sobbed.

"That's kind of you, Dr Ziggefelde, very kind. Forgive our anger. Dr Beamish was so good to us, arranging this placement in the hospice and you and the staff have all been so caring of Malcolm. I just know that he couldn't have been in a better place. We're just confused and so dreadfully upset. One day we have a fully fit sporting young son and the next he's diagnosed with something awful and well," her eyes filled with tears and she stuttered, "just leave us for a while then we will make our way home."

"Yes, I'm sorry. For the record, Mrs Grant, I regard you as fine parents and very brave indeed. We all loved Malcolm too, for his courage and lively sense of humour. I know that it is perhaps just a little premature, but as you know there is a funeral parlour not two miles away. We obviously have close contacts to many parlours, but this one is a kind of associate to the hospice. You've donated generously to the hospice and it would be our privilege to pay for and make all the necessary arrangements for the cremation service. It is the least we can do."

"Oh, but we did really want to have him buried, Doctor. We've never been that happy with cremations."

Dr Ziggefelde gave a thin smile that disguised irritation.

"But cremation really is such a good thing," he said quickly and almost clumsily. "Churchyards are so crowded these days and it's much nicer, I think, to have a loved one's ashes spread somewhere beautiful, eh?"

Mavis persisted. "Thank you, but we have a plot sorted with our local church and that's what we want, Doctor."

Dr Ziggefelde frowned, steepled his fingers and stared directly at her.

"Okay then, but in that case please let us make all the necessary arrangements for you through our associate funeral parlour. He shall have the best."

"Thank you again. We want everyone to see him before he's is buried." Mavis dabbed her nose lightly and Jim, now composed, sat up straight.

Dr Ziggefelde put his arms up almost automatically.

"Ah! Please don't do that. It's all the drugs he has been given recently. You see, I must warn you that the flesh has started to deteriorate already. I am so very sorry to tell you, but he is not a very pretty sight. No funeral parlour can change that, no matter how hard they try Take my advice, it is best to remember him as he was."

He leaned forward and touched her shoulder reassuringly and she looked up at him. It was now getting all too much for her.

"Oh dear," said Mavis, "oh dear, oh dear, my poor Malcolm. So be it then. Seal him up properly. I won't explain to everyone. That would be too much."

She turned to her husband. "We'll just do as the doctor says."

Jim nodded silently and Dr Ziggefelde led them slowly down to the chapel of rest where Malcolm's body lay already sealed in a coffin. As he showed them out of the waiting room, his foot crushed a small yellow rosebud that had fallen from Mavis's spray of flowers brought for her son, leaving a damp stain on the carpet.

China

Chin Kwok stood at the corner of a large grey apartment block in Kunming, in the southern Yunnan province of the People's Republic of China, hunching his shoulders and trying to look inconspicuous. Kunming is the provincial city of the province and he recalled his parents describing it as historic and cultural. They said that because of its beautiful gardens and greenery it had always been known as 'city of flowers.'

Today they would have been disappointed, it was anything but beautiful. He earlier watched as twenty frightened and confused prisoners were taken in chains to ritual public humiliation at a local football ground in front of television cameras and members of the public. After sentence they left the stadium. Each prisoner's hands handcuffed behind their backs and bent almost double, frog-marched by two uniformed guards to a white bus parked in a courtyard nearby. With extended mirrors on either side, each arching forward like eyes on stalks, the bus looked like an enormous white slug.

Chin remembered seeing buses like these at other locations. He recalled sending a picture to his boss, Jane

Kavanagh, and her horrified reaction to it. The Chinese government owned a fleet of eighteen new mobile execution chambers for prisoners sentenced to death in the Republic. He knew that each one was equipped with a sophisticated system that administered lethal injections, supervised by medical staff ensuring a quick death. The whole process would take no more than thirty minutes from sentence to carrying out the execution. It was considered a better system than the old-fashioned bullet in the back of the head; at least the relatives didn't have to pay for the bullet.

They were kept busy.

He watched a body being transferred from the white bus into a JAC K6 refrigerator truck parked nearby. Its noisy engine was running in anticipation of more to come. As the vehicle doors were opened, cold air spilled out and met the warm air outside turning it into clouds of mist that seemed to reach out and carefully embrace the victim. Chin had the personal details of all the condemned prisoners – you can buy anything in China. It showed one or two drug traffickers and murderers, but the largest number comprised people whose only crimes had been those deemed to be against the Chinese people such as extortion, slave labour, fraud, corruption and bribery. He also noted the inclusion of those whose political or religious ideology countered communism. His chest tightened at the background intelligence that revealed that about fifteen thousand prisoners are executed in China every year. In the province of Yunnan such trials were a regular occurrence.

Chin looked to one side and saw relatives waving frantically to get a prisoner's attention before they entered the bus – one last wave, one last glance, before death claimed a loved one. If they wanted the body for a family funeral then they would normally have to negotiate with the authorities, sometimes they would be successful, but more often, they would not. There were few people watching the transfer, the stadium audience had now left, and most of those who happened to be in the area, anywhere near the guards or the bus itself, simply sloped their shoulders, put their hands in their pockets and walked on quickly, looking at the ground as they did so.

Eventually, all the bodies were loaded into the JAC truck, the doors were locked and someone got in and revved the engine hard. Chin ran to his Chinese manufactured Citroen Fukang and set off in pursuit. The truck drove erratically through the suburbs and out into the countryside, and Chin was amazed it hit nothing. Luckily the truck's top speed was only 100 kph and he kept up easily.

The Yunnan scenery was spectacular and Chin looked at the Himalayan mountain range and thought it resembled a large granite wave in an ancient frozen sea, with fluffy clouds atop, looking like froth. Local people he spoke to considered the province to be the last steps to Tibet and the roof of the world. Yunnan in Chinese means 'south of the colourful clouds' and he was told that seeing this was meant to be an auspicious sign; it was certainly not the case for the poor souls who ended up in the truck.

The beauty of the panorama paled into insignificance.

Chin drove for an hour deep into the countryside and arrived at a town called Song Yang. After negotiating numerous narrow streets, he followed the truck east, as if leaving the town. It slowed at a small, gated compound and drove in. He could not follow and parked fifty metres away, alongside a line of waste bins outside a shabby garage. The compound had a grim, scruffy appearance of a labour camp, with fences topped with razor wire. He looked past the grey buildings and saw beyond them a smaller and very much smarter modern white structure with large tinted windows and a lot of external pipe-work and cooling towers. He could just make out the sign on the front of the building: 'The Hang Soy Institute.' The truck approached the building and skidded to a halt on the gravel outside two large metal doors. They opened as if on some given command and a dozen green-suited staff wearing operating masks filed out with stretchers and began to gather the bodies of the executed prisoners.

The leader shouted, "Let's go, be quick now."

It took the staff only twenty minutes to unload the cadavers on to small trolleys and take them inside the building; it was all so matter-of-fact. When they finished several of them stood outside talking and smoking. Chin felt sick at the thought of the human bodies thrown around like sacks of waste; he wondered about the lives of the people who had been so cruelly executed. What did they do to deserve death? What were they like? Who did they leave behind to mourn for them?

As he crouched down low in his driving seat, he noticed two young women and one rather ugly man with a distinctive dragon shaped scar on his cheek directly under his right ear, standing smoking a cigarette by the double doors. The man's scar was so large it was visible from some distance. The girls were teasing him and he seemed annoyed and walked away.

Chin considered the situation carefully. If the bodies were to be handed back to relatives for a traditional burial, then that would have been done at the stadium. There was something sinister happening on the execution circuit.

His mission was to observe and report back what he saw - he had much to tell already.

England

Dr Johannes Ziggefelde, attended Malcolm Grant's funeral which was well attended by family and friends. There were tears and a eulogy, and everyone spoke of the sudden loss of an otherwise fit and healthy young man with a lively sense of humour, well loved by everyone. Generous mourners donated money to the Maria Cresswell Hospice. They were impressed by the care and tenderness shown to Malcolm and grateful to the hospice for the organisation and generous payment for the lavish funeral arrangements.

The mourners were sad to hear of the death of Dr Jack Beamish. Everyone was totally shocked. Discussion over cucumber sandwiches in the local village hall moved from the poor deceased Malcolm to the stresses that doctors were currently under, and the supposition that Beamish committed suicide due to the strain of looking after his wife. They thought it too much for the man.

Dr Ziggefelde put his hand on Mavis's shoulder. "I really am very sorry for your sadness, Mrs Grant. You have my deepest sympathy. If there is anything else the hospice can do please let me know."

He talked to everyone and gave his condolences to Jim Grant, who sat red-faced and silent on a chair in the corner of the hall, then said farewell and left the building.

After turning his car back towards the local church, he parked outside the lych-gate. The churchyard was deserted.

Evensong was two hours away and he hoped that the gravediggers had done their job properly. It was a short walk across damp grass to Malcolm's grave, situated in a new plot surrounded by young yew trees to the east of the cemetery. He stood looking at the earthen mound, then went to it and damped down the soil with his right foot, almost as though he was finishing the job, putting the final seal on the tomb.

There were times like this when exposure to religion in his early years left him remorseful, but the terribly hard times spent in a broken eastern European country hardened him sufficiently to be able to make excuses.

He took out his mobile telephone, dialled and left a long clear message.

Ted Sanderson got home much later than he expected. His senses were greeted by a waft of warm sweet smells – baking! Alison came out of the kitchen, looking mid-way between awful and happy. His heart melted. Without saying anything they embraced and held each other for what seemed like ages.

She looked up at him and started to speak, "Sor..." and he quickly interjected, tenderly putting his fingers to her lips.

"Don't say anything. It's okay, really, it's okay."

This was an automatic response that wanted the incident forgotten, no discussion, just the familiar urge to move on.

He looked at the kitchen table, filled with fruitcake, scones, and a sugar-dusted sponge cake. Each delicacy was presented to look good with eye-catching detail. The message was clear: *these are your favourites and they are for you.*

After a few moments in each other's arms, he gave her squeeze.

"Smells good. Is it my imagination or is that cakes I see before me?"

"Your imagination, be damned. It's your nose for a good feed. Yes, it's cake. I made a mess of it actually, but perhaps we can salvage something."

This meant that some small thing had not quite gone right, something unnoticeable by a hungry bloke: the top not quite level, icing or jam inserted a little unevenly, a bubble here, a bubble there. Nevertheless, the cakes would taste wonderful, as always. He nodded sagely and Alison knew what he was thinking. She huffed playfully.

"Well, you taste them – you'll eat anything."

She gave him a wan smile and he kissed her forehead. It was always the way, when things seemed to get back to normal, he grabbed the chance for tenderness with both hands, yearning for everything to be the same as it had been in halcyon times; but it never seemed to last.

Later they ate a simple meal of spaghetti bolognaise followed by a piece of the fruitcake, which was as tasty as he thought it would be.

"How about watching, *Sleepless in Seattle*, you know, that lovely cheesy romance with Tom Hanks and Meg Ryan."

Alison smiled. "Yes, why not, I need a feel-good moment."

He put the DVD on and took her in his arms. They settled back for a quiet evening. Alison cuddled up to him, resting her head against his chest.

Throughout the film, he made mental notes on the Beamish suicide case; after all, he knew the plot backwards.

It was Alison's warmth he wanted next to him, not entertainment. The junior hero in the film, Jonah, played a key part in bringing the two people together; Ted wished there was a third party to help him through his personal maze.

The large meal and the events of the day took a toll on both of them and they felt drowsy. Ted could not get the vision of the bloody, headless corpse out of his mind. What on earth would possess anyone to commit suicide by hanging? Then he shuddered and realised all too well what a sense of hopelessness can do to anyone.

Alison dozed and began to purr, which made him smile.

After a couple of hours, wrapped against her body, Ted felt himself stiffen. He pressed against her and held her tight, feeling the blood flow, so much so it was almost painful. The vision of Patricia Lenahan, dressed in a cream skirt and blouse with her blonde hair moving in a breeze crossed his mind, but he loyally forced it out. He just wanted to live this moment, to embrace it and pretend that everything was all right. Alison was here in his arms and felt soft - he wanted her like crazy. She smelled of bath oil and a light perfume, probably her favourite, *Fifth Avenue,* from Elizabeth Arden. His left hand reached down her body and gently along the smoothness of her thigh, whilst his right hand softly moved the hair from her face, just as the penultimate emotional scene in the film showed Meg Ryan coming out of the lift on top of the Empire State building to where she thinks Tom Hanks will be.

He looked at Alison and tenderly kissed her ear, muttering to himself, *come back to me...*

Sadly, Hanks and his son Jonah weren't there. She's late and they've gone, and she looks forlornly around her. The screenplay was artful and the feeling of disappointment visceral.

Suddenly, Alison woke with a start. Ignoring his firmness against her, she waved away his hand irritably. "What are you up to?"

"Oh, just wondered..." Ted replied.

"Wondered what?" she said, straightening up and wriggling from his grasp. Her whole demeanour was different, as though the gentle evening had disappeared like a soft mist dispersed by an intrusive breeze, as though it never happened.

He searched for an excuse and clumsily blurted, "Oh, er, just wondered if you needed to take more pills."

"Ah, pills. Yes, of course. The bloody pills. I'll take them now," she huffed. Yawning and without looking at him she added carelessly, "I'm off to bed," stood up and went upstairs.

The blood drained from his loins.

Ted closed his eyes, resigned himself to the solitude and put his feet up on the arm of the couch to watch the end of the film. Ryan, Jonah and Hanks had now met and were walking away, with linked arms, and background music heralded a happy ending. He switched off the set box, breathing deeply to keep his heart from pounding hard against his chest. The emotional twists and turns of the day had taken their toll. Settling back, he recalled the image of the petite Dr Patricia Lenahan and deliberately let it stay a while – a long while.

Then the blood flowed again.

3

Jane Kavanagh let her hands glide over the smooth wooden steering wheel as she moved her face gently left and right in the summer breeze that flowed over the windscreen of her open top Jaguar XKR. Driving this car made her feel totally at ease and relaxed. Today, she needed that feeling of wellbeing. The past few weeks had been frenetic and complicated, but emerging information had given the case a jump-start it needed. Her dark green eyes flashed in the rear-view mirror and her hair fluttered outside her sailing cap in the warm breeze. She felt good.

The countryside was resplendent in the spring sunshine. Patches of bluebells added colour against the woodland and long brown ploughed fields, flat in the Anglian landscape. Seagulls hovered and bobbed around a tractor ploughing its way slowly across the land, in the hope of something to eat as the soil was turned over in large strips.

Jane realised her mind was wandering. *Focus on the job, Kavanagh,* she remonstrated with herself. Over-confidence leads to mistakes and mistakes are dangerous. She frowned and reminded herself that investigative work in the UK was straight forward, but elsewhere in the world the utmost care was needed, because she and her fellow operatives were always on their own. It was made very clear to her that if apprehended, they were not part of MI6, Europol or Interpol, or even the bloody Co-op. This was why they were so well paid, or at least so the argument went.

For all that, Jane enjoyed the work and accepted this corporate excuse. She contrasted her current salary with what she earned as a second lieutenant in the British Army; her days in uniform only just paid her mess bills.

After thirty minutes of pleasant motoring, with her stereo loudly playing her favourite jazz music, she approached the seaside town of Cromer and followed directions to the police station.

It was time for patience, diplomacy and lots of listening. She was, after all, entering a highly charged, male dominated arena: the Norfolk Constabulary.

"Here we go," she thought, "lots of testosterone to deal with!"

Det Supt Ted Sanderson walked up to Mike Daniels and Nicola who were sitting at a desk that was groaning with box files and papers and said, without the nicety of a morning greeting, "Anything interesting?"

Mike didn't look up. "Well, yes, there is actually. Amongst all this NHS trivia we found these." He pushed two pieces of paper across the desk.

Ted was in no mood for guesswork, he had been told that the chief constable wanted to see him and just wanted facts. "No, just tell me, Mike."

"Okay, it's interesting that these bank balances show that Beamish has over £40,000 in his current account and £250,000 in his deposit account. I know that GPs recently negotiated an increase in salaries, but I didn't know they could easily amass this kind of cash. It was transferred mostly from salary. Interestingly, he doesn't seem to have spent anything from his current account on food or any kind of expense that you and I would normally arrange. You know what I mean, direct debits and that sort of thing. He must have paid for absolutely everything in cash. He could have paid from another account that we don't have a record of, but I doubt it. So, the question is, where did the cash-in-hand come from, you can't live on thin air?"

Ted stroked his chin. "So why commit suicide? With so much cash sloshing around it's more a case to live if you ask me."

"Ah, there's the rub, Guv," said Nicola. "His wife is in a very bad way in an expensive nursing home. All his assets are in trust to keep her comfortable for the rest of her life. His local solicitor has power of attorney. There seems to be enough to see her through, so to speak. If this was his goal, he achieved it."

Ted probed absentmindedly.

"What else?"

Mike leaned back in his chair. "We still have to wait for the forensic and post mortem reports, but having had the dubious pleasure of seeing Dr Beamish's face I have to say that he was mighty upset just before the time of death. It was tearstained and, well, the whole process of his suicide was badly planned almost like it was a sudden decision. He's a doctor for Christ's sake. Couldn't he just take an overdose or a lethal injection?"

Nicola looked up. "Yeah, guv, perhaps we should consider analysing some of the patient records for inconsistencies. Remember that Dr Lenahan said Beamish was becoming a little absent-minded and vague. I thought I might check his record keeping. Let's just see what comes to light."

Ted allowed himself to smile. Nicola was one of his prodigies and he was impressed by her diligence.

"Well done, Nicola. I look forward to that. For now, I have to do a report for the chief constable and the press about the incident. On my way in the duty inspector whispered that there was some excitement being generated. I get all the good jobs, eh?"

Mike gave a wry laugh. "Yeah, right boss. Now go before we get too jealous and ask for time off in compensation."

Ted turned away. Sometimes he didn't know what he would do without good work colleagues.

China

Two blue wicker chairs on the wooden veranda of a small boarding house in Sang Yong had been pulled together and Chin Kwok sat in one, using the other as a footstool. Even at his age he half expected his mother to appear wielding a broom, to remonstrate with him to remove his feet.

The boarding house was close to the building where the bodies of the executed prisoners had been delivered the previous day. His room was comfortable and simply furnished with items made of rattan, and the plasterwork had been painted sea green. He ate breakfast in the house, but turned down other meals offered daily by the proprietor, who didn't often see people from out of town. It was better to use restaurants, because he would be able to meet local people and talk to them about what was going on in the grey stainless steel and concrete monolith across the street. His mission was to look for clues relating to the disposal of the bodies of executed prisoners, a bit like playing Trivial

Pursuit – you simply never knew what information would be revealed or how you should play your hand. However, he knew he had to be careful and resolved to ask general tourist questions relating to the architecture and planning of the town.

Later the same day, he was lunching at a local restaurant and recognised three girls he had seen at the institute, as they sat eating and laughing at a nearby table.

A plump girl, with a red scarf around the top of her head laughed as the waiter took her order. "Noodles in chicken soup and some dumplings to start," she nodded towards her friends, "and Dragon Tattoo over there can have duck's feet."

Her companions stared and laughed, making flapping motions with their hands.

Dragon Tattoo simply stared back at them and took a long drag of his cigarette. His expression was so dark the girls turned away uneasily and started to chat about an upcoming music festival.

This man was an outsider of the group. Time to work on him.

Chin moved closer to the man and pretended to accidentally knock over his drink.

"Hey, watch out," said Dragon Tattoo gruffly, squaring up to Chin. It was clear why the man was shunned by his workmates.

"Oh, sorry. That was stupid of me," said Chin with a smile, not backing away and facing down the belligerence with a determined look directly into his eyes.

"I should punch you," said Dragon Tattoo with an angry scowl.

Chin took a bold step. "I wouldn't do that if I were you. I can take care of myself pretty well and I'd beat you easily." The man sat back in his bamboo chair and looked at him sternly with a half-smile on his face, summing him up.

Before he could speak, Chin reached out a hand. "I am Chin Kwok. I come from the south, close to the province of Hong Kong. Let's be friends, not fight over a spilt drink. What are you drinking? I will buy you two."

Dragon Tattoo paused for a second, then shook Chin's hand and laughed, revealing gaps in his brown stained and broken teeth; they were in such bad condition, he would have been better off without them. He told Chin that he was not working on shift until the afternoon of the next day. Chin realised that it was going to be long night.

The next day Chin awoke with the biggest headache he had ever had in his life. Rice wine didn't suit him and his brain was doing its best to cope despite his ears ringing and his optic nerves wobbling. He recalled the evening's events.

Dragon Tattoo was horribly drunk. He had difficulty focussing and his glass often missed his mouth as he attempted to swig more rice wine. He smiled crookedly and said, "They were criminals, enemies of the people – I feel nothing for them. We unloaded them like pigs from slaughter. That's my job and only that. But I know where to look and see what's happening."

He tapped his nose with two gnarled fingers conspiratorially, then swilled down another glass of rice wine splashing some on his shirt. "I look through a crack in the wall. Nobody sees me. The bodies are taken to a large room with lots of tables and they are opened up like sardine tins. Organs are removed and packed in boxes."

Chin had tried his best to look disinterested - inside he felt morbid. The man made it sound like stripping cars for spare parts. At first Chin thought it was the wine talking and he was pretending to be clever, but a sickly feeling came over him when he realised that he was likely to be telling the truth.

He wanted to vomit.

"What's left is fed to the dogs," said Dragon Tattoo, pretending to snarl.

Chin realised that he was trying to shock him. He knew it was untrue because he had seen a large industrial incinerator behind the main building and occasionally detected a pungent smell when it noisily fired up - in any case there were few dogs.

Before Dragon Tattoo passed out, he told of small air-conditioned wagons that would turn up to collect various items packed in containers. That was interesting and pertinent.

Chin's training in the Hong Kong Police Force did not expose him to death on such an industrial scale. His work in London sorting out several of the city's Chinese gangs was never as gruesome. It was, however, dangerous and badly paid. So, he left to earn more money, enticed to assignments working on the fringes of international policing. This was not what he really wanted to do, but at least the pay was good.

Today Chin would let his head repair itself and drink nothing but water. Then he would wait. Wait to catch one of the air-conditioned vehicles arriving and leaving the complex – then follow it.

England

Ted Sanderson straightened his tie and brushed a few toast crumbs from his trousers as he stood in the corridor outside the office of the chief constable. Alec Ayers was a small, spry man who demanded high standards and everyone knew that he was particularly irritable when his officers appeared scruffy. He had no patience with camouflage and his subordinates had to get to the point and leave out the frills when briefing him.

He was uncomfortably irascible and habitually fashioned lines of argument around indisputable everyday facts, in such a way that to think anything different was utterly stupid. Full of his own self-importance, he controlled the world around him. Ayers was the last of the breed of red-meat-eating senior policemen; unreconstructed and unrepentant, and for his last year in the force everyone knew that he would remain every bit the 'old-fashioned copper'.

Ted could only assume that today's interrogation concerned the Beamish suicide – what fun that would be. He sucked in the stuffy warm air of the corridor and knocked on the door of the outer office. The personal assistant, Marjorie Bloom, called him in.

"He's waiting for you - now," she said, getting up and scuttling him into the chief constable's office. It was conservatively decorated in green and cream wallpaper, with team and group photographs, and award certificates adorning the walls, including one of Ayers holding his Queen's Police Medal. There was a large mahogany desk around which eight chairs were placed. The room smelled of Sandalwood. Ted had been here several times before for everything from thanks to upbraiding. He was no stranger to the senior man's mercurial moods.

As he entered, he stopped, surprised at the sight of a woman sitting at the table making notes in a Filofax. She was slim but not skinny and wore a light grey suit. She did not look up.

The chief constable sat at his desk and appeared to be signing various documents. He looked over his reading glasses. "Ah, Ted. Come in, come in, I want you to meet someone."

He got up from behind his desk and walked towards the woman, beckoning Ted to follow. She stood up, smiled pleasantly and extended her hand to Ted, who was captivated by her almond shaped green eyes.

"Jane Kavanagh," she said, finally locating his fingers. "Pleased to meet you, Ted. I've heard a lot about you."

Her hand felt softer than it looked. He muttered what sounded like a thank you and they were ushered to sit at the committee table.

"Yes, yes, good man our Ted. Now let's get down to business."

The chief constable put his hands together and looked directly at Ted.

"Okay then, first things first. Jane here is going to work with you on the strange suicide case, that Dr Beamish chappie."

Ted frowned.

Jane smiled, and gently interjected. "Yes. I know it's a bit strange. I'll explain what my presence is all about. First off, I run a team of investigators covering the illegal worldwide trade in human organs. We've reason to believe that Dr Beamish could be implicated."

Ted swallowed and took a deep breath as she began to speak. Every man knows instinctively when he has let his work drift, existing in a comfort zone, padded by the loyalty of colleagues and the protection that longevity in a post brings. But then comes that moment, a sharp jolt to the senses, when a bell rings and a 'general alert' sounds that something is up. That something was Jane Kavanagh. Her very nature, precision and confidence made him feel like an amateur. She looked and sounded sharp and he had not encountered anyone like that for some time.

She looked directly at him. "Surprised?"

Ted weighed up the situation quickly and chose the high ground.

"Actually no," he said, feigning a casual tone, "prima facie, it seems as though the man committed a straightforward suicide. However, we noticed several factors, particularly the odd way he managed to sustain his life-style to make provision for his wife who is in a nursing home, he has very substantial savings and a healthy current account balance. Otherwise, we are concentrating on his work where several medical records in his files don't look quite right, but it's early days yet. We knew something was odd. Above all, the big questions are what was he up to and why top himself?"

The chief constable looked pleased, sat back in his chair and smiled broadly, "Good show," he said loudly, clearly pleased that Ted was, 'on his team.'

Feeling confidant and more in charge of the situation, Ted unwisely added, "If you don't mind me saying, I am surprised to see that we have a visit from, what, the Metropolitan Police?" He looked at Jane and splayed his hands. "Couldn't we be trusted to follow our lines of enquiry and advise on what we find? If the man is an international criminal, couldn't we be told?"

He put his hands in his lap and then noticed that the chief constable and Jane Kavanagh exchanged looks. Ted sensed he had blundered.

The chief constable looked awkward. "Ted, I'm sorry. I should've introduced Jane in more detail. I was coming to that. Jane represents MI6, who are working with Interpol and Europol. This is a serious case, Ted. It isn't something that can be handled lightly at local level and from my reading of the brief it needs the utmost care. I understand that Jane is an experienced agent and we must work together to get a result. So, she is definitely not with the Met."

Jane interjected. "Ted, I would be as upset as you if I thought my patch was being trampled on, but it's as your boss says. It's a complex case with international dimensions and very difficult to grip, but we now have a chance to follow a lead that may take us to the ringleaders operating this disgusting crime. For the record, I'm here on a hunch from recent surveillance of a local hospice and purely by happenstance, only just learned of the Beamish suicide. A quick check by our in-house people put Dr Beamish in the frame. I want to meld the two investigations. It has Home Office clearance. I'm aware of your length of service and am really glad to be working with you, Ted."

Ted gave her ten out of ten. Experienced leadership uses recognition, support, teaming and encouragement to win the day; she peeled away his suspicion and antagonism, like that of an orange skin, exposing the delicate core of his personality, putting him and his boss completely at ease.

He opened his mouth to speak, but closed it again - he was outclassed.

"Here's the crunch. Human organs are big money. It's becoming easier for hospitals to legally obtain them, as countries call for its citizens to make a positive statement or carry donor cards to avoid delays. The sad fact of life is that demand is rising. Increased selectivity, especially in the USA, about the age and condition of organs, makes organ transplantation a tortuous business. In some religious countries, it's completely banned. This leaves a void, which is unsurprisingly filled by unscrupulous criminals. The major consumer of organs is the USA. It's illegal for citizens to negotiate the sale or purchase of organs on American soil, however, heavy fines and threats of jail are no deterrent. It's difficult or nigh on impossible to catch buyers or agents."

Ted sat back, now fully engaged in the details of the brief and interjected. "Yeah, that would be difficult. But I bet that desperate people simply go on holiday to get their operations done. Listen, I don't want to appear ghoulish, but if people want to sell their organs, should they not be allowed to do so?"

Jane stiffened. "Ted, that's true in some respects. But this trade needs to be regulated and overseen by medical experts to avoid catastrophic life-threatening outcomes. This is where we focus on the so-called donors. You see, some people are kidnapped, drugged and have their organs removed without their consent – it depends where you live in the world. On the other hand, if you are unlucky enough to be sentenced for a crime in China then the chances of a quick execution and a bountiful human organ harvest to meet a predetermined shopping list are high."

Ted winced and nodded, accepting the ugly facts. The chief constable squirmed in his chair.

Jane went on to explain that improvements in cool storage and development of Cyclosporine, an immunosuppressant drug that prevents rejection of organs by the recipient's body, had opened up opportunities to increase the availability of organs.

"Donors are paid pitifully low rates in Pakistan, Turkey or Egypt, say six hundred US dollars, and organs are sold on for over ten times that figure. Importantly, the demand is high, which of course is what fuels this hideous trade."

The chief constable looked up, "Where is it all happening?"

Jane reached for a slim paper file.

"Here are some reports that give the statistics on where the harvesting is most prevalent. As you can see," she flicked the pages, "it really is a worldwide business with differing dimensions depending on location and, frankly, market need."

She flopped the files on the table in front of Ted and the chief constable.

"Nice little scams circumvent national laws. Livers, spleens, pancreas, kidneys or brains go for anything from seventy-five dollars to three hundred dollars for a spinal cord. We squeezed that out of a suspect, but sadly that was all. Anyone we question goes into complete silence. Let's cut to the quick – in 2014 it was estimated that the illegal trade in organs and tissue of all kinds generated between $840 million and $1.7 billion, and that's only 10% of the traceable transactions. That's bigger than the drug trade – as I said, it's big business."

The chief constable and Ted skim read the content.

Ted looked up. "And the local focus?"

"Ah, yes, Dr Beamish. Well, it's really quite simple. Our agents staked out a so-called health clinic in Romania and a vehicle arrived from the UK and delivered a consignment. We don't know what was in the packages, but we do know that the Romanian hospital concerned is suspected to be in the forefront of organ transplants. Well, we followed the van back to the UK and traced it. It's a private hire chap who does all sorts of deliveries to Eastern Europe. This particular consignment had customs documents that indicated the items were delicate hospital instruments to be transported in coolers."

Ted looked up from the papers in front of him.

"Where from?"

"From the Maria Cresswell Hospice here in Norfolk. On my way here yesterday, our boys in the back-room did some low-key information-gathering it appears that the late Dr Beamish has had a lot of dealings with them, as indeed have several other doctors throughout the region."

She paused for effect. "The common factor is, they all needed money."

Downstairs in the station's main office, DS Nicola Bradbury carefully sorted out piles of notes and forms from the mess she found in Dr Beamish's practice office. She apprised Ted Sanderson of the major observations prior to his appointment with the chief constable. Now she was looking for obvious clues, mismatches, or patterns in diagnosis. Nicola was professional in her approach and knew that it was all about keeping an open mind and patiently sifting the information in front of her. An experienced local GP was nominated to be the police medical adviser and he would help to review some of her results and carry out a perfunctory check of Beamish's paperwork. She intended to extend the agreement to review the practice records. A little charm goes a long way.

Eager to please and get on the good side of his new boss, DC Hovens looked up from his desk, "Oh, sorry, I forgot to say that Dr Beamish's home computer is being 'plumbed' by experts. They look for child porn or anything that could generate such a feeling of guilt that would lead someone to commit suicide. Apparently, the possibility of being found out often drives people to distraction. Do we need to put something in the notes that it went to IT today at about 1000 hrs?"

"Thanks, yes, do that. I wonder what they will come up with?" Nicola made a note. Was Beamish into child porn, or drugs perhaps? Some suicide notes arouse suspicion, but Beamish's read:

To whomsoever finds my body: I leave this world a weary and sad man. I know I have done wrong and may God forgive me. My conscience is too heavy for me to carry on living.

For now, I am happy that my dear wife Angela is well provided for and should records be lost or confused, this note signifies my dying wish that all my estate is held in trust for my wife to cover her residential home fees for as long as she shall live. After she dies, the residue should be donated to Cancer Research.

May God have mercy on my soul and damn those who tempted me into a horrible mess and to work against my oath.

Jack Beamish, MD.

Nicola put her fingers either side of her brow and turned to DC Hovens, who was also looking at a transcript of the note.

"That's interesting. What temptation, and what did he mean, '...to work against my oath...'? What had he done? The post mortem found no signs of drug abuse, although he had been drinking a lot on the evening he died. The report also showed that he had no nasty sexually transmitted diseases."

DC Hovens unwisely cracked, "I wonder how the medicos worked that one out."

Nicola shot him a stern glance and continued. "He was not suffering from any life-threatening condition either. On the other hand, his bank records showed that he did have a very large cash balance. So why commit suicide?"

The day drifted on and she pulled together other information from her team of detective constables. Beamish had been left no legacies, nor was he, so far as she could ascertain, named as a beneficiary in any recent last will and testament. The conundrum remained that he spent none of his salary whatsoever. It was a mystery, but Nicola was determined to solve it. She was ambitious and this focused her energies – it earned the nickname, 'Pushy Nic".

The photographs of the body at the scene of the suicide were horrible. Some of the young constables cracked dark jokes. She couldn't really stop them – it was all part of the macho culture. Besides, it was difficult enough getting to grips with her promotion and supervising these young bloods, not that they were that much younger than her, without alienating herself unnecessarily.

She got up from her desk to stretch and get a hot coffee, just as DI Mike Daniels came into the office with a large cardboard box, which he tipped onto an adjacent table.

"Hi," she said, "any luck at all?"

Mike grimaced, "Dunno. Strange chap. His whole life was wrapped up in visiting his wife Angela in a residential nursing home and providing a trust fund for her. She has Alzheimer's disease."

"Yeah, I know. It's sad, he seems to have been totally focused on her needs. He's beginning to come over as a nice bloke." Nicola frowned and shook her head. "Seems crazy to be so suspicious about him really."

A couple of young DCs swaggered over to see what was going on and to get close to the scent of 'Pushy Nic'. It was widely understood that the first to 'get there', so to speak, would receive a magnum of champagne from his peers; although considered to be a 'mission impossible' it was worth a try.

"And so, esteemed ones, what have we here?" said DC Gerry Winters the youngest and brightest of the group, brushing his curly blonde hair back, his blue eyes flashing to accompany a broad smile at Mike, but more so to Nicola.

Nicola politely smiled back; she was ambitious but not stupid. She knew what was going on. In her early police career, she had had the same bet with female contemporaries on a handsome male boss, as she rightly suspected the boys in her team had on her. However, she was comfortable with the compliment and was happy to play along. Oddly, it gave her a strange feeling of power over them.

Mike irritably moved the items around the surface of the table, pushing a girlie magazine to one side. In the old days, Nicola used to blush, but that was very much a thing of the past, as was boyish banter of a sexual nature. She could see that the DCs itched to make saucy comments, but would not, wary of disciplinary action. Any form of sexual banter was banned outright in today's police force, even the most innocuous comment could be seen as 'acceptance'.

The items on the table comprised notebooks, diaries and a few grainy photographs. They were the family kind, with Beamish and his wife, Angela, looking happy and content. He was certainly slimmer back then. It seemed as though there were no children. Other items included pens, paperbacks, receipts of all kinds and a large round brass paperweight bearing the name Artaxis along the bottom edge, and a five-pointed star surrounding the Leonardo da Vinci drawing, 'Man.' in the middle.

"I fancy the paperweight," said Farmer, which earned him a stare from Nicola.

"Farmer, have you checked all the witness statements?"

He winced and knew that she was dismissing him, and playfully touched his forelock in mock salute as he went back to his desk.

The mood in the team room was lazily casual and without focus and this irritated Nicola. Mike seemed uninterested in the case and had earlier indicated that it was, 'just a bloody suicide'.

A team brief was scheduled for the next day. Nicola was determined to research all the angles; besides, she had a definite itch about the suicide of Dr Beamish.

4

Ted and Jane sat at a corner table in the canteen. It was quiet and the sun shone into the room from a window that needed a good clean. Opposite, police staff chatted noisily and the sound of the catering service provided privacy.

"Ted. We need to keep things simple. We have clearance to set up a small team and you are the expert on who to include. Can I suggest that I be introduced to the team straight away so that I can explain the big picture? It's going to be challenging melding the two cases and I want to make it clear what an important part they will be in an international investigation."

Ted agreed. "Yeah, good idea. We also need to underline the fact that the investigation has to be carried out in absolute secrecy and information needs to be tightly controlled. We can't have leaks to comrades or the press for that matter. The world at large must believe that we are assigned to clear up the suicide attempt and that it's all straightforward and above suspicion. To avoid compromising further opportunities and, for form's sake, we'll return all the paperwork to the medical practice after taking photocopies of course."

"Can we hack into the medical centre computer system?"

Ted thought for a moment and made a hurried note. "Yes, but high-level approval is needed, but it can be done."

They agreed that the remainder of the work should start from square one. Ted would lead the team and Jane was to provide essential support and feedback to Europol and Interpol. A separate office had been allocated to the team and was being set up with a security lock on the door and screened IT links.

Jane quickly added, "To avoid prying eyes, the team will have to do all their own cleaning."

"That'll be popular. Still, if we grab their enthusiasm, they won't mind."

Ted decided to keep his small team to those already working on the case. DI Mike Daniels and DS Nicola Bradbury were good value and the two young male officers, Farmer Hovens and Gerry Winters, had shown aptitude on other cases and, importantly, could be relied on for their loyalty and confidentiality.

He worked with Jane to prepare a brief and an hour later they sat in front of the new team, ready to go.

"Okay, listen in. I want to introduce you to Jane Kavanagh. Jane works for MI6."

The team straightened at once and looked at her.

"The nature of the Beamish suicide had a new dimension and you've been selected to form a special investigation team." He paused to let this remark sink in. "It would appear that our good GP, Jack Beamish, could have been involved in rather murky stuff involving the illegal removal and sale of body parts. More of that later. We need to do a lot of admin to set up a team infrastructure and Nicola I would like you to lead that. For now, I'll hand you over to Jane for the big picture."

Jane began, quietly, and covered the background information, along the lines explained to the chief constable, but this time with much more detail about her role, adding the international and political dimensions. It was gory and hard-hitting. The most interesting part was the suspicion that there was something going on in the local Maria Cresswell Hospice, to which the late Dr Beamish had links.

DI Mike Daniels was interested, but clearly not excited. On the other hand, the three younger officers hung on Jane's every word. Ted saw from the looks on their faces that they were like coiled springs ready to dive into the task. He envied Jane's ability to connect with the team so quickly.

Jane paused and Ted chose to make his mark.

"Okay, guys. I can't emphasise enough the importance of secrecy in all that you do. You only need to say one word, just one word, to your colleagues out there," he raised his arm in the direction of the main office, "and it will find its way to the local newspaper and bingo, the cover is broken. The case would be severely compromised and we'll look stupid, at home and to other crimes agencies. To be trusted and brought into this investigation is a real compliment to the local force, so let's live up to it."

Before he could continue, Jane made a new point and effortlessly resumed her brief. Ted was mildly irritated. He knew it was unreasonable behaviour on his part, but felt a bit like a schoolboy whose game has been interrupted.

Jane had the team's undivided attention.

"Look, this is an unusual case for you guys. I know that. We've loads of snippets of information from various sources, but as yet there is nothing concrete. In your world, a crime happens, you garner the clues, then sort out suspects and you create a narrative and then investigate. Well, this is different, we've not one or two, but thousands of victims, and we don't have direct leads to the possible mastermind and key players. So, we have to break things down into key components. We must first research the information in our possession, that's to say, what we know about Dr Beamish, and the Maria Cresswell Hospice. That's going to be difficult, but just keep asking questions, turning information over in your mind, testing all the time. Then we need to broaden the investigation to include other doctors in the region, especially those with links to the hospice."

Nicola spoke up, almost excitedly. "What about the worldwide picture?"

"Don't you worry about that. I'll give you all the information you need and keep you up to date as to where your local investigation fits in and what is going on elsewhere in the world. But let's get this crystal clear. I have to get to know you much more, to trust you. I want to do that. Frankly, the hospice is our hottest lead in the UK and that's where I think we should focus our immediate efforts. It's exciting, guys, don't underestimate your role in this mission."

After that, it was easy going. She made her mark clearly and logically, without hectoring or barking as if in a cheap television police drama. The team was motivated. They now knew the investigation was well beyond the normal range of police work and the excitement was palpable.

Jane had been outstanding and Ted felt like a resentful bystander.

Ted arrived home just as it was getting dark. He wondered whether or not he should be pleased at his new task or disappointed that he had extra work to do. Over the years, he had quarried a role for himself in the local force and earned promotion into a job that he coveted. In his youth, he loved the fascination of ploughing through piles of data and evidence to find clues to gradually unveil the truth. Now he left all that to junior officers and only really became involved in the presentation of the final result. He did not relish all this international stuff. Experience taught him that operations like this led to either success or frustrating failure, with the odds stacked hugely in favour of the latter.

He parked his car outside his home and strolled up the lavender-lined pathway, taking in the soft scent as he brushed past the flower heads. As he opened his front door, he had a strange feeling of foreboding. The house was quiet, no noise from the radio or television. The vacuum cleaner lay on its side in the hallway with a torn dust bag nearby. A picture of a baby lay on the floor, its glass shattered.

"Alison. Are you okay?"

There was no response.

He walked into the kitchen, then the dining room, but there was no sign of her. Then he went into the lounge and gasped. Alison lay on the couch, pale faced, clothes askew and one leg draped over the edge. Ted rushed to her side and immediately felt her pulse. To his relief, there was just the slightest trace. As he reached for his cell-phone he saw a brown plastic pill bottle with its familiar printed label on the side lying open – it was empty. He dialled 999.

"Hello, yes, er, emergency and ambulance please. It's an overdose," he said, his throat tightening as he used the term. "Ambulance, yes, overdose on Prozac. No, not Paracetamol, it looks like Prozac. 9 Granby Close." He gave his mobile number, adding, "Okay, yes, I'll try and wake her and get her to drink. Be quick, please."

Putting his phone on the coffee table he quickly pulled Alison's body into a sitting position and gently slapped her face. Thankfully, she groaned.

"Get up, get up, Alison," he said urgently.

When she failed to stir, he pulled her frail body into a standing position and half-dragged, half-walked her to the kitchen. Her legs began to move and took a little of the strain. Propping her against the sink, he ran the tap and filled a glass with cold water. Tipping her head back he let some water pour into her mouth. She gurgled, and his spirits rose. He made her drink more and she began to writhe in his arms. Suddenly, she vomited loudly. He dragged her back to the couch, and satisfied that she was now conscious, cleaned up the mess.

The front door bell rang several times and he hurriedly opened it.

"Christ, what the hell do you want?"

Jane stood there aghast.

"Well, fuck you too Detective Superintendent. I was just bringing you this." She held up his A4 Filofax and glared at him. "You left it on the bonnet of my car."

There was a squeal of rubber against the gritty road behind her. She turned and saw an ambulance. Two paramedics got out and rushed up the path.

Ted put his right hand to his head and addressed them. "In the lounge, she's not in a coma, but isn't very conscious."

The paramedics ran straight into the lounge.

Jane's face softened from anger to concern. "Ted, what's going on?"

He pursed his lips and grimaced, looking over her shoulder he said, "My wife, Alison, took an overdose," adding tightly, "I'd be grateful for your complete confidentiality on this please."

Without giving a reply, she moved past him, gently taking him by the arm and closing the door.

The hospital waiting room was rank. It smelled of disinfectant and urine. The disinfectant was excusable, but where the urine came from was a mystery. The usual array of customers, some looking vulnerable and others agitated, because they weren't allowed to smoke, sat around the waiting room in badly repaired chairs. Jane sat down beside Ted and held out a polystyrene cup of weak tea from a dispensing machine. He screwed up his face at the taste.

"Okay?"

He half looked at her. "Yeah, okay. Sorry I was such an oaf. When I saw you at the front door, I was expecting a paramedic. You rather threw me. No excuses, it was unforgivable."

"Forget it, I would've done the same." She paused and said, carefully, "Was this a surprise?"

Ted looked at her as she crossed the boundary into his personal arena, but he was now beyond pride.

"I guess so, but then again I guess not. I don't really want to talk about it."

They sat in silence until the doctor came and told Ted that Alison was going to be all right and needed to sleep the night through. He looked relieved. Jane had driven him to the hospital and now she led him out. When they reached the fresh air, it was obvious that Ted had had enough and his normally handsome chiselled features cracked into a grimace. She watched him move to a quiet corner and his shoulders shook. Keen to preserve his dignity and privacy, she politely turned away.

Back home Ted tidied up the lounge. Jane watched him and did not let her concern register. A close-knit and tightly focused team was needed to carry out the UK investigation, to add to work done in Europe, the Middle East and Asia. Jane was weighing up the predicament she was now in. When Ted finished tidying, he turned and beckoned her to sit on the sofa.

"Look, sorry about earlier. It's been a long haul. I seem to be saying sorry a lot, so perhaps I should at least tell you a bit about our lives. There was an accident and I don't want to go into it, but the long and short of it is that we've been unable to have another child and it's been a running sore."

He paused and it was obvious that he was searching for the right words. She filled the awkward silence.

"Ted, don't feel sore at breaking down in front of me. I've been through the mill too you know. When I was undercover in the army, in Northern Ireland, I saw a little girl blown to bits when a mindless Protestant threw a pipe bomb. That just did it for me. I had a nervous breakdown and was in hospital for a time. You should've seen me and a rather large Parachute Regiment sergeant bawling in each other's arms – it was quite comic. You don't have the monopoly on emotions, my friend."

Ted smiled at the ease with which she drew a parallel between their emotions and at the same time let him know a bit more about her past.

She went on. "Later, when I recovered and left the army, I accepted the offer of international intelligence work and went undercover in Bosnia. Since then, I've buried myself in work with all sorts of security agencies, Europol, Interpol and even a bit outside the fence, so to speak. It keeps me sane. I just want you to know that."

Ted sat back and sucked in air. "Thanks, for that. Look, Jane, I didn't like you at first. Sorry, it was jealousy, I guess. Alison's condition always stopped me from doing anything exciting or different and I suppose I was envious from the moment I met you. What a chump, eh?"

He ran his hands through his hair. "I just want to get back to the copper I was."

Jane looked around and spotted a bottle of Jameson's whisky.

"Now then, my Irish ancestry wholeheartedly approves of your choice of the hard stuff. It's early evening, so why don't we have a tipple or two?"

Relieved to have unloaded a little, Ted collected two glasses and opened the whisky. He sat down on the couch heavily and Jane enticed him into conversation.

"So, tell me, how did you get to be a copper?"

"Oh, it's all very ordinary really. My mother encouraged me to be academic, mind you she had plenty of space since my dad spent most of his time in front of the television. She gave me a focus. It sounds really cheesy, but a few things about my school days left dark shadows in my mind, perhaps even shaping my character. I remember as a gawky teenager, standing by when a soft, foppish young boy was physically and verbally abused by some of the rough farm lads at school. The image of the face slapping and humiliation always leaves me empty inside. I desperately wanted to intervene, but I turned away. I just wasn't brave or big enough to help. I got fitter and bigger from a fair bit of gym work. As I got older it just seemed the right choice of career for me." He paused and added ruefully, "Not sure where I am now!"

"Well now, Ted. Since we are on the same team, let's share. My story is simpler. My parents doted on me, but however nice that is, I felt suffocated. They wanted me to stay in Dublin, get married and have children. I rebelled. I'm too headstrong for normality. The rest is history. Anyway, I usually grow hostile towards anything that reminds me of me. So that's all your getting!"

Ted smiled gratefully. After an hour and a fifth double whisky his eyes began to close and he slowly drifted off to sleep. Jane got him a blanket and tucked him up on the sofa and he soon began to gently snore. Looking down at him, she felt a little jealous of his love for his wife. It suited her to be without a partner, but occasionally flirted with the notion that sharing her day with someone would be nice. However, for now, immersing herself in work was the tonic she needed and, importantly, she was in control.

Jane saw the real Ted. He was clearly a compassionate man, dedicated to helping people and judging by his current rank, successful, but was concerned that he appeared marooned and directionless. She was compassionate for his fractured life, yet already considering what pit props to put in place to stop the roof of the project from caving in - it was decision time. In the morning, she would need to have a difficult conversation with the chief constable.

She left quietly closing the front door

DS Nicola Bradbury was keyed up. She enthusiastically worked late into the night on the data they had collected from the medical practice with DC Farmer Hovens.

"Farmer, this stuff is interesting. There are regular numbers of patients, about three a month, directed to the Maria Cresswell Hospice. All of them diagnosed with leukaemia by a consultant oncologist at Norwich General Hospital. The same consultant signed all the letters, it was, let's see now, here we are, Rado Ilovic. What do we know about him? The letterheads show the hospital address as, 'The Royal Norwich Hospital'. Hasn't that changed?"

Farmer eagerly flipped his notepad open. "Well now, I made a quick call to the Primary Care Trust and they said they changed the hospital name three years ago, and don't use the logo that was on Ilovic's recent letters. Mr Rado Ilovic is a visiting cancer specialist from Bulgaria who was given the use of two small offices for research work. He is not directly connected to the oncology department and his Medical Institute in Sofia paid the Trust very handsomely for the use of the small office space. The hospital administrator was a bit trite and said it all worked well and money was short in the NHS these days, and it was also good to have an international dimension."

Nicola registered the loose grip on accountability displayed by the hospital. It stank of something more sinister.

"Farmer, you're a hero. I can't wait to tell Jane."

Farmer leaned back in his chair and smiled. "I think that you're out to impress our Europol lady," he said, adding, "she's a bit too old for me."

"Everyone's a bit too old for you, sprog," she retorted and he winced. "So where are we on the money trail then?"

Farmer reached for more notes. "As for this little lot, so far I've found forty-three receipts. They are all for cash for everything from shopping and fuel to purchases for clothes. This guy likes paying in cash. Oh, and even his utility bills are paid for in the same way. He takes cash to the bank or post office and raises a money order, or pays over the counter. I guess as we move towards a cashless society and carry out more checks on money laundering, this will become more difficult. However, he was so well respected and known by everyone in the town that he was able to pay this way without anyone commenting."

Nicola nodded and Farmer continued.

"The bank manager reviewed Beamish's personal account and was mortified. They were friends and because of this he never really saw a reason to suspect anything, but he did say that with anyone else he might have asked questions."

Nicola put her hands to her face.

"Farmer, do tell me you told him to keep this line of inquiry absolutely confidential?"

He flushed with boyish anger.

"Yes, of course. I do wish you wouldn't do that."

He stood up and strode away, saying over his shoulder. "I'm a good guy one minute and a dummy the next. You wouldn't have asked Gerry that. I'm not stupid you know."

As he stormed out of the office Jane came in.

"What's up with him?"

"Oh, me. I guess, I was a bit clumsy."

"Good thing that you said that. When we can't recognise when we've made a mistake, we keep on making them. Buy him a beer later," said Jane. "Keep your team on side, Nicola."

Nicola was quick to spot the opportunity to learn from Jane, who was competent, strong and had such a lot of experience - a woman in a man's world, displaying confidence and ability. She would always look to the superior who could do her the most good and was not going to get a conscience about that. Ted was a nice guy but he had let a number of things slip. She briefed Jane on the evidence so far. As hoped, she was impressed and told her so. Nicola felt good. There was more to do to tie up loose ends and she was determined to deliver.

Marjorie Bloom, personal assistant extraordinaire and self-appointed forecaster of internal storms saw Jane Kavanagh leave the chief constable's office with a determined look on her face. She decided to take him a cup of coffee straight away. He sat behind his desk twisting his fingers, his face red and the veins on the side of his neck throbbing. He didn't even look up or say 'thank you' and she knew that it was best to make a hasty retreat. She had well-tuned perception and put out a warning to all the senior officers in the station to beware for the rest of the day.

Jane walked slowly back down the stairs to the special operations office. Her ankle hurt where she twisted it on the rough pathway after a run that morning. It was probably the copious amounts of whisky the night before that had made her careless. Her discussion with the chief constable had been forthright, it was the only way to deal with a misogynist. There simply wasn't time to do other than outline Ted's situation – this conflicted with her personal integrity and mission focus; inevitably, mission came first.

The conversation with the chief constable was made easier when Mike Hancox called and bluntly explained what the Home Secretary had agreed regarding the management of the operation and that Jane's needs were paramount. The poor man was unused to being upstaged, least of all by a woman. Jane was firm without being rude.

She made her way back to the main office just as Ted was entering at the far end of the room. He talked to DC Gerry Winter, who pointed to the ceiling, which could only mean that Ted was being summoned. He looked towards Jane and smiled in recognition and understanding. She responded with a wave and hoped that he would not be disappointed in her.

Gerry caught up with Jane just as she reached Nicola and Farmer in the temporary team room. DI Mike Daniels ambled over and joined them. They sat around a large table laden with papers and charts.

"Right then, let's get down to work," as she spoke her eyes caught sight of something in the box of items removed from Dr Beamish's office and home. It was the brass paperweights.

"Something up, guv?" said Nicola Bradbury.

"Yes," she lifted one of the paperweights up and examined it. "This company paperweight is from Artaxis, one of a small number already under covert investigation by the FBI regarding illegal organ transplants and links through their associate companies to some dodgy clinics. Well, what do you know!"

They talked easily and freely, as Jane drew them closer.

"I am really excited about the situation so far, guys. The case is gaining traction. Our observation of the contact between the Maria Cresswell Hospice and a Romanian clinic, and poor Dr Beamish's suicide offers up routes to more information. But I need to repeat, we really must keep everyone, and I mean everyone, believing that this is an open and shut suicide. We don't want it known that our investigations are deeper. While I'm at it, I also need to explain that Ted Sanderson will not be around for a bit. He is on temporary compassionate leave. Mike, the chief has agreed for you to take his place."

"Okay with me," said Mike, smiling with understanding of the unspoken reason for Ted's absence.

Nicola blurted excitedly. "Yeah, it's so good about the progress. A friend of mine came back from Kerala in India and said she had heard that many poor people sell their babies for organ donation. Can you believe that?"

The boys grimaced.

Jane frowned. "Nicola, it's not just India, it's worldwide."

They didn't notice Ted Sanderson exit the station by the side door. He left Jane a note.

Jeremy Radcliffe was damned if he was going to be given the run-around. He had been a civil servant of high rank in London and just because he was retired and living in rural Norfolk didn't mean that he could be taken advantage of. He sat in a waiting room at the Maria Cresswell Hospice holding his wife Agnes's hand. She needed him now more than ever. During his working life he spent all his time in various ministries doing his duty, being loyal. Over his retirement years he tried to repay her love and support. Now some foreign doctor had diagnosed her with something awful and he wasn't going to let her down. She needed care until the end and was damned well going to get it.

The door to the waiting room opened and Jeremy stood up.

"Hello, Mr Radcliffe, I'm Dr Ziggefelde, Johannes Ziggefelde, I am the visiting consultant surgeon. What can we do for you?"

"It's quite simple. Our local GP Dr Jack Beamish sent my wife to see a consultant, Mr Rado Ilovic. Or should I say the late doctor, as I understand it. His suicide is terrible. Mind you, not surprising really. He had enormous strains on him with his wife ill with Alzheimer's and all. Anyway, as I say, he took us to see Mr Rado Ilovic without delay. That was terrific. But the news was," he stopped, appeared awkward and almost choked the words, "well, grim."

His wife was not so old, but looked as though she was carrying an enormous burden. He smiled at her thinly.

"He did say that he would make arrangements for my wife at the hospice. It was promised." His voice trembled slightly, but he was going to fight hard for a place at the hospice for Agnes against all the odds if he had to. "He said it would be arranged. We've heard absolutely nothing. It isn't good enough, you know."

By now his face was reddening. He was agitated, but determined to call up the Beamish promise.

Dr Ziggefelde put his hands on his hips and sucked his cheeks.

"Look, Mr Radcliffe. I need to check a few things out. But from what you say, you understand that there have been pledges to help you. We respect those with whom we work, like Mr Ilovic and the late Dr Beamish. Let's sort this out straight away. Give me a moment, please."

Dr Ziggefelde left the room and Radcliffe could see him talking to the hospice manager. He returned barely ten minutes later and announced that three rooms had been vacated that very day and Mrs Radcliffe was welcome to select one that suited her most, without delay.

Jeremy Radcliffe felt his face slacken and the tension drain from his body.

Her hand felt soft as he touched it and she was led to the rooms, to inspect them and make her choice. He had been the scourge of the Civil Service Departments in London before he retired, relentless in all that he did.

He achieved his aim, and as a bonus a choice of room for Agnes. The old Radcliffe grit had not deserted him. In addition, there were no fees, but merely a request for a donation for as much as he would be able to afford, as her treatment and care took place. Unusually for him, tears formed in his eyes. He was a great administrator, but a poor house-person and carer. Now, when she needed it most, she would receive the best attention possible.

He took a deep breath, satisfied that only he could take on bureaucracy and win.

5

Jane arrived at a cottage, which was a special place in the Norfolk countryside, made to look like a bed and breakfast boarding house. The sign always indicating, FULL. It was a safe house run by Graham and Margaret Ogden, who were ex-MI6 agents. Rumour had it that they finished their time in Eastern Europe under trying and dangerous circumstances and nearly lost their lives. Without anywhere to live, they were offered the job of managing this safe house, which provided support undercover for resting agents. It was well equipped with fully functioning, secure communications. There were dozens of sites like this in the UK. The Ogdens were the right people for the job and accepted the task with alacrity.

Jane parked underneath a long yew hedge, beside the small cottage. The FULL sign swayed gently in the breeze and she felt comfortable even before entering the doorway. Margaret Ogden was drying her hands on a blue striped tea towel and looked up.

"Hello there. Long day?"

"Oh, so-so, I just need to stitch a few things together. Any chance of a large house speciality, one of your white wine spritzers?"

"Coming up. The conservatory caught the sun today and it's lovely and warm, so why not go in and make yourself comfortable?"

Margaret was dressed in a smart flowered day-dress and looked very much younger than her 56 years. Her English-rose beauty hid a multitude of professional secret service experience – she looked more like a vicar's wife than a spy.

Jane didn't need telling twice and made her way to the back of the house. Sitting in the comfortable lounger was just what she needed after a long day. As soon as her head leaned against the cushioned seat, she felt drowsy and started to doze. Her mind was full of the different strands to this complicated investigation and her concern turned to the situation in China. In her half-sleep she recalled her visit to Beijing to talk to the Minister of the External Relations for the People's Republic of China, Madame Lom, a truly inscrutable and formidable woman, the archetypal Chinese diplomat. The first meeting was undramatic, more a game between two professionals based on ancient historic ritual. First came the three-day wait for an audience. It was part of the culture and one had to pretend that it hadn't really been three days at all, merely a short while. Finally, Jane was formally summoned to Madame Lom's presence.

The large marble auditorium-style room that was Madame Lom's office, had high ceilings, pillars and red banners emblazoned with golden Chinese characters. Behind a single large mahogany desk sat Madame Lom, dressed in a plain high collared white suit, with embroidered black letters on the collar. She wore her straight black hair long to her shoulders, and curled inwards at the bottom and her face was plainly made up except for her lips, which had a light cover of bright red lipstick. Her black-rimmed spectacles gave her a severe, fiercely attractive look. She looked as though she had been sculpted.

"Good morning," she said in faultless English, with a slight Chinese edge to it. "I understand that you want to discuss our procedures for removing organs from the bodies of condemned prisoners to give them to loyal Chinese people who need them. I am confused by your concern. I read much about the death of adults and children in Europe waiting for donors and the way you allow the guilty to be lightly punished only to offend again. One of us has it wrong, I believe."

Jane thought for a moment before answering.

"No, of course not, I ..."

Madame Lom broke in. "We have had regulations since 1990 for the use of organs from bodies of condemned prisoners. More recently, we have banned the sale of human organs and restricted transplants given to foreigners – we need to deal with the medical demands of millions of people in China. This is our policy." She put her pen down with a flourish and looked straight at Jane.

Jane was aware of the tactics of 'first strike – then sit back' and responded quietly and courteously.

"Madame Lom, I have not come here to comment on your country's civil rights, your processes for organ donation, or anything else for that matter. It is not in my gift to do so. What you do in your country is not my business. Crime is my business - international crime, that is. You see, our worry is that some people in China, like many other countries, may get tempted to provide organs for profit. If this happens, in an uncertain world such as ours, Madame Lom, then the poor and disenfranchised can find themselves exploited, or worse. Criminals will find a market that needs feeding, that's for sure."

Madame Lom smiled, almost imperceptibly and nodded slowly. She recognised that Jane had deftly moved out of China's system of punishment, to the evil actions of the world outside its borders. It was a deft touch. China is a country of contrasts and never more so than in the twenty-first century as capitalism flowed across the land like a heavy morning mist. Times were changing.

A servant brought a tray containing a large white decorated teapot and two small white bowls. Jane was amused as Madame Lom went about the process of delicately filling the bowls, dabbing the sides with a napkin, before she raised one to her lips and slurped the liquid loudly.

Jane explained the situation from a worldwide perspective.

"Madam Lom, some bad people are harvesting organs in a variety of ways, almost always illegal and often cruel. Who knows where it will end, it could, after all, be one of your family members who could suffer – couldn't it?"

Madam Lom remained passive at this attempt to personalise the situation. She was a difficult person to engage in conversation and blanked almost all of Jane's attempts. Jane gave a few more details about the work in Europe but avoided the American connection.

After another cup of green tea, Madam Lom sat back in her chair and smiled.

"You are unusual. I mostly get visits from men, political men, security men, but lots of men. You must be good at your work."

Jane thought hard about what to say. "Well, yes. I am good at my job. Most of all I get the luxury of doing work that I believe in. In this case, people are being cynically exploited and robbed of parts of their bodies and even their lives by organised crime. That's wrong. I will win this conflict, Madame Lom. I will catch the evil-doers."

From that moment on Madame Lom's attitude changed and she started to talk; about the greatness of China, how times had changed and the challenges they faced. She asked about Jane's family in Ireland – she was certainly well briefed – and Jane actually enjoyed telling her of her university studies and freely outlined her military work.

Eventually they parted, understanding each other's difficulties without actually saying so. Madame Lom was aware of China's image in the world and its poor reputation for civil liberties, justice and aggressive attitude to other cultures in those annexed provinces close to her borders. Ironically, winning the right to stage the 2008 Olympics, and making such a success of it, was considered the cornerstone to a new beginning, but of course, it opened the country up more than ever to tourists and commentators. Life was getting more difficult for this old lady of the east.

Jane dreamt about the journey back, remembering the notes she had made of the situation in China. Madame Lom had given nothing away. Jane knew that it was not the practice for government officials to lie – the cultural tendency was to dissemble. Despite their good relationship, Jane was aware that she must, nevertheless, send in an agent to check Madame Lom's assertion that things had changed. In a country as big as China it was impossible to control every agency and individual. There was evidence that something wasn't quite right. It was not important what Madame Lom had said, rather what she had not said. She said that they banned the sale of organs from executed prisoners and *restricted* transplants for foreigners. What a strange thing to say.

As she dozed fitfully, she heard a loud tinkling and imagined hundreds of bright Chinese lanterns waving in the wind.

She awoke with a start.

Leaning towards her rattling ice-cubes in a tall glass full of white wine and soda was Margaret.

"Well, that was a quick snooze, Jane."

Jane sat up and rubbed her eyes.

"Yes, by golly, I must have been tired."

She took the glass and drank a third of the cool liquid. Margaret left the conservatory. Jane turned her thoughts to the present. There was nothing for it, but to try and get information from within the hospice. Great care was needed. The problem was that the local coppers were very visible in the community – everybody knew everybody in Norfolk. She knew exactly what she had to do and would call London in the morning.

The rest of the spritzer tasted wonderful.

Nicola Bradbury's instructions had been straightforward: ask a few questions of the hospice, the medical centre and neighbours, but make it quite clear that the police considered Dr Beamish's death was nothing more than a straightforward suicide due to stress and overwork. The team was sad to hear that Det Supt Ted Sanderson was out of action for a while, but Nicola was pleased, she liked Jane Kavanagh. She was so experienced. It oozed from every pore in her skin, her every word was so logical and exact. Nicola was in awe of her.

She bundled her notes into her folder and prepared herself for her task according to a work plan devised in Ted's absence. Farmer and Gerry were allocated tasks for the day and she would catch up with them later.

Nicola drove her VW Polo from the Norwich police station to North Walsham, and Dr Beamish's practice. After parking her car, she walked up the path, aware that she was the focus of attention.

"Good morning," said Elaine Harmer, acting as if she didn't know her. "Can I help you?"

"Hello, I am not sure if you remember me, I'm DS Nicola Bradbury. I just have a few questions for you regarding Dr Beamish's suicide. I hope you don't mind? It won't take long, I promise you," she said, raising her warrant card as she spoke. The head receptionist barely glanced at it.

"It doesn't matter if you do. We've hardly any patients these days. I'm afraid that the rumour mongers in our society started to put it around that our lovely Dr Beamish was up to evil things and that's why he killed himself."

She huffed and raised her head high. "But I know different. I was quite friendly with the doctor and I know just how he suffered because of his wife's terrible affliction. I know, I really do."

Nicola regarded her carefully. It was evident that the suicide had had a bad effect on patient numbers and she surmised that this woman felt her status had waned with the passing of the doctor, with whom she clearly had a good working relationship. Mrs Harmer dismissively waved a hand at the junior receptionist and led Nicola into an office behind the reception area where they sat awkwardly as if discussing an embarrassing medical affliction.

"Tell me, Mrs Harmer, did the doctor ever give you any inkling whatever, that he was so stressed that he might take his own life?"

Elaine Harmer looked upwards and repeated her mantra. "No, but I knew him well you know, very well indeed. You don't work with someone for eleven years and not know them. Anyway, I could see well enough he was stressed. I just wish I had done something about it. But then I only had the other doctor to talk to."

Nicola noted the word *other*. She also suspected that Elaine Harmer was playing up to the situation rather than thinking objectively. It was a common habit by those seeking to gain attention in these circumstances. She was mindful of instructions to keep it simple and told her that the police would await the coroner's decision. Perhaps it was due to stress from having to work hard and worrying about his wife.

The door opened and Dr Patricia Lenahan came in and introduced herself. Nicola was sure that she had been listening to the conversation. Dr Lenahan walked between Nicola and Elaine Harmer, who stiffened as the doctor turned her back on her, and said patronisingly, "It was such a pity. I overheard Elaine earlier and I agree that it was such a stress for Dr Beamish. I think we are all to blame for not noticing. It's had a bad effect on the surgery. I now only work here three days a week and we'll have to lay off one of our receptionists quite soon. It's so unsettling for the staff."

She added negligently, "But that's life. I must go now. If you need to contact me then the staff know my mobile number."

With that she was gone. Nicola was left with, *the staff.*

"Elaine, did you notice anything going on in Dr Beamish's life that was unusual or different?"

"No, not really. I suppose though, come to think of it, there was a big change in his personality about two years ago. That was about the time he joined a local golf club. It's an expensive one, too. Anyway, he had a golf partner who was a foreign businessman. I really didn't like him one little bit." She folded her arms in front of her ample bosoms and looked upwards and to one side. "No not a bit. He had a 'glad eye' if you know what I mean."

"You don't know who this man is?"

"No, only that he played golf regularly with the doctor."

Nicola made a note then looked up and stabbed in the direction of internal politics. "Did Dr Beamish get on with Dr Patricia Lenahan?"

Elaine Harmer smiled, looked at the open door, and whispered, "She's been a partner for almost two years now. I suppose it's a man thing, well, a 'past middle-age' man thing, but I think he was in awe of her. She's very clever, I'll give her that, and pretty of course. Frankly, she rules the roost. I think with all the stress he suffered that he just didn't want the bother of solving day-to-day problems. I know he was grateful to her once or twice when he felt a little low. She was helpful, I suppose. He said that she had a place by the sea and a boat, and promised to take him off for a break." She smirked, "Nice for some people!"

"I know you liked him, but was Dr Beamish a good man?"

Elaine Harmer stiffened and replied steadfastly. "Oh yes. He was very well liked indeed. I don't think he was truly appreciated. It was the good things he did for people you see. Like when people needed cancer care. He would take them to the Norfolk Hospital himself and virtually bully a consultant into seeing them rather than relying on the National Health Service waiting lists. He also took a close interest in the lives of people whose diagnosis was awful."

"Oh, was that his special relationship with the Maria Cresswell Hospice at Honing?" She felt a sting of regret at inadvertently telegraphing interest in the hospice.

"Why yes, how did you know that? He was so kind to people with a terminal illness. I think it was probably because of his own situation. That's the kind of man he was."

"I know this will be sensitive, but did he have a drink problem?"

Elaine Harmer's face reddened. "No," she said emphatically, "definitely not!"

Nicola stared at her. "Just a nice chap then?"

"Yes. I hope you don't mind, but all this is a bit deep, isn't it?"

"Oh, not really, we just like to ensure that we cover everything, that's all."

Nicola stood up to go and brought a business card out of her Filofax. "Here's where to find me if you think of anything of interest. We are about to wrap this case up so if there's anything else you remember or want to tell me then just give me a call."

Elaine read it absentmindedly and casually put it into her handbag.

Nicola returned to the office and immediately sought out a probationer DC, Annie Deakin, to accompany her to Dr

Beamish's detached red brick house, not more than a mile from the practice in North Walsham. It was an unassuming house in need of a lot of attention. The brickwork needed repointing and a gutter was broken in the middle, allowing water to drip down the front wall and over a window, leaving an ugly brown streak.

"Why are we here, guv?" said the DC.

"Annie, sometimes it's necessary to visit a scene just to get the feel of things. That way you get an all-important view for the person concerned, how they live and so on. Sometimes clues are found, sometimes nothing. That's the way it goes."

Nicola opened the front door, pushing it hard because it had stuck slightly at the edges, and was almost barricaded by piles of junk mail. They stood in the hallway and looked around, feeling the fuggy stillness of a house that had already forgotten its owner.

"Annie, I need to explain for your experience, that it's procedure to always be accompanied by another officer when carrying out a search. Please touch nothing. In simple terms, your role is to ensure that I don't get accused of planting evidence or removing anything without properly noting it down."

Mindful of the introduction, the probationer nodded her understanding and walked around with her hands behind her back, craning her head this way and that looking at the rooms, hoping to find something of interest.

The house was simply furnished and there were no colourful pictures or other things that made it a place to relax in. The furniture was dated and by the damp smell and cobwebs in the corners of the rooms it appeared that only the study had been used. This was confirmed by the presence of several discarded take-away trays and unwashed cups. The faded edges to the wallpaper curled up in some places. In the hall, a new set of golf clubs leaned against an old-fashioned dark wooden coat stand. Otherwise, there was nothing significant about his surroundings, other than its untidiness. Beamish was, more or less, a solitary man and according to the neighbours he had no friends they knew of. In fact, that was just it. There was nothing noteworthy about him at all.

Beamish's private papers had already been removed for closer examination and many of the cabinet and desk drawers were left half or fully open. This made the study look like a tooth without a filling. As she turned to leave, she saw a round, brass paperweight on the windowsill. On it was engraved the outstretched Da Vinci's 'man' and the letters: Artaxis. One of many pharmaceutical freebies, she supposed. She realised that she had seen it somewhere before. She indicated to the probationer she was removing the item to an evidence bag and, after making a note and getting the DC's signature, put it in her briefcase.

A bell rang at the front door of the cottage and Margaret Ogden shouted, "I'll get it."

Jane recognised the voice in the hall immediately and shouted. "Jenny Willis, you rogue. You made it."

They hugged, smiling effusively, glad to see each other. Jenny held Jane's shoulders at arm's length and regarded her in mock seriousness. "Bloody hell, lady Jane, you're looking very grown up and serious. What the hell has happened to you?"

"Away with you, girl, I'm on a case and it reflects in my looks. All work and no play at the moment. Jenny, it's so good to see you again. It seems an age since we worked together on that, what was it now, oh, the paedo gang in Manchester?"

"Yeah, that's right. You stopped me from pummelling the ring-leader. Good job, otherwise my career would've stalled."

The Manchester case had been dangerous. Jenny's short fair hair and neutral features gave her a kind of anodyne look, uniquely forgettable. This young woman was used to blending in. However, she was able to change her appearance to meet the needs of any role asked of her.

Margaret brought them cool spritzers and smiled broadly at the way they chattered and how Jane brightened in the company of an old friend. After considerable banter and a deal of laughter, Jane brought matters down to earth outlining details of the mission.

"We're onto something big, Jenny. But staking out the Maria Cresswell Hospice is hopeless in the short term – it will take ages to get anything near a substantial piece of evidence and I don't do patience."

"I remember!"

"Okay, then. Here's the plan. The current receptionist will be befriended and slipped a debilitating drug that will take some time to leave her body. The hospice uses a local recruitment agency and your name has been added to the database, showing that you have the exact qualifications and skills needed, and are ready to start at a moment's notice. It's a long shot but might just come off."

"I damned well hope so," said Jenny. "We can't keep slipping receptionists Mickey Finns!"

Jane laughed. "Let's be serious now. There is a suggestion that there are some bad people involved with this lot, you know, the kind with a big 'M' in front of their name, so take very good care of yourself."

Jenny sighed and replied playfully, "Bad people, oh goody!"

Jane thumped her gently on the shoulder. "I said be serious! Now listen carefully to my brief about equipment and then we'll go through the background to this particular investigation."

Jane reached behind her and brought a small cardboard box to the table and opened it. She reached inside and brought out what looked like a cord.

"Now then, this is a nylon diamond grit coated thread insert which you can place around the top edge of your knickers."

Jenny convulsed with laughter.

"I knew that would happen! You may laugh, my friend, but I used this to saw into a Serbian leg as he was about to drown me. Boy, was I glad of that! The beauty is that it has a multitude of uses."

Jenny held the wire-like item up to the light and inspected it carefully, reluctantly agreeing to insert it into her underwear whenever she could.

"One last piece of kit, now look at this little beauty," Jane produced a credit card that had a camera embedded. "It won't produce award winning photos, but can capture basic evidence when needed."

After the items were wrapped and Jenny had put them into her holdall, Jane explained the broader background to the case and the importance of gaining information that would ascertain the operation of the hospice in illegal organ harvesting and trading,

"It's important to look for written evidence, observe on the comings and goings, the personalities and so on. Of course, the hospice could be in the clear, but my instincts tell me that we are on to something."

Jenny took it all in and was now concentrating on notes that Jane gave her. When Jane told her the full story about Katrina Anatov the Bulgarian prostitute and her narrow escape, the mood changed.

"Oh God. You mean people are being hijacked for their bits?"

"You got it. Once upon a time a girl had to guard against Rhohypnol in her gin and tonic, and being shafted by some weirdo rapist. Now the reason you wake up with your knickers on back to front, is because someone has pinched your kidney or ovaries."

Jane threw a file down on the desk. "Read this and you'll understand why I've held on to this brief for so long, and why I need you to help with surveillance. You're the best, Jenny and I need your skills."

Jenny sipped the house speciality, ice-cold spritzer.

"You're such a smoothie Jane. Tough as old boots when you need to succeed, but soft as goo when needs must. I accept. Now, why don't we pop down to a pub and get some real drink inside us?"

"Great idea. Why not, it'll take some time for things to come together. Let's do it whilst we can, besides, I could do with letting my hair down a bit."

Jane and Jenny handed their key documents, keys and other items to Margaret for safekeeping. She agreed to drop the two of them at the Barley Mow public house nearby and pick them up at closing time. As they made their way upstairs, Margaret sighed and remembered her own days of surveillance and the camaraderie in local pubs. Those days were now a long way away. Now they were owned by the younger generation.

The Barley Mow public house was five miles from the guest house and well away from Cromer. Jane and Jenny struck up a conversation with the owner, who was an ex-copper and his line of jokes included every non-politically correct one-line comment in the book. They hardly stopped laughing.

Jane was just finishing a large gin and tonic when she caught sight of DC Gerry Winter and a young girl entering the pub. She deliberated about waving to him to join them and in the end decided it would be good to get to know him. He caught sight of her and came over.

"Hello, Jane, this is Mandy, my girlfriend."

"Hi there, nice to meet you, Mandy, this is Jenny, a colleague of mine."

Jane caught Jenny giving Gerry the 'come on' and kicked her gently under the table. It was easy to see that Mandy was sweet, but not very worldly-wise. Jenny would have won the seduction contest with consummate ease.

They had been drinking and talking for about thirty minutes when suddenly the door burst open and three scruffy men barged in. Two of them walked unsteadily to the bar and one of them stood looking around the pub menacingly, before ordering a beer. The publican reminded them to behave themselves.

Gerry recognised them instantly. They were so-called travellers from a local site, these men were the sort that do anything but travel and everything illegal, and were well-known to the local force.

The man standing away from the group was called, Liam. His gaze fell on Gerry, who tried to turn away and avoid him, but it was too late.

"Hey, fellers, it's the pretty police-boy. How ya doin' pretty boy? Where's that arsehole of a boss of yours, Detective Superintendent Sanderson, the white crusader?"

The men laughed. The publican chastised them for their language, but they simply ignored him. They gulped down some beer and shuffled towards the table, looking menacingly at Gerry and the women.

The publican went to the back corridor and reached for the telephone.

The man called Liam arrogantly regarded Gerry and the group, squinting with a sneering expression. He was a tall with a shock of wavy black hair and dark eyes set in a chiselled face with a ruddy complexion. He turned to his mates and gestured at the table in front of them. "Michael, for the love of God, tell me how it is that a poofter like this police-guy ends up with three good looking women."

He turned to Gerry. "Tell you what, Gerry boy, you pick one and we'll have the other two - deal?"

Jane saw Gerry stand up and squarely face the men. He said calmly, "Look boys, you're disturbing the customers and making the girls here anxious. Give it a rest, huh?"

They put their drinks down and came towards him. Liam snarled, "Now, you know that's not very friendly? You boys in blue, constantly harass us poor, innocent travellers.

Yes, that's it, harassment. You breach my bloody human rights, that's what. It's hard to make living sure it is."

The men laughed and sneered.

"You and your ponce of a boss really piss me off," said Liam as he pushed his face closer to Gerry's, swallowing his beer in one gulp, belching loudly. "In fact, I'm very annoyed. I don't like going home to my caravan annoyed. It means I can't sleep. I have to blow off steam see."

Jane saw that Gerry was courageous, but sometimes courage is not enough. Emboldened by the odds, one of the men stepped forward and prodded Gerry in the chest. Several customers quickly left the bar for the safety of their cars and an early journey home.

Jane flashed Jenny a look and received an almost imperceptible nod in agreement. She sprang up, moving to the right of the table.

"Hey, feller. What's your problem? We just want a quiet night, so why don't you just move back to the bar and enjoy your beer?"

Almost unseen, Jenny quietly moved around to the left of the table.

The smaller of the men, but nevertheless the bulkiest laughed. "Look at this, boys, a bossy little tart. How I love those, I really do. Do you shout instructions when you orgasm, darlin'...ooh, left a bit, right a bit, do as you're told...oh, ah?" He gyrated his hips in vigorous circles and his mates egged him on, guffawing and shouting.

Gerry had had enough. "You know I'm a police officer and I am telling you to..."

Liam grabbed him by the throat, "You'll do what, pretty-boy?"

Before he could tighten his grip, Jane brought her right fist horizontally around in a wide arc and hit him on the lower left side of his rib cage just under his kidney. He yelped with pain and was winded so much that he couldn't talk and fell to the floor. The largest of the men moved him out of the way and glared at her.

"You shouldn't have done that you tart."

He lumbered towards Jane and she assumed a defensive karate stance, legs apart, even balance, with one foot slightly in front of the other, arms half-raised and ready to repel a blow. The man didn't even recognise the position or suspect what was coming. As he swiped at her she pushed the blow harmlessly across her body and brought her knee up into his crotch. He groaned and half sank to the floor. But he wasn't down and out and he started to get up. As he did so she punched him in the face twice with the extended knuckles of her right hand, elbow close to her body jerking her shoulder to force each blow forward very quickly, then kicked his legs out from under him.

Meanwhile, Jenny was dealing with the third man, holding him in a straight arm lock to one side and slightly behind her, whilst raising her left foot so that her heel hit his face several times - blood from his nose dripped to the floor. She smiled at Jane as if to say, '*This is fun!*'

Gerry stood as though he was frozen in ice – not frightened but just shocked, surprised at the efficiency of the violence from the two attractive ladies. Just as he was about to utter something intelligible, the doors opened and four policemen burst in, illuminated by the blue flashing lights of their cars. The publican pointed to the fracas and they came straight over.

Jane and Jenny moved silently to the back of the bar leaving Gerry to explain the situation as he was proffering his police identity card. They saw Margaret's car pulling up outside the pub and grabbed their coats. It was time to leave. Gerry turned and smiled agreement to them, waving them past and they exited by the back door.

In the back of Margaret's car, Jane turned to Jenny. "Who on earth taught you to arm-lock like that?"

Jenny looked up to the ceiling, "My boyfriend since you ask," adding, tongue in cheek, "On me of course. Actually, it's quite nice."

Margaret looked up from the road ahead and into the rear-view mirror with a feigned mock expression of surprise, "What the hell are you two talking about?"

Jane and Jenny convulsed with laughter.

Ted sat by Alison's bed looking at her pale expressionless face that gazed out of a window at the green fields and hills. It was a comfortable nursing home, clean, tidy and not at all like the Victorian mental homes of yesteryear; but the stigma remained. She had a mental illness – that is what depression is; cloying, debilitating and illogical.

He knew that the treatment could push her further into herself. It was supposedly a kind of self-fulfilling therapy, but it was, nevertheless, dependence. He had seen it all before and was ready to deal with the inevitable aftermath: calmness, contrition, blame, guilt and the slow climb back to normality – ready for the next fall.

When they were first married, they had been so well in tune with each other. It was the family joke that one would often talk for the other, or even guess what the other was going to say next. They played tennis and squash together and enjoyed a good party without a scintilla of jealousy if either was flirted with.

Their sex had been simply the best. Ted often joked with her that her sexual athleticism and inventiveness contrasted with her overly hygienic demands. She simply laughed at him and continued in her own way. Then came the joy of giving birth to a baby girl and the happiness of her first two years of life; she was called Madeleine and made their life complete. They bought clothes, toys, designed a nursery and then a bedroom for her. Plans were made for her education and they held high hopes for her future.

The completeness was shattered when a drunk-driver ploughed into their stationary vehicle at traffic lights. The scene was like a nightmare, each element of it set in their minds like a slow-motion movie: the impact, the screams, the sound of metal and glass shattering, then the silence and smoke, before the emergency vehicle arrived amid a cacophony of sirens and flashing blue lights. They clung to hopeful thoughts that, *it's going to be all right.* But it wasn't all right at all. Little Maddy's neck was broken instantly and she died at the scene.

She was dead. She would never come home.

The impact on them both was devastating; the pain, physical and mental, was unbearable. Every nerve in their body was numb and their hearts ached. It took them months to recover enough to even live a normal life. There could be no blame attached to them, but they still re-ran every aspect of that awful day: if they hadn't got up so late, taken a detour to the supermarket, driven down a different road and so on.

They pointlessly clawed around every conceivable fact to try and explain a terrible random event. Grief is absolutely necessary, but unchecked, it can be corrosive. No more so than for Alison. It ate at her. It wrapped her tightly in a cloak of misery. Whilst Ted had gone back to work which helped to move the painful images to the back of his mind, Alison stayed home and became more remote. Inevitably her spirits plummeted.

Over the next three years, Ted was often incredulous at the passion with which she catalogued her inadequacies and no amount of persuasion as to the ridiculousness of some of her statements improved the situation. She was impenetrable and mentally whipped herself, and this led to a damaging lack of self-worth.

Then intimacy stopped and conversation became stilted and jagged. They lived together, apart.

All these years on and it still hurt like hell.

Here she was then, her face waxen and expressionless, and he knew that he would do what he always did - be there for her, come what may.

"How are you doing?" he said softly.

At first, she ignored him and then tears filled her eyes.

"You should've let me go."

He held her hand lightly, "And what about me? You think that's what I would've wanted?"

Ted expected her to recite the already familiar lines that set his nerves on edge, *this is not about you; selfish bastard; I am my own person; you don't understand,* but she didn't.

She tenderly took his hands in hers and whispered, "I know you care. I know I've been a cow. I can't help it and I want to get out of this bloody red mist but it's so difficult. Doing that, with the pills and everything, that's just not me, it never has been, I don't want it to be me..."

Her face crumbled and she broke down and sobbed. Ted got up, leaned across her body and held her tight.

"The boss laid me off for a while, so that I can help you. Now hear this: I'm not going back to work until I am completely satisfied that you're all right. Do you understand?"

Alison stopped crying and looked at him, her eyes heavy with tears. She had always been quick to criticise his work, how he put it before her sometimes, how he loved it more than her. She once yelled hysterically that no one seemed to be mourning as much as she was. But she knew in her heart that it was all bunkum. All the painful words she conjured up, to throw at the world around her, didn't change the situation. It didn't bring Maddy back. She held her hands tightly on her lap.

"You must go back to work. I'm well looked after. You'll die of boredom. I'm okay. Please, for me, go back to the office."

"Then it's a deal you want? Let's just say a couple of weeks. Improve, get better, do what the shrink wants, he looks a soppy little sod anyway, and sure, it's a deal."

Alison attempted a half-laugh that sounded more like a splutter.

"Do everything he says, take your pills, stick them up your bottom for all I care, but just get nine out of ten from Doctor Strangelove out there. Then tell me that things are okay. Do that and I will for sure go back to work."

He kissed her lightly then held her face in his hands. "Thank you for thinking of me when you are feeling so bad, darling. But that's just like you."

Alison nodded. "Okay, you win."

It was a masterful approach and gave her something to aim for: a determination to see her man back in action, rather than focussing totally on herself. Ted knew that it was important to give her confidence and make her understand just how much she was wanted. He was re-energised seeing her respond positively and it made his heart sing. His earlier anger and frustration evaporated and he now thought only of her return home.

Ted muttered the phrase he had used so often: "I'll never give up."

There was a knock on the door and it opened wide, without acknowledgement in walked a sprightly elderly doctor with slicked grey hair swept tightly back on his head and wire-framed tinted spectacles. Ted looked at Alison with amusement in his eyes and without a word they acknowledged the presence of Doctor Strangelove!

After the doctor left the room, Ted lay on the bed and Alison curled up against him. They talked about a thousand and one things and the pressure of recent events lessened.

Ted listened with admiration as Alison admitted that she had hit rock bottom and decided that this was her 'last chance saloon'.

She was determined to get better.

6

The special incident team room in the Cromer Police Station was quiet and the securely locked door prevented unauthorised entry. Intermittent shafts of sunlight flickered down to the desk from a roof hatch, illuminating dust particles hanging in the air. The notice boards attached to the walls were resplendent with charts and 'spider' diagrams, showing links drawn from one clue to another, to try and piece together Dr Beamish's links to The Maria Cresswell Hospice and beyond. White curtains that kept the information covered had been partially pulled to one side. Only two officers were at their desks today.

DC Gerry Winters picked up the telephone, then smiled broadly.

"Okay, that's great. I'll tell the DS and we'll pass it on to Jane. Be careful, won't you? I was going to say, look out for yourself, but that's a bit redundant, given your performance the other night. Cheers now."

He put the phone down and turned to Nicola. "That was Jenny Willis. Sure enough, one of the receptionists at the Maria Cresswell Hospice has been taken ill and they need cover. The manpower agency took the bait and Jenny has been called as an urgent replacement. She obliged, at a moment's notice, which pleased the hospice. Will you call Jane?"

Nicola felt distinctly uneasy knowing somebody was to work under cover. She had no experience in this kind of thing and was unsure whether it would be dangerous or not. However, her ambition took over and she knew that if she rose to senior rank, decisions like this would need to be made without delay. Gerry told her of Jenny's combat prowess, but all the same, there's not much room to swing a karate kick behind a receptionist's desk.

Nicola dialled Jane's mobile.

"Jane K."

"Hi, Jane, it's Nicola. Some news, Jenny is in the hospice, so it's all go, I suppose."

"Great. Let's hope this is the beginning of something good." Jane paused. "What's up, Nicola, you sound unsure?"

Nicola turned away so that Gerry Winters could not see her. "Sorry, but, well it's very new to me, that's all. Isn't it dangerous?"

"It's good you feel like that and that you don't just take it for granted. Yes, frankly all undercover work is dangerous, but there's no other way. Jenny is experienced and knows what she's doing. Our role is to monitor things closely and be there if she needs us. We need to avoid sensitivity and remain focused and clear-headed."

"Yes, I understand. Sorry, I feel a bit silly now."

"Don't feel that way, it shows you recognise the risks and it'll keep you on your toes."

Nicola put the phone down. Her fears had been allayed and she appreciated the comments Jane made about her not taking things for granted. There was room to be human as well as professional after all. Jenny was an experienced operator, what could go wrong?

Jenny Willis decided to dress flamboyantly. She wanted to be considered a bit dizzy and not the sort to cause concern, but even the hospice manager's eyes spun at the discordant mixture of colours.

"Well, good morning. Dawn Clarke, I presume?" said the manager, Bobbette Grainger, without disguising her horror at Jenny's sartorial display. Jenny used the name of an old school-friend on various missions. It helped to use the same one, because this fixed a temporary persona in her mind and allowed her to respond quickly in answering off-the-cuff queries and shouts for assistance, without the tell-tale second's delay.

"Hello," she said girlishly, nodding her head like a model dog in the back of a car. "I am so glad to be able to help here. What do you want me to do?"

The manager took the parent-child posture and showed her where everything was, craning her head forward and carefully outlining each simple task several times.

"Now, do you understand everything, Dawn?"

Jenny played along by asking her to repeat things thus establishing her as a slow, dizzy personality.

"That's that, then," said the manager. "Now for a couple of very important points. Firstly, we need you to dress much more soberly. This is a hospice, Dawn, not a hotdog café. We have some clothing in the rest room, but tomorrow, come to us in a white blouse and dark skirt. We'll provide the jacket. Okay?"

Jenny nodded and played the chastised child.

"I also want you to understand that your job is to take calls and pass them on to the correct extension. According to your CV, you appear to know your way around the telephone exchange, so that's good." She craned her head towards Jenny smiling like an overpowering elderly aunt.

"Most important of all, just distribute the mail into department boxes. Please note, the hospice departments undertake administration. Do not, and I repeat do not, go beyond the blue-carpeted area. This limits you to the reception areas, rest room and toilet. Is that perfectly clear?"

The manager clasped her hands together and Jenny was sure that she would be given a chocolate bar for being a good girl.

"Yes, Miss Grainger. I understand everything. When can I start?"

A start time was agreed and the manager stayed a while to ensure that her new receptionist was up to speed. Jenny deliberately made a few errors and was able to correct them showing an aptitude for learning; she knew that the work would be mindlessly boring, but it was uncomplicated enough to give her lots of time to observe and gather evidence.

After changing into a spare white blouse, she deliberately left one button undone to expose her ample cleavage, supported by an expensive push-up bra'. Sooner or later, a honeybee would take the bait.

During the day, she took a number of calls and successfully connected them with the right departments. She received the mail and separated it into the various mailboxes, without opening it. It struck her that she wasn't specifically told not to open the mail. If she was to exploit this opportunity offered by the loose description that '*departments undertake administration*', she would need to do it soon. The mail comprised a mixture of letters coming in from the USA and Eastern Europe as well as the UK.

After a short break for lunch, Jenny resumed her place behind the desk beside the mail racks. Just as she did so, a tall man with thin fair hair and a pale expression stopped to talk to her. He was immaculately dressed in a beige suit and open necked white shirt.

"Hello there, you're new here, aren't you?" he said in a thick foreign accent. As he spoke, he nervously clicked his knuckles.

"Yes, temporary, sir."

"Well, let's hope that we see more of you. I'm Dr Johannes Ziggefelde and you are?"

"Dawn Clarke, sir. I am glad to be working in such a worthwhile place."

"Yes, my dear, it is worthwhile. Enjoy your time here. If there is anything you need to know, just ask me."

He said all that without removing his eyes from her chest.

China

Chin Kwok grew bored with the occasional drinking sessions with Dragon Tattoo and watching the Hang Song Institute building. It was a mental trap; his head either throbbed with the effect of too much rice wine or with sheer boredom – the greatest enemy of all observers, making them lax and prone to mistakes. He remembered only too well when working in a London bar observing Triad gang members, he was lost in his thoughts and found himself, leaning on the counter with his hands on his chin thinking about football, but jolted back to life when he realised he was staring directly at gang members. He leaned on the balcony overlooking the dusty rubble strewn road to the Institute and let the warm mid-afternoon breeze brush against his face.

Breakfast that morning had been rustic, boiled eggs and rice pancakes, accompanied by green tea and bread. He longed for western food again: bacon and eggs, fish and chips, steak pies, and almost dribbled at the images in his mind. Chin let out a low sigh then looked around the balcony and upbraided himself; he had to guard against unusual mannerisms.

The manager of the house, a small bespectacled man with a bad hunch came to his table. "Hello, where you from and where you go?"

"Hello. Near Hong Kong, I am heading north east to Shanghai, but in no hurry," he squirmed, grimaced and put his hand to his stomach. "I picked up a stomach bug and must stay a few days."

The manager took one step backwards as if the bug would jump onto him from Chin.

To corroborate his story Chin visited the local herbalist and a small bag of what looked like items collected from the forest floor sat to one side on the table.

"I would be grateful if the cook could boil up the contents and then strain the disgusting liquid into a bottle for me. This was recommended."

The manager smiled politely, but not effusively, and stretched his arm towards Chin who handed him the bag. "Yes, of course," said the manager and he scuttled away.

Chin laughed to himself. *"If you think I'm drinking that forest piss you're joking!"*

Tonight, he would meet with Dragon Tattoo again and doubtless they would demolish a few more bottles of rice wine. The thought of losing more brain cells filled him with dread; how that man could drink! Perhaps he could doctor the man's wine with 'forest floor' – that was worth considering!

Dragon Tattoo, dressed in green denim jacket and jeans, joined him at about seven p.m. Chin tried a different tack.

"Friend, let's not get straight into the wine tonight. I want to talk to you and get to know you more. We are friends, are we not?"

Dragon Tattoo lit a cigarette, leaned back in his wicker chair and regarded Chin with interest. He said nothing. Chin carried on regardless, now familiar with the silent moods of his new friend.

"I am passing through and will be gone quite soon. I want to be able to say that I met this great guy and we drank a lot of rice wine together. We were friends and we had a lot of laughs, yet I don't really know much about you. Can we change that?"

Dragon Tattoo thought for a while. Slowly but surely a smile came across his face. He didn't speak for about a minute.

"Why not? My name is Zhan Soo and I am one of ten children born to a father who was a farmer in the western province of Szechuan. When I was ten years old a terrible drought came. You may remember, that was 1972, I think."

Chin nodded sagely although he hadn't a clue about the disaster.

"Anyway, he struggled to make the land workable and died of exhaustion, brought on by working too hard. It was a case of leave home or die with my brothers and sisters – there was no other choice. I tried the army and had to leave after two years. They said I was too stupid to learn how to use weapons or do anything interesting. The years spent in the countryside didn't equip me for work that needed an education. But I have always been good with my hands. I came to Sang Yong and worked as a labourer for a Communist Party chief who wanted to build the Hang Song Institute in that compound over there."

He pointed his nicotine-stained finger towards the window and in the direction of the Institute building. "I am a good worker and well paid. One night I got drunk and my co-workers left me in a tattoo parlour with instructions. The tattoo artist did this and you know something? I even had to pay for it – the evil dogs. It was expensive and I hated it at first. But now it gives me some notoriety, I think. I don't have many friends here in Sang Yong. They don't like outsiders and feel that I had taken a job away from a local boy. They also tease me because I am ugly. Perhaps it's my teeth?"

He smiled and flashed his few remaining, disgustingly stained, teeth. The man would never win a beauty contest.

"Then I landed a permanent job as a janitor along with several other young men and women once the Institute building was completed. I am very lucky compared to some other people, I think it was because the Party Leader knew me and was also the son of a farmer. He was an outsider as well. He looked after me. I helped build it and now I work in it."

"That's so interesting," said Chin, building the bond.

He then shared his own experiences, all of which had been carefully scripted by his handlers. Dragon Tattoo listened with an implacable expression. It was a script that could be tuned slightly so that it melded with any situation and Chin did this adroitly.

"My father was also a farmer, how about that? We had no money and they scraped to send me to school, but I was bullied and eventually left to work in a fabric mill in Shanghai. I keep myself to myself and have no friends to speak of. So, I make time away from work to leave my home and visit relatives, or sometimes just go to different places to meet new people. That was why I am here in Sang Yong."

After about forty minutes, the atmosphere had changed considerably and they exchanged even more stories of life in rural communities, problems with parents and how luck had been with them through difficult times. They shared so much that it was as though they were lifelong friends.

Chin had done his job well. One more day and he would begin to ask questions about the Institute; but for now, there was nothing for it but to raise yet another glass of rice wine.

England

Jane sat outside one of the many coffee shops on the Strand in the city of London, enjoying the mild spring temperature. A mother walked by with two young girls who chattered excitedly and nearby, a street musician played an accordion for pennies. A waft of scent from an adjacent flower stall was delightful and seemed almost out of place in streets full of vehicle fumes. It was days like this that she wished she were footloose and fancy free, able to do the museums, art galleries and bookshops with a friend, with no pressures and no priorities.

She sipped her black coffee and corrected herself. Pressure was precisely what she thrived on, as well as the excitement. You cannot have it both ways. Leaning against the back of the metal chair she observed the world through lightly tinted sunglasses, her stockinged legs extended in front of her.

Several times well-dressed men stopped to talk on some pretext or another, but she moved them on with a polite smile and a response that said, *thanks but no thanks.*

It was important to gather her thoughts before meeting with her boss. Mike Hancox's mantra was: do nothing until you are certain and even then, chew on it for a bit longer. But time was not on her side. She also thought that he was having reservations about the whole project. Sure, there was a shed-load of information coming in about the illegal harvesting and sale of human organs, but the prime suspect, Artaxis Incorporated, remained outside the fire; until now. Then she had seen the emblem on a paperweight from Dr Beamish's office. It could be legitimate, but maybe not. It was her job to convince Mike that they were making progress. She hoped the email she sent him about the next step would be accepted with enthusiasm.

Dear old Cromer town was the cherry that she had been waiting for. Somebody, somewhere was going to make a mistake; some clue would emerge and make that all-important link and she was going to be ready for it.

She stood up and smoothed the silky material of her chic Versace bottle-green two-piece suit and strode towards the entrance in a nondescript building near the jazz bar, Smolenskys on the Strand. Swinging her small handbag loosely, she rehearsed the words she would use.

The corridor to Mike Hancox's office was dull and reminded Jane of her thankfully infrequent visits to the MOD years earlier. Marked beige walls begged to be refurbished and brown nylon carpeting tiles bravely clung to each other, some stubbornly raised at the corners. Hancox's office door was open and he beckoned her in. Its expensive decoration and furniture contrasted with the corridor.

Mike Hancox was six foot five inches tall and possessed a body that was built to launch ships. His dark hair and old-fashioned straight moustache gave him the appearance of an ex-army colonel. He was known to be tough on UK Interpol and Europol agents seconded to his department, even those he 'bought in,' and expected high standards.

As Jane entered and sat down, Hancox carelessly tossed his reading spectacles onto papers in front of him.

"Nice to see you, Jane. Now then, what's all this in your email about a visit to the USA? You clearly think the budget for this mission is bottomless."

Jane smiled politely and did not rise to the remark.

"Mike, I know you're aware from the brief that several firms in the US are being covertly investigated by our FBI colleagues. Let's focus on Artaxis. They had some dealings with the late Dr Beamish. I expect Jenny Willis to uncover the same in the hospice. But I just can't wait for that."

Hancox twiddled his thumbs like rotating windmill vanes and frowned.

"So, the budget increases. How can I be sure that this will be useful?"

"I can't. You can't. But there's a slim thread that needs pulling. The Belgrade clinic situation that led to Katrina talking to Interpol and the late Dr Beamish suicide must have spooked the guilty party. It's worth getting a knee-jerk reaction from the most likely candidate."

Hancox probed further, nit-picking and biting his pencil, irritating Jane. She tried to hide her impatience, a negative personality factor that had stayed with her since childhood. When his questions moved about aimlessly, she reached the limit of her patience and blurted almost angrily, "Mike, I know that you think I'm hurling myself at anything and everything, but there is method in my madness. Each snippet of information, every possible clue, adds up. I'm absolutely determined to solve this case. I want to visit Artaxis and spook them – simple as that. Do I know specifically know what I'm going to do – well, no, I don't. Do I even know that Artaxis is actually the major player? No, I don't know that either. But frustratingly, they are neither in, nor out of the frame and that irks me. I just want focus."

Hancox was now quiet.

Jane continued, more calmly. "The simple fact is that straightforward policing, working by the book and politics doesn't always work. Take for example the situation with the missing children in Brazil in the late eighties, when international crime agencies were pushing to investigate the situation. As time went on corruption and gang culture made investigations difficult and complex. So, what did they do? They closed the case down, that's what they did."

Jane did her best not to lean across the table at Hancox and added, "Well, we're not doing that!"

Hancox raised his hand. "Enough. I think I've tested your patience long enough, Jane. I was half-sold anyway and just wanted to be sure it wasn't a whim."

Jane squinted at him, flushed and clutched her hands on her lap, but said nothing.

He continued unabashed, almost as if his objections were a mere pause for thought. "I want you to consider a possible strategy," he handed her a large envelope. "A well-known investigative journalist called Caroline Redbridge returned from the Congo with a dose of Eboli – nasty affliction. Anyway, we got to her before it became known to the wider world and had her placed in a very good, but remote nursing home. She will be spaced out for at least a month."

"But, how..."

"Let me finish. You look remarkably like her and could take her name. So, I agree, let's plan on sending you to the USA. The question is, how can we use this woman's reputation to get you anywhere near Artaxis?"

Jane fought off the intervention in her mission focus and mild loss of control, but did not want to lose momentum. Her mind raced to meet the new scenario.

"Got it!" she exclaimed. "I'll read some of her professional papers and try to copy her style in a blog about the illegal trade in human organs. Probably best to allude to several US companies who could provide information, but include more about Artaxis. I'll put good money on them getting in touch with me for a chat, if only out of curiosity."

Hancox smiled, convincing himself that he had placed her foot on the accelerator.

For her part, Jane's irritation dissipated in the face of planning factors that she could personally take control of -

besides, she was inwardly relieved that continuum of the investigation was now implicit. She was happy to venture in or close to the lion's den.

They sat in mutual silence as it all sank in. Then Jane added a new dimension. "When I go to the states, I want to take Det Supt Ted Sanderson with me."

"Why?"

"Because it would be good to have a 'watcher', someone to look out for me. It's also useful to have two people. We can pose as a couple if need be to divert attention. The added dimension is that it's good for teamwork. The coppers in Norfolk have been doing a great job and this would ensure inclusion and keep them feeling a key part of this mission. Anyway, boss, I'm aware that I'm just running through ideas and don't want to waste your time brainstorming. Can we leave it for now."

Hancox recognised that she now wanted to be left to get on with the planning. There were enough elements in the box, so why not. He contentedly let the control slide back out of his hands.

"You have it, Jane. I look forward to seeing positive results. We can sort out the admin bits and pieces later. Finally, and interestingly, rumour has it that you really got through to Madame Lom of the Chinese People's Republic. She is a bloody hard nut to crack, but apparently, she liked you. Is there no end to your charm? I only hope she doesn't find out about our chum, Chin Kwok. Of course, he's acting alone and not on our books."

Jane winced at the corporate blind eye being turned. Nevertheless, she returned him a silent, polite smile, happy to have achieved her aim. Today, she had had enough of

Michael Hancox and just wanted to get out of his office and get on with the job.

An hour after Jane left the office, Hancox stood mulling the case over when his phone rang. He moved his hand around in an arc and answered it.

"Hancox."

"Hi, Mike, howya doin' buddy, John Kowalski here."

"John, my dear chap. Glad you called. I was going to call you today to update you. We're sending your old Bosnia buddy to the US to observe on Artaxis. I haven't a clue when or how, but I'll let Jane work that one out."

"Oh, that's, er, great," said Kowalski awkwardly.

"You sound uncertain."

"Oh, well I guess I'm just a bit spooked. Just a note of caution, my friend. One of our agents placed as a temporary admin operative in Artaxis mysteriously went missing. She was later found in a down-town boarding house. Dead."

"Bugger!" exclaimed Hancox.

"Cute phrase, my friend, Anyway, she was very popular, so we're a bit upset. On a practical note, we don't know whether she talked or not. It was made to look like a lover's tiff with the perpetrator absconding in the middle of the night. Artaxis showed concern and wanted to know details of next of kin so they could provide support. I suspect that the hair on the directors' necks are standing up straight."

Hancox held back icy thoughts of incompetence, sandwiched between sympathy and mission focus. They chatted about the situation and emerging evidence elsewhere in the world, but concluded that Artaxis was now definitely in the frame. This case was not without its risks.

"Okay, John, but we're determined to go ahead. You know how good Jane is. Will you do me a favour? I'll send you details of her itinerary when it's sorted, so keep an eye on her for me. I should mention that she will be accompanied by a male copper."

"No problem, Mike. We'll look keep her on our radar and look out for her. But do tell me your cop won't wear one of those silly big hats, eh?"

Hancox laughed. "Okay, Yank, if you insist. I'll get him to leave his truncheon behind as well. Thanks."

His demeanour at the friendly exchange diminished as he put the phone down - the news of the missing FBI agent began to sink in.

Ted worked hard on Alison over the next week and a half in the hospital and was determined to continue for the next few weeks until he saw a good result. He resisted moves to have her sectioned for her own good and insisted that she was strong enough to fight back. They talked, softly, reminiscing about their past, those halcyon days, visualising it all, eyes closed and holding hands, recalling events, years, days and even times, laughing at the silly things and rejecting memories of the manic moments. They consigned the bad things to a mental dustbin never to be opened again and kept the cherished ones.

He attended every meeting with a counsellor – at Alison's request – even though the medical staff wanted her to undertake them alone. Ted grew to know more about Alison than he ever had before. Maddy's death hit them both like a steam train, but police work enabled him to pull himself together again. For Alison, it had been agonisingly different. The sessions revealed her overwhelming depth of despair. He started to understand how a groundswell of neurosis that started with a first miscarriage, the attempt to grow another little Maddy, accelerated out of all proportion until she felt it stuck to her like glue, contaminating her every thought and movement. He needed to get her out of this psychological rut.

Ted learned a lot about himself too. He was, in many ways a typical man. Despite his fifteen or so years of marriage, which equated to one hundred and eighty menstrual cycles, or, put another way, over nine hundred days of pre-menstrual tension, he had learned little about chemical imbalances, moods and women's needs in general. It didn't make him a bad husband, just one who was forced to react all the time instead of taking the initiative. It meant his compassion sounded hollow, he recognised situations but not the reasons – he was aware that it left him outside the problem looking in with a kind of unsympathetic tenderness. His support had become rote and arm's length and he knew he had some work to do too.

For all that it was a rehabilitation centre, the ward resembled a three-star hotel room and was comfortable enough for two people to relax in. Ted arranged for a small fridge to be installed and stocked it with a few bottles of wine and mineral water.

It was late in the afternoon and they had enjoyed a good lunch and a pleasant but damp walk in the woods nearby. Ted started to open a bottle Chardonnay and saw Alison struggling with the zip on her blouse.

"Let me do that."

He reached out instinctively but she pushed his hand away.

"No, I'm not an invalid!"

"For sure you are not, but that's not why I asked," he put the bottle on the sideboard.

Alison cocked her head to one side. "Then pray tell me why, detective superintendent?"

He placed his hands gently on her shoulders and looked into her eyes.

"Simple, my lovely lady. Undressing you is one of the things I truly love to do. Any excuse. Call me stupid, call me randy, or call me..."

Alison stopped his lips with her fingers and gazed back at him, reassured that her man still fancied her after all their travails. Her eyes glistened.

"I won't call you any of those things, I'll just call you...a time-waster!" She pulled his head closer to her and kissed his lips, at the same time edging him towards the bed.

They sank onto the soft sheets and slowly became one again. The wine would not be touched for some time.

The days that followed were the most constructive and useful in all their years of marriage. They talked of their courting days, her intent to pull him off his pedestal when he got high-minded. For him, he recalled Alison's maddening attention to detail in all that she did and her personal values, citing a thirty-mile round trip to return a purloined hotel towel.

On a particularly mild day some weeks later, they were lunching on the patio outside the room, with Alison looking radiant and better than she had done for long. She turned to Ted and touched his upper arm gently.

"I think it's time."

He smiled at her. "What? To catch a train?"

"No, nutcase," she touched his hand lightly and looked directly into his eye. "Time for you to go back to work. You've been great, really great, and I couldn't have come this far without you. But I need some space now to be myself and work out my route back to normality. This is my battle and I'm going to win it."

He looked concerned.

"It's not a rejection, Ted. It's the opposite. I'm doing fine, really, I am. What I did shook me to the core. I've really worked hard to take stock of my life. See it as a first step to success. You're the best. But as I say, it's time."

Ted smiled at her and squeezed her hand. He knew that she was right. The time they had shared together had been so good with many happy memories flushed out from the past. Now he needed to move away and let her deal with her gremlins. For his part, the Beamish case nestled in its own space in his head, but was trying to escape. It was enveloping his psyche, pulling him back to his desk.

Jenny Willis, aka Dawn Clarke, the new receptionist in the Maria Cresswell Hospice clocked on for her first full day's work. She dutifully passed calls to the various departments without error and met and greeted people coming to visit or, sadly, bringing relatives or friends into the hospice. She lived the reality of it all and was touched by the tenderness shown by relatives and staff to those who had to be looked after until the candle of their lives was gently allowed to dim, then go out.

The quietest time of the day was around three o'clock. That is the time when most workers feel drowsy. The

English are not like some of their European contemporaries, who recognise the value of the siesta. Time to act.

Jenny held back the morning's mail. She brought a dozen manila folders from home, each with a sticky label on, pre-prepared with departmental titles to save time. She proceeded to quickly open the mail and put the contents in one pile. With the utmost casualness, she walked to the photocopier.

When she was about half way through the task, the photocopier grinding out copy after copy, quietly and efficiently, Dr Johannes Ziggefelde strode in through the front doors. He saw Jenny and approached her. She froze. Her right hand quickly undid the top buttons on her blouse and she walked deliberately away from the photocopier towards the reception area and he veered towards her.

"Good afternoon, doctor, and how are you today?" she said, coyly.

"All the better for seeing you, Dawn," he replied with a broad smile, "I just need to get some envelopes from the cupboard behind you."

He squeezed between Jenny and the stationery cupboard, lingering a moment longer than was polite. She responded by leaning forward slightly.

"Oh, sorry, sir, it's a bit crowded behind this desk, isn't it?"

Ziggefelde nodded gratefully. He found the items that he wanted, or at least pretended to want, and moved back to the front of the reception desk.

"I'm just trying to think of new ways of supporting the departments and of course you, sir. You must be ever so busy. Whatever I can do to make things easy, I will," said Jenny.

Ziggefelde smiled and acknowledged her comment. "Well done, Dawn. Perhaps you and I can talk about such things together some time in the near future. Keep up the good work. But for now, I must go. I have an appointment." He half waved a goodbye, a gesture that said, *I'll be back.*

As soon as he was out of sight, Jenny shuddered at his attention. He was creepy. She was always squeamish about using sexuality to gain a foothold, but reluctantly accepted that it often yielded results. She put it out of her mind and gathered the copies of the letters, folding hem as flat as she could. Then she opened her blouse fully and stuffed them inside a vest that she wore that day for this purpose. The vest kept the papers flat, but she tapped her tummy several times to make sure; the process took thirty seconds.

Jenny now turned her attention to sorting the mail. Each letter was duly placed into a pre-prepared folder for the appropriate department; this was her excuse for opening the envelopes. For those that she was uncertain about, she put into one marked 'miscellaneous', then put the folders into the mail racks. She knew there would be hell to pay. It was now three forty-five. In just over an hour, she would be out of the building and safely home with the photocopies.

She wondered if they would contain anything interesting.

DC Andy Crouch sat at the bar of the local pub, the Kings Arms, near the Cromer police station, with a pint of best bitter to one side, idly pretending to do a crossword. It was about six thirty p.m. and a favourite watering hole for station officers. He was always on the lookout for scuttlebutt or gossip. More particularly, he wanted to be in on every case that involved anything remotely exciting and was aggrieved that DS Bradbury had not regarded him highly enough for whatever it was that was going on now. 'Going on' was what the station police staff called it. A suicide case had been concluded with indecent haste and an operations room set up in a different part of the building to discuss heaven knows what. Even the doors were securely locked and it was impenetrable – there was not a chance to look at tell-tale white board sketches or presentations. Tellingly, there was no record whatsoever of the work being undertaken on the police HOLMES II data management system.

He sidled along the bar, up to DC 'Farmer' Hovens.

"Hi matey. What's news?"

Farmer regarded him as everyone else did, with great suspicion. In any case, he was aware that when on any kind of special mission, pubs frequented by other officers should normally be avoided. He unwisely chose to ignore this rule.

"Oh, not much. Bit o' this and a bit o' that."

"What are you drinking," Crouch waved to the barman who came over to them, and said, "Same again?"

Farmer could never resist a free drink and nodded. The barman obliged and pulled the perfect pint: cool, golden brown with a quarter-inch head on top in a straight glass. Pure magic.

After supping the top quarter Farmer put the glass down and the two boys bantered as boys do, about football, the girl in the corner with a great body, politics – especially the Human Rights Act – and work.

"So, you must be chuffed with your current operation then? God, you're a lucky so and so I wish it were me."

By now they were into their fifth pint. Farmer was not usually given to incautious language, but under the influence of best bitter caution momentarily deserted him.

"Well, actually, if I say so myself, I am lucky. But it's hush-hush mate, so I can't tell you anything." He tapped the side of his nose as he spoke and drained his beer. Andy Crouch waved to the barman to bring them two more.

"S'okay mate, I respect that. Christ if everyone knew then where would we be? But I'll tell you what buddy. That Jane Kavanagh is a looker if ever I saw one. From what I hear she did a good job on a couple of travellers the other night who tried to carve up our Gerry."

Farmer smiled with that sense of ownership that some fools think they have by associating themselves with a successful event or famous personage.

"Yeah," he took the new pint of bitter and supped the cool head, "she's quite something. But then with her background I suppose karate is just one of her skills. She's ex-army, seen service in Northern Ireland and in Bosnia and God knows what. Her mate is with that other lot, the wotsit, y'know, Interpol or Europol. I can never tell the bloody difference myself."

By now he was full of bravado and swaying against the bar, his right foot trying its best, but failing, to locate the brass foot-rail. Andy pressed harder.

"Oh, yeah. I heard that there was another little lady on the case too. Does that mean we see two new beauties back at base? Lovely old job."

"Think again, Casanova," said Farmer, eyes by now glistening. "Firstly, Jane will not often be seen at base and secondly our new little beauty is here for a bit of hush-hush observing. Then I suppose she'll be off to other exciting things."

With all the insouciance of a bragging drunk he tapped his nose with his left forefinger again, looked left and right and incautiously added, "She's observing at a hospice not too far from here. Enough said, pal, 'kay?"

Andy assured his pal that all was safe with him and ordered a couple of packets of crisps and they bantered some more. In his mind though, he was sorting out the information: two Interpol officers, not working from base and one undercover at the hospice. This could only be the Maria Cresswell Hospice at Honing. It was time for a bit of undercover work of his own, to see if he could dig up some useful information.

This could lead to a pat on the back and who knows, perhaps even promotion?

It was five o'clock and the regular receptionist arrived to take over the evening shift at the hospice. Jenny was about to leave, satisfied with her day's work, the papers crinkling against her warm rib cage, but as she approached the doors, she heard a loud shout.

"Dawn Clarke, what the hell has been going on?"

It was Bobbette Grainger, the hospice manager. She was striding towards Jenny, her faced flushed waving some papers. Two large men dressed in grey suits stood towards the back of the reception area and looked quite menacing.

"What's the matter, Miss Grainger, what have I done wrong?"

"I told you specifically that you were to simply put the mail into the correct pigeon hole for each department. I did not tell you to open or read it."

"But I didn't read anything miss. Not at all. I promise I didn't"

She added a few tears for good measure.

Grainger went on. "How do I know that? You opened the mail, Dawn, and you shouldn't have."

"Miss Grainger, you didn't say don't open it, you really didn't."

Just then Dr Ziggefelde came into reception on his way out and overheard the exchange. He clicked his knuckles several times before walking towards the fracas.

"You just said to put the mail directly into the pigeon holes. Well, I thought that I would help the departments by opening the mail and sorting it out into folders, properly like. It took me bloody ages too. I really tried to improve things. Now you're shouting at me. It isn't fair. I really want to make a success of this job, I really do."

Grainger squared up to her and half raised some of the mail, menacingly. To Jenny's enormous relief Dr Ziggefelde intervened.

"Bobbette, I think that I am to blame too," he said and Grainger turned towards him with a look of surprise on her face. "I spoke to Dawn this afternoon and she was saying that she wanted to improve the administration if she could. I didn't dissuade her and she must have taken that for a green light so to speak. I suppose that it is partly my fault."

There was a long pause as Grainger tried to weigh up the risk in what had happened and whether or not to use the two heavies standing nearby. After a long pause, she half-turned and nodded to them and they quietly moved back into the hospice corridors. Red blotches on her neck and face gave away the fact that she was seriously stressed about the situation.

"Dawn, look. The hospice has very strict rule about confidentiality. We observe it at all times. The departments are responsible for their mail and no one else – that way we can ensure there are no slip-ups or embarrassments. Doctor Ziggefelde and I can discuss this some other time. I'm sorry to alarm or worry you. I appreciate that you did your best to improve things. Thank you, but in future please let me be the judge of any administrative changes that you suggest. You can go now."

Jenny made a big issue of blowing her nose and dabbing her eyes. Then turned and walked head down towards her car. After a few steps, she looked back and saw Grainger and Ziggefelde in animated conversation, as they walked along the hospice corridors. She remembered her Daddy's favourite skiffle song by Lonnie Donnegan in which a US wagon on a train track gets through a state customs line and the driver sings: *Fooled you, fooled you – I got pig-iron, I got pig-iron...*

She laughed, turned the key in her car ignition and drove home, with the photocopies tickling her belly.

DC Andy Crouch sat in his bedsit putting together what he considered to be the bees-knees in observation kit. On the bed lay dark waterproof clothing and a black woollen hat, black gloves and a thin scarf for his face. He had bought himself a small black rucksack, torch and general-purpose knife. Ex-army binoculars completed his James Bond garb.

What he could not do, however, was to be caught in possession of a police identity card. He put this with his wallet on his dressing table. Instead, as part of his cover, he went to his computer and printed a professional style identity card, showing him to be a freelance journalist by the name of Adam Critchley. He used his laminator to seal it before cutting it into shape. To give it all some authenticity he put a couple of notebooks and pens into the rucksack, remembered that it was likely to be a long haul and added some orange drinks.

He dressed in the kit he had bought that day and stood in front of the mirror, moving this way and that, posing, raising a hand holding an imaginary pistol James Bond style. Satisfied so far, he pulled down the hat and covered most of his face with the scarf then turned off the light. He was all but invisible.

Perfect, he thought, *and now for the hospice.*

7

After a home-cooked meal, courtesy of Margaret Ogden, Jane sat at a well-worn office desk in the conservatory and looked out at the darkening sky. She worked well at night as it suited the rhythm of her body. Reviewing two separate files was the order of the day: one outlined the progress of the whole of the project and the other was labelled 'UK/Hancox/Controller'. Mike Hancox, was such a mercurial character. He could be as hard as nails or good fun, but his experience was beyond question. He has been instrumental in getting her out of several scrapes and she owed him a great deal of respect. Nevertheless, she was angry with his attitude at her previous visit.

After his agreement for her to plan a visit the USA, she read as much as she could about Caroline Redbridge and her journalistic crusade on every aspect of social justice championing people who were in no position to look after themselves. Jane began to admire the woman. Her work to highlight the reported culling of feral children in certain South American cities, the abandoning of baby girls in the rural areas of India and the thoughtless destruction of regional environments in some states in Africa that disenfranchised local people, had been highly commended by the UN.

However, she made enemies and it was inevitable that her successes were not enthusiastically heralded by international business as much as they were by academics and social activists. There had been two attempts on her life in six years. For now, she was out of action in a remote private hospital. Interpol had arranged payment for this through a third party. Caroline Redbridge would never know the source and had been told that it was a Christian organisation that wished to be anonymous. She was very ill indeed and was advised to take her time getting well. In the meantime, it was convenient for her identity to be used to spook Artaxis.

Jane scribbled a rough outline of an article on the illegal sale of body parts throughout the world and considered how she would weight the text. It had to focus on the evidence that people were being robbed of or selling their organs illegally to third parties. She would allude to the large sums of money that were being made and the likelihood that it would need a single organisation to control this trade and it was likely to be based in the USA. She tapped her chin with the top of her pencil. There had to be a way of casually dropping some clue or another into the text, that would raise the temperature and cause mistakes or unwise decisions to be made by Artaxis. A few examples of the horrors experienced by donors around the world would be thrown in for good measure to gain the shock-horror effect; that would not be difficult. Then there was the tricky question about what to say about the need to champion action to stop the illegal trade altogether. She looked at a fatter file on the left-hand side of her desk. It contained the terrible story of Bulgarian prostitute, Katrina Anatov that had opened up the whole can of worms.

She sipped her coffee and recalled meeting Katrina, and the frightening events that followed.

Bulgaria – reflection

The Bulgarian taxi-driver looked at Katrina and could not believe his luck. He had had a bad week with hardly a decent fare to provide food for his family or pay for his fuel. If he had not got involved with delivering small packages of drugs around Sofia, then he would not have survived. He had drunk far too much of the local beer and was feeling quite miserable - until now.

The good-looking near-naked young woman in the back of his car was looking at him contemptuously, but he did not care. Sex was the last thing on his wife's mind these days and he was certainly not going to turn this chance down. He stopped leering at her and said menacingly.

"You want embassy, I want you – deal?"

The taxi driver was sweaty and his face greasy and unshaven. Katrina hesitated then reluctantly agreed. She pointed to the wound on her left side and said, "Be careful of this!"

He joined her in the back of the taxi and she recoiled at the smell of tobacco on his breath, then he turned her to one side to look at the wound, but took little care.

Sated, he got out of the taxi and urinated against the rear wheel. Katrina curled up in a ball on the back seat and prayed that he would do as she asked in return. He reached into the side of the door and pulled out a bottle of beer then opened and drained it in four swallows and threw the empty bottle into the car park. He turned to her and said sneeringly in Bulgarian, "You are not English! I could of course take you to some friends of mine and get a good price for you?"

Despite her fear, Katrina responded calmly. "Unless of course you choose the ones I escaped from. I will tell them that you helped me and changed your mind. Trust me, make the wrong choice and your balls will be decorating the front of your taxi. It's up to you. Besides, I am a prostitute, and the price wouldn't be worth the chance. So just cut the crap and take me to the British Embassy as we agreed. You've had your way. Now honour the deal."

The taxi driver looked to the sky, considered his options, and then shrugged. He got into the vehicle and drove off at high speed. After about five minutes the taxi approached the gates of the British Embassy. The roads were deserted and looked slippery after a short shower of rain.

He looked into the rear-view mirror where Katrina sat with her knees up under her chin, shivering with her arms wrapped around them and eyes wide with anticipation.

"Okay, you tart, I'm not stopping," he sneered, "I will slow the vehicle and you choose when to jump out. If you don't jump, then you will travel on to somewhere where tonight's services will be repeated so many times that you'll lose count."

He laughed scornfully and slowed the vehicle as it approached the gates.

Katrina was so scared she felt dizzy but she didn't think twice and opened the door to the taxi as the gates came into view. She knew the fate of girls that fell into the wrong hands and this was enough to propel her out of the vehicle. For good measure the taxi driver sadistically put his foot on the accelerator, roaring with laughter as he did so, and her body spun out of the rear door, rolling over several times before crashing into the kerb in front of the embassy.

Two Bulgarian guards looked at the helpless body of the girl, scratched from the fall in the road and with a wound to the left side that was now bleeding profusely.

She looked up and pleaded in English that she had learned from in school days.

"Embassy – quick - I'm British."

The guards were confused at first and then both decided that perhaps she was really English and carried her inside. One of the secretaries called for a doctor and wrapped her in a woollen blanket, then led her to the embassy first aid room. She lay on a bed feeling the crisp sheets against her body and the cool hand of the middle-aged secretary stroking her forehead and proffering warm tea.

She burst into tears of gratitude and relief.

The days that followed were uncomplicated and unthreatening, as she outlined the facts honestly to the officers who questioned her, and admitted that she was a Bulgarian citizen and not British. This posed an enormous dilemma for the embassy. She was not claiming asylum and they were not empowered to allow her to stay in the building.

Percy Walsh, the First Secretary, was incensed by her story when briefed. He was one of the few people who, promoted from within the lowest levels of the civil service, broke into high rank in the Diplomatic Corps. The Corps was almost exclusively manned with Oxbridge graduates, mostly from wealthy and more often than not, aristocratic families. He was well liked and renowned for his distaste for the cloying culture of 'expediency' that was at the heartbeat of all national embassies., and colleagues also knew of his sharp social conscience.

That morning he had a bruising encounter with the ambassador. After an hour's discussion, they retreated on reasonable terms with Percy charged with sorting something out. Otherwise, Katrina would be shown the door.

After lunch on the second day, Percy made several calls, before coming to see Katrina. He had a kindly face, a straight dark moustache and was tall and good-looking. He put her instantly at ease.

"Hello, Katrina, how are you feeling today?" he asked warmly and sat down beside her, not too close and yet near enough to make her feel comfortable.

"I'm okay, very sore all over, but okay. Thank you for getting a doctor to deal with my operation wound."

"Yes, I was concerned about your operation wound. I'm so glad it has been sorted out. Your story is very upsetting, Katrina, very. I have to tell you that it's been difficult sorting out what to do next. Let me keep it simple. The British Embassy is in a quandary as to what to do, but luckily, I have some good contacts in your government and they want to help. Your country is embarrassed about the situation you find yourself in. Some good people want to help and will not let you down. Without them it would've been much more difficult, I can tell you. Most important of all, I managed to secure the services of one of the best human rights lawyers in your country, Dimitar Kurntov. I am not sure if you have heard of him?"

Tears welled in Katrina's eyes. "You did this for me, a prostitute?"

Uncharacteristically, the First Secretary touched her shoulder gently.

"No, because you are a human being, Katrina," he said, "a human being."

The days that followed went quickly and a sensitive Bulgarian government immediately closed the nursing home and arrested the staff. Katrina was relieved that she had gained enough notoriety to be safe from the dead hand of government that would have wanted to hush things up had she not gained access to the British embassy. The question of what would happen to the staff of the clinic and who were the paymasters of this ugly trade hung in the air, until Percy pulled a masterstroke. He called Interpol and the embarrassed Bulgarian government agreed to work with the agency to investigate and take the necessary legal action. Percy's call was just what Interpol had been waiting for. This was the first key piece of evidence needed to kick-start a full investigation.

Two weeks later Katrina was allocated an apartment outside Sofia and Jane Kavanagh turned up. Jane was experienced enough to carry out a full appreciation of the situation. She was concerned that although the Bulgarian government had arrested the hospital staff and given Katrina the apartment, there may well be others who would be extremely put out that the operation had been closed down. Her safety was paramount and proper security had to be arranged.

"Okay, then, Katrina, time for you to relax and we can wait for the next scene in this tragedy. My job is to get to know you and keep you safe and I promise that I will do that."

Katrina smiled meekly. She was not a weak person but the clandestine and dangerous nature of events left her in a dangerous limbo.

"Thank you. You are very kind. I have not had much kindness in my life. There's not really much to know about me. I come from a poor family. My mother was sick from the day I was born and I guess I carried that guilt - you know, being born and causing your mother such illness. I took any job I could get to earn money to pay medical bills and to live, but missing so much school to look after my mother cost me an education. Eventually, I became a prostitute. Not nice but there was money in it."

"Don't feel embarrassed, Katrina, it's the oldest profession in the world and you did what you had to do to survive. I certainly don't judge you. How did you end up in the clinic?"

"After I confessed my financial position to a customer, he offered to help. The next thing I know is that a woman contacts me and offers to arrange to sell one of my kidneys for a large sum of money. It all went so quickly. She put me in touch with someone else and then I was in the hospital and counting down the anaesthetic. You know the rest."

Jane wondered just how many others were in the same awful position in the world. She spent time with Katrina gently pursuing each fact to tease out some important but hitherto forgotten clues. On the second day, Katrina was entering into the spirit of things.

Jane grew surprised when Katrina asked, "Why don't we trace the woman who recruited me for organ donation. I'm sure I can recognise her. She will give evidence. What do you say?"

"Oh, dear, Katrina. I'm sorry. I didn't want to worry you. The police followed up your description of the lady and the other day a senior detective told me that a female body matching the description had been found in the river Iskar on the outskirts of Sofia."

Katrina was shocked, dropped a glass she was holding and it shattered on the floor. She grew flushed and began to tremble, holding her fingers to her lips.

Jane sat her down and put her at ease, and told her that a security operative would be assigned to her soon. This improved Katrina's mood - but she was still scared.

Two more days drifted by with no further useful information coming out of their conversations. On the fifth day, the telephone rang, when Katrina answered it there was no one there. Jane grew alert and as dusk approached, put the bedroom light out and closed the curtains, leaving a small opening. The apartment lounge remained lit with the curtains closed and she left Katrina curled up on the couch reading a magazine. Taking a cup of black coffee into the bedroom, she settled down to watch the road outside through the gap in the curtains.

At first, she thought it a pointless exercise. However, after about an hour, a large black car stopped outside the apartment block and two large men got out. They stood looking up at the flats. Both men wore black leather bomber jackets and one wore sunglasses despite the dusk. She telephoned the police department and they undertook to immediately investigate. Nothing happened for thirty minutes. Then she saw one of the men answer his mobile phone, He looked up at the apartment while talking animatedly to his accomplice. Then they both moved quickly towards the front door of the block. Jane realised that her request had been intercepted.

She sprang out of her seat and ran to the lounge, half-falling over the dining chairs. Katrina looked up in surprise and dropped her magazine.

"Katrina, get up now, get up. Let's get out. Quickly. Don't ask. Run," Jane yelled. "Go, go, go."

They scrambled out of the door and Jane took Katrina's hand and pulled her up the stairs. Adrenaline flowed and seemed to give them energy. They took the grey, dirty steps two at a time. Eventually reached the topmost apartment. Jane turned to Katrina. "Knock on this door and demand to be let in. Say that you are the police, be stern and make it work or we're done for. Be quick."

Katrina hesitated for a brief moment then pummelled the door and demanded in stern Bulgarian that the door be opened. There was an exchange of words, but the door opened just a little. It was enough to let both of them burst inside. Luckily, the occupant was an elderly lady who stepped back, frightened and bewildered at what was going on.

Jane closed the door carefully so that it didn't make a sound, whilst Katrina gave the woman a hug and explained that they were afraid of some men and they had to hide, it was the only thing they could do and she was sorry for yelling. The elderly lady, frail though she was, understood, half-smiled and accepted the situation.

To Jane's surprise, the lady nodded sagely, straightened her back defiantly, took her hand and guided her towards a bedroom.

Katrina whispered, "She is brave. She said that she survived the horrors and uncertainties of the communist era and is toughened to fear."

The lady beckoned them into the bedroom and opened a large ornately carved wooden wardrobe full of musty old clothes, they got inside and she shut the door. Just as they did so, there was the sound of a door being smashed in and shouting somewhere on the floor below, then crockery and glass being broken.

Katrina's body was shaking and she held on tightly to Jane.

Jane hated hiding and felt more vulnerable because of it. There was silence, then came the sound of banging on the doors of other apartments below, more shouting and ten minutes later the men pounded at the lady's door.

The lady opened the door slowly and confronted two heavily built men who went to push past her, but she valiantly stood her ground. There is something about a strong-willed elderly lady who looks frail and weak, and yet refuses to budge, no matter what faces her. It is the defiance of a butterfly against a bullock, and yet, the bullock stops, unwilling to do what it can do so easily. These men were the toughs of today, young criminals who wanted money and reward, nothing else. They weren't the communist thugs of yesteryear, who were content to dispense rough justice to anyone who got in their way as their political masters directed. These men weren't into bashing old women.

She spoke to them quietly and solemnly - then the girls heard the door softly closing and the lock clicking.

They cautiously crept out of the wardrobe and walked towards the lady who spoke to Katrina. "I told them I had nothing to hide and they were at liberty to search, but had to be gentle with me because I was frightened and no different from their own grandmothers."

Katrina kissed her on both cheeks and cried into her shoulder. Jane looked at the way the lady held Katrina's and realised that she was doing just what any grandmother would do, despite the frightening experience of the night.

After waiting for an hour, Jane and Katrina exited out of the back door of the apartment block, hailed a taxi and went to a hotel in central Sofia. She was fuming and berated the police department about their lack of assistance, then demanded of government officials that Katrina be allowed to leave the country. Initial refusal met with the threat of an investigation into police corruption as to how her call was intercepted. Reluctant officials were persuaded that it was in the country's best interests for Katrina to leave until the fracas settled down.

Katrina was now hot property and was speedily moved to London.

England

Jane yawned widely as she slowly flicked through the pages of the file that contained the results of Interpol work in Bulgaria. The closure of the hospital in Sofia resulted in detailed interviews of every member of staff. Evidence was now rolling in, but it was slow going. It had been touch-and-go, but when some pretty hefty European Commission incentives were placed before Bulgarian government officials together with heavy hints that it was time for the country to work hard towards dealing with organised crime and corruption the enthusiasm was thereafter unbounded. Key facts began to emerge. Two men were caught, questioned and indicted for the murder of the female intermediary, found in the river with her throat cut and the clinic doctors, now out of work, sang loudly. Most important of all was the fact that there was sufficient information which led Interpol to believe that a large medical research establishment somewhere in the USA was implicated as the central focus in organising the receipt and sale of body parts. Yet again, all they had were references to intermediaries and small clinics on the margins of society. Frustratingly, there was nothing absolute, no real proof, just enough to start the file and justify further funding for the operation.

Pushing the file to one side, Jane reached for the one marked, 'UK/Hancox'. She poured some more hot black coffee and adjusted the swivel arm of the table light. The file was getting thicker already. What a great hunch it had been to follow up the lead that a van had recently travelled to the Romanian hospital from the Maria Cresswell Hospice. The Beamish suicide added another interesting dimension. No substantial evidence was yet to hand, just observation. Jane's thoughts turned to Jenny Willis and her undercover work at the hospice. She also solemnly contemplated the work of Chin Kwok, recruited from the Metropolitan Police in London because of his Hong Kong Police experience. With his cheerful and lively demeanour, he was now their key under-cover agent in China. In one of those strange ways that stay with everyone from childhood, even when many go on to eschew religion as they grow older, she prayed for their safety.

It was emotionally tough work managing a large project with a number of operatives. Jane much preferred individual investigation or observation tasks. In these situations, she was in control of herself and the mission in hand, and was responsible for no one else. Worrying about friends and colleagues didn't sit easily with her, especially not when she had been instrumental in putting them into the field in the first place. To be a good controller, the kind of person Mike Hancox was, needed strong character with an absolute focus on the mission. Whilst friendly and supportive, he would move agents like chess pieces to achieve success; she strongly suspected that if necessary, he may also ditch them.

Over the next two hours she constructed a short article for her blog in the style of Caroline Redbridge, citing the terrible state that many people found themselves in, having been robbed of their organs, and the vast profits that could be made from all kinds of body parts. She exhorted readers to be on the lookout for such activity and challenged those who read her blog to respond to her with evidence of malpractice and to join her cause. It was a passionate call to arms.

Stretching her arms above her head, her neck cracked as she straightened and she realised how long she had been hunched over the desk. The illuminated hands of her desk clock showed two a.m. She closed the files and put them into the secure safe. It was all taking shape, but still far too slowly.

For all that, Jane knew from experience that things had a habit of changing – sometimes very quickly.

8

Ted's discussion with the chief constable had been tense. He knew that his boss felt out of control on the Beamish case and didn't like it one bit. Ted accepted, for form's sake, that he was notionally heading up the inquiry and Jane Kavanagh was seconded to the team, but she took the lead in terms of sorting out how to best use the information gathered. That made sense. Although he was not prevented from working on the case, he got the impression that his boss was now completely uninterested in the outcome. Eventually, the chief constable dismissed him with a wave of the hand, without even asking after Alison. He said they would talk again.

Ted left the office biting his tongue. He always understood the value of expediency, but there were times when patience wore thin and today was one of those days. He walked to the operations room, keyed in a code and entered. Jane was sitting in the corner and looked up, registering surprise. She stared at him as he walked across the room towards her and held her pen between her hands, putting it down gently as he reached her desk.

"Hi, c'est moi. I return to the fold," he said, and he held his arms half open.

Jane looked straight at him at first, and after a few seconds smiled politely. "So, how's Alison?"

"She's fine, we spent a lot of time together. Frankly, we spent more time talking in that place than we ever had over the last three or four years. Thanks, for asking."

"So why are you here?" she said, directly.

"Alison insisted. It's a really good sign. She felt good enough to kick me out of the door. She wants to get her head right so that she can return home. I'm really proud of her."

Ted walked to the coffee percolator and poured himself a cup of stewed black coffee. He sniffed it and decided to take a chance.

"So, how's it all going? I need to know so that I can get back up to speed." He put the cup to his lips and flinched as the hot coffee burned.

Jane thought for a moment. "Okay, Ted. You're not stupid, you know that coming back is going to be disruptive for a short while and, take it from me, your DS Bradbury has been simply superb. She's enjoyed the freedom and has stretched herself to achieve some great results. Now don't you go changing that balance." She added, "You just have one obstacle."

"Yeah?"

"Yes. I think your chief constable has gone lukewarm on the investigation from a couple of things he has said. He did rather get a flea in his ear from the Home Office. Anyway, from what I see around the station there's already jockeying for position."

"Jane, he's just miffed. His nose has been put out of joint and he feels out of control in his own manor, but I am absolutely certain that he'll do nothing to hamper the work of the team. Perhaps the route to a calmer life is to keep reassuring him about the mission, alluding to the tributes that will arise to the Police department, and of course, himself. We should badge this as a fitting swan song for his retirement - hoping, of course, that the case doesn't go into the next millennium. As for young Bradbury, I'm delighted that she's finding her confidence. She's good value and it's obvious that you've brought out the best in her."

He eased himself into a small armchair. "Let's get things straight. I'm totally committed to solving this case and more than happy that we work together as a team to do so. I am not going to get in the way of anything you have set up - I'm only too glad to be back at work. You have nothing to worry about."

Jane leaned back and smiled. "You are on the right track, Ted. Sure, I'm a little bit concerned, but I've a more jaundiced view of your master, so watch your back. Besides, it's his local approval I need for some things, otherwise this is just a forward office for Interpol and MI6. Harsh but true."

Ted laughed inwardly, Jane had a way about her, a kind of 'no frills' approach to problem-solving. He liked that - it was refreshing. He took the same tack.

"Whilst we are on the subject of support, Jane, I would like to meet your boss in London. I think I should be trusted more. I mean, brought into the wider picture."

Jane nodded in agreement and thought, *that will be an experience for you!*

Nicola Bradbury was pleased to see him, she looked and sounded completely different to the person he left behind weeks ago. She had a discernibly sharper edge to her now. He was careful to ask for a briefing on the situation and the work in hand that wouldn't take any more time than a bullet-point format and a verbal run-through. He explained that he was the one having to catch up and did not want to add to the workload. Nicola came back thirty minutes later and gave him a clear, professional point-brief and was ready to explain progress to date.

"Nicola, this is a good brief, thank you. So much work has gone on in such a short time. Just one thing, the undercover agent, what's her name, let's see," and he flicked over the pages of the point-brief, "Jenny Willis. What's she up to?"

"She is under-cover in the Maria Cresswell Hospice, guv. And by all accounts, despite her size, packs a punch. The objective is to find one, or hopefully more, pieces of paper that implicate the hospice in the sale of human organs, or better, links them to Artaxis Incorporated in the United States. So, I guess it is a lot of observing until the right moment comes along."

Ted nodded thoughtfully, *Jane is right, Nicola, you definitely are sharper – good luck to you, young lady.*

He reflected on Jane's comment about watching his back and realised that his return to work had been received in a neutral kind of way and his role had hardly been endorsed; he resolved to discuss the situation with his boss in the morning to clear the air.

The chief constable's personal assistant looked a little ill at ease as Ted entered the outer office. He waved her away and made his way straight to his master's office without stopping. The door was open and he was surprised to see that DI Mike Daniels was briefing on a number of matters. *Mike of all people, briefing the chief. Now there's a strange sight?* he thought to himself.

The two men looked up and regarded him with surprise.

"Sir, I wondered if we might talk about my role on the Beamish case. We didn't really conclude matters yesterday."

Mike shifted uneasily and said to the chief constable that he would leave and come back some other time, feigning some urgent problem or another. The chief agreed, but looked at Ted the way that a headmaster does to school prefect reporting someone in form 4B for smoking. His demeaner was different today.

"Ted, good to see you back. I missed your good counsel," he said, disingenuously.

They both headed for two armchairs by the window. As Ted passed the desk, he saw the titles of two of four files. Grimewood was one and Turnbull the other. He grimaced; both had been cases where he could have done better. They had been active when Alison had been going through some particularly bad times. It occurred to him that he could chart his worst performances to her mental outbreaks.

"Problems with some old cases, sir?" he said inquisitively, arching an eyebrow as he said it.

The chief constable regarded him knowingly, without expression. "No, Ted. Your DI brought a few things to my attention, that's all. I don't think he expected you back so soon. Don't think too badly of him. He's probably just realised that time is running out and there might just be a promotion contest soon, if you have to retire that is."

Ted knew only too well where the problems were in both those cases and one or two others. They were clumsy and untidy errors, nothing more. His trusted DI, Mike Daniels, had had the privilege of hiding them; perhaps now they were being dusted off.

"And?"

"And nothing, Ted. I'm too busy to piss around digging up old ghosts when they have been sent on their way already. I was about to announce that, when you came in. Now let's talk about you. There's some interesting stuff that I would like you to get involved in."

Coffee had soundlessly been delivered by his PA as they made their way to the chairs and the chief reached for a cup. Ted had to think fast, as visions of burglaries and schoolground vandalism formed in his mind.

"I have a request, sir. I want to stay on the Beamish case and see it through." Ted sat back and let it sink in.

"No, I don't want that, Ted. We're understaffed and I really want you to take the reins locally and sort a few problems out."

He slurped his coffee loudly. Ted remembered that he always did that when he wanted to mark the end of an issue, but Ted wasn't going to let go and his mind raced to find the right angle – which came easily.

"Sir, I think we could kill two birds with one stone here. I know that Mike Daniels probably feels that he is getting a little long in the tooth and I heard downstairs that we are getting short on the management side," he lied, "so, with respect, why not give Mike a leg up? He's a sound officer and I hold no grudges against his earlier machinations. In fact, I want to admit here and now that without him supporting me in the past things might have been a lot different. Frankly, life has been pretty tough."

Ted felt the time was right to give the chief more details about his home life and the pressures that he had been under with Alison's depression, then outlined her current situation. The chief nodded and seemed to take it in.

"Alison doesn't know yet, but I'm going to take early retirement. Before that I want to be sure that this station receives a lot of credit for the work that is being put into this Beamish case. You need to know, sir, that when it's all over, we're likely to be marginalised and the hard work done by your officers will be lost in the noise of applause for the bigger crime agencies like MI6 and Interpol. That wouldn't be fair at all."

The chief put his coffee down grasped his hands together and frowned at the table. Ted knew that he had hit the right button. *'Attaboy, take the bait!'.*

"So how are you going to do that then?"

Ted knew that the one thing that had eluded the chief was a state honour.

"I think it's a case keeping me involved so that I can brief you on developments as they occur. Things are heating up. There could be a result in weeks. It's imperative that we are properly involved with the final press release and reports. You know what I mean, television and radio reports, newspapers, interviews and so on. I guess the Home Secretary will need to know about our contribution. So, sir, it's important that I continue to represent our interests – we do, after all, play a large part in the case. I need to meet with Jane Kavanagh's boss to establish our position."

He held his breath. The chief constable looked straight at him.

"Well, not that I think that press interest is the be-all and end-all, of course. But I do want the station to get its fair share of the praise, we deserve that, don't we?"

The chief constable pretended to consider the question more deeply by looking at the ceiling, then, bingo. He reached for his coffee cup and slurped it loudly.

"Okay, Ted, on balance, I agree. Good man. I think your plan is very sound indeed and if you're sure about Daniels, then we can proceed. Yes, get right into the system, and keep the force visible. I think we have a good plan here."

Ted stayed for another half an hour, during which he explained his intention to start a new venture after retirement, something that wouldn't involve long hours of work and which was a tad more creative. He was seven years older than Alison, at just forty-five years old and it was time for a fresh start. Since the chief was about to retire there was a lot of synergy in their conversation. They went back a long way and it was not really difficult to seal the deal and walk confidently back downstairs knowing that he had got his own way.

As he passed Mike Daniels' office, he popped his head in and greeted him.

"Mike, hello. Listen, I want to stay with the Beamish operation because it's 'touch and go' at the moment and I've invested so much time. I'm sorry if that appears selfish. I've secured a permanent position on the case. This means that you will soon be moved, but it's not bad news, I'm certain it will be on temporary promotion, but don't quote me. Good luck my friend."

He tapped his nose and said that he hoped that it would be the start of something good for Mike

Mike stuttered his thanks and looked awkward. Ted helped him.

"Look, Mike, I'm sorry for my absentmindedness, Alison's struggle has been tough on me and I suppose I've not been that good at handling it. But I am on track. I really appreciate your support and the way you've covered for me."

Mike looked relieved.

Ted reflected that doing this made him feel more secure in himself than anything he had done in the past. There was a knock on the side of the office door and the chief constable's PA came in to say Mike was wanted upstairs.

Ted gave him the thumbs up and waved him on. He watched him walk down the corridor, nervously adjusting his tie and brushing sandwich crumbs off his suit.

After a beer and lunch at the nearby pub, the Kings Arms, Ted walked down towards Cromer pier. The sky was clear and the same seagulls that had feasted on poor Dr Beamish's flesh now circled and swooped, looking for tourists with ice creams. He stopped by the entrance to the pier and put his hands on the warm railings. A tap on his shoulder made him jump.

"Wow, someone's on edge," said Jane.

"Oh, no, not at all. I was deep in thought. This case has so many elements to it, quite intriguing really. Oh, and by the way, for what it's worth, you've made a heck of a difference to Nicola. She's really stepping up to the plate and it's good to see."

Jane nodded in agreement and handed Ted a piece of paper. "Here are details on my boss, Mike Hancox, including telephone and email contacts. He's happy to meet and bring you up to speed. He doesn't always to do this, so make the most of it. It's important that we work in harmony, Ted, but have a care. Just one slip and we'll alert the enemy and poof, the case is scuppered!"

They walked back up the hill to the station and Ted was pleased at Jane's interest in Alison's situation. She had buckets more empathy than his boss. Sometimes, it's reassuring to know that someone else understands your problems. He watched her drive away. After glancing at the notes, Ted took out his mobile phone and dialled Mike Hancox's number.

Assistant Nurse Annie Briggs pushed the trolley containing the body of Hermione Radcliffe down the long, carpeted corridor from the private rooms in the Maria Cresswell Hospice and along the practical linoleum covered hallway that led to the room where bodies were prepared for funeral. Annie knew that the end was inevitable in a place such as this and worked hard to make life as pleasant as she could for all those with whom she came into contact. Hermione had been gentle and patient with everything that she had to suffer. She was patient too with her arrogant and controlling husband. Annie was certain that he loved her and yet she had the feeling that this was a late sensation in their lives. He seemed to be making up for lost time and she wondered whether or not it was a kind of 'love conscience'.

Annie was disappointed. Hermione never seemed that sick, then gradually, and yet almost imperceptibly her energy sagged, she passed into a coma and then died. Annie touched Hermione's blanket-covered feet gently as she pushed the trolley slowly, singing softly some of the songs of her native Jamaica. Occasionally she would point this or that out to Hermione, as though her spirit would gratefully acknowledge the trivia. The body was cold, and yet, *not deathly cold*, she thought to herself.

The trolley wheels squeaked as she turned into the green room with its black rubber-covered preparation table and ominous looking side tables on which all manner of different instruments lay, gleaming in the florescent light. Annie winced.

"Here we are, Hermione. I won't go until someone comes in, honey. I promise you that."

Just as she finished reassuring Hermione's body, the doors at the back of the room burst open and two people entered dressed in green gowns.

Dr Johannes Ziggefelde was doing up his facemask as he strode towards the table. He regarded her cheerfully. "Good morning, Annie. Keeping our customers happy as usual?"

"That's right, Doctor. Now this lady is something lovely, so you folks make her look good now, d'yer hear?" she wagged her finger playfully at him.

Dr Ziggefelde raised his hands as if in surrender. "Annie, if you say so."

When the main door to the corridor closed behind Annie, Hermione's body was slid gently onto the table. The nurse went to the door and locked it, then returned with a tray of instruments. When the blankets and clothing were removed, Ziggefelde reached between the body's thighs and looked at a thermometer that was connected to the groin. It registered a slight reading showing that the body was as close to death as it could be; but with the overdose of drugs pumped into the body over the last couple of weeks, that wasn't surprising. This meant that all the organs were still in a good state - including the brain. This mean that the body was sentient.

Despite the physical senses being down to almost zero, Hermione was aware of tugging and ripping of her bodily skin but could not shout *STOP*. Voices, tinny and distant, talked about kidneys, heart and so on. Her mind was in a whirl; *What was happening to her?* Cloudy vision meant she could only just make out a grey fuzzy light through half open eyelids. The muffled voices used words like lens and cornea - suddenly the right eye-lid was pulled up and white light burst in.

Coming towards her central vision was a bright silver scalpel.

China

Chin Kwok sat with his elbows on a blue painted wooden breakfast table in a small restaurant in Sang Yong and nursed yet another hangover. He wondered just how it was that Dragon Tattoo could consume so much rice wine without it affecting his senses. After laughing and joking they parted company at about two a.m. He was becoming quite good company and Chin hated deceiving him. This was normal in undercover work where relationships develop quickly, but it has to be guarded against. Familiarity with people who had to be used to get information quite often led observers to drop their guard. It was just as likely that someone who was being used to gather information would turn nasty if they found out. He would take no chances and his mind returned to the job in hand.

One thing was niggling at him. For a few days, he had the unerring feeling that he was being watched. Call it experience, intuition, whatever; he simply knew it. In fact, he also thought he knew who it was. During the week, a young woman turned up who looked like an outsider. She was small and attractive with unusually pale skin and wide round eyes, quite unlike the country people around Sang Yong. Although she dressed like everyone else, her clothing looked as though it was new and had been deliberately washed to age it. He considered her style of dress and also noticed she had a very rounded, full figure that could only be a product of a good diet and an absence of physical labour. Bored with the dull assessment of it all, he playfully imagined what her breasts were like and the shape of her rear. *Ah, back in London I would make it my priority to target you my beauty and I would win for sure.* He raised a cracker to his mouth and crunched it noisily.

She also made the mistake that Chin had long since learned to deal with through personal experience, that of occasionally looking around her taking in the objects and the people in the hotel, as if her agenda was different from everyone else's. He held his round tea bowl in both of his hands and when she looked up smiled at her. She responded readily, then continued with her breakfast. It was the wrong thing to do. Country Chinese are very private and rarely smile at strangers until they get to know them better.

Who was she and where was she from?

She disappeared as quickly as she had arrived. She was not at breakfast the next day and certainly wasn't at any of the local restaurants. He reasoned that perhaps she had travelled to another town.

Today, Chin had more important things to consider. Dragon Tattoo was still friendly, but he had a strange look about him. At first, Chin thought it undisguised malevolence, but he knew that his friend had sustained a severe wound to the cheek some years back, that had the effect of suppressing a smile and other facial expressions, turning them into something less cheerful. Facial expressions are considered good indicators of temperament, friendliness or danger, but those with unusual or damaged features are always difficult to read.

At three p.m. he met Dragon Tattoo for tea at a corner shop. They regarded each other politely. Then his friend said, absentmindedly, "Another consignment tomorrow."

Chin tried not to look too interested, but was wary that it was being clumsily introduced into the conversation. Had he developed a personal rapport with Dragon Tattoo that transcended boundaries of secrecy and sensitivity?

"Oh, machine parts or what?"

"No, stupid southern man. You know, you saw them didn't you, a week or so ago. The bodies of executed prisoners. They are brought here to the Institute for examination and preparation for cremation. They are criminals and so denied a traditional burial."

"Oh. Bodies eh? Can't be a nice task to have to unload that cargo."

"Not bad really." Dragon Tattoo slurped his black tea noisily. "It always makes me feel glad to be alive, I suppose.

The girls are strangely nonchalant about it. That always surprises me, but then nothing should surprise me about women. I think they are born scheming and stupid."

Chin remembered some of Dragon Tattoo's tales. He had been teased mercilessly at school but even more so at the Institute by the other female janitors, the ones he had seen unloading the truck when he first arrived. Young girls don't deal with ugliness easily in any society, least of all in China. Recent freedom of expression and ability to purchase and travel outside China removed young people from the traditional standards of behaviour expected of them by their elders. Chin could forgive Dragon Tattoo for his abrasive comments.

He ordered some sweet cakes.

"I'm sorry you have to do that. It can't be easy for you. Each of those people had a life with parents, a family and friends..."

Dragon Tattoo cut in with what seemed like the party line. "They are criminals and as such deserve nothing. They steal from the Chinese people, lie and cheat and there is no room for that. They are as bad as the Falun Gong."

Chin winced. Propaganda about the Falun Gong movement, which was dedicated and devoted to the pursuit, through meditation and philosophy, of truthfulness, compassion and tolerance, was distorted and invoked terrible violence against them. Tens of thousands had been tortured and imprisoned. Worse was the overwhelming evidence that many Falun Gong had been executed and their bodies probably used to supply China's organ transplant needs. Dragon Tattoo's views bumped heavily into Chin's social conscience. He unwisely pursued the point.

"Oh, Falun Gong. But weren't some of our officials indicted by Argentina and Spain with accusations of illegal use of the bodies, or something like that. I do remember they encouraged UN Special Rapporteurs to investigate the treatment of the group."

Chin wished he had not risen to the comment. He was aware that next to China's state censorship of the press, this human rights matter was a national scandal and yet it had been superbly managed to ensure that anyone who was a member of the Falun Gong was considered a threat to everyday life and national security.

As expected, Dragon Tattoo became incensed, half standing to make his point. "The Falun Gong are scum, Chin, and you read too many western newspapers. But it does not matter, all such people end by facing death. Like those in the shed."

Chin tried to put the reports that he had read about the repressive methods used against the Falun Gong practitioners to the back of his mind, but they lingered. He feigned indifference and poured more tea.

"Sorry, my friend. I can be so stupid."

Dragon tattoo sat down and continued. "Anyway, I know what happens to these people. I know."

He grinned maniacally and let this sentence hang in the air. Chin waited a few moments before pursuing it.

"Oh? I suppose they spring back to life and are turned into loyal party workers then?" He laughed, but Dragon Tattoo didn't share the joke.

"No," he said, almost seeming to catch his breath, "No, not quite as cheerful as that. They are cut up."

Chin realised he was getting close to a revelation.

"Cut up? But is it not practice that some organs are used for transplants for Chinese people? That's fair use of parts to save lives, isn't it?"

He felt sick at saying it.

"Yes, I used to think so, Chin, but..." he began to falter and Chin mentally egged him on, "well, I observed through a rear window one day, that teams of people dressed in green gowns opened up the bodies and removed everything. I mean everything. Flesh of all sorts was taken out and packed into cool trays or boxes, even bones seemed to be removed and labelled as if for use. They took pieces from the eyes, lumps of flesh, skin and all sorts. What was left was packed into a blue truck and taken out to the incinerator to be burned. There is a large filter on the top. You can see it from here," he pointed almost absentmindedly over to his left. "This probably reduces the stink of burning flesh."

Chin remembered the earlier rice-wine-induced remark about body parts fed to dogs. They were both quiet. Chin desperately wanted more information but Dragon Tattoo was lost in his own thoughts.

After a while Chin spoke, "But where do they put this stuff? I can imagine that research can be carried out, but from what you say, together with the regularity of consignments, there must be a lot to use up."

"It doesn't stay here," his friend replied. "I see small refrigerated vehicles come and collect cooled boxes and take them away. Who knows where they go?"

Chin ordered more tea and cakes. He was desperate to keep off the rice wine for just a little longer and his expectations rose. At last, Dragon Tattoo too a long drag on his cigarette and offered up a priceless piece of information: they expected another consignment of bodies in a day's time. Chin took note and didn't pursue the matter further in case he raised suspicion.

It was time to let the facts sink in and decide what his next move would be.

England

Jeremy Radcliffe sat in the hospice chapel. The staff had left him alone with Hermione's body, which was dressed neatly in a white robe. She had been made up and although a little sallow, looked serene and at peace. This pleased Radcliffe. He bowed his head and did what all people did in such circumstances – he wept tears of regret. Regret that his career had always come first; regret that they had never had children; and above all, regret that he had been irascible and stubborn, often forgetting that his loving wife Hermione frequently needed to be made to feel special. He had known that, but stubbornly put it to one side. In the twilight of their marriage, he tried to mend the damage, but it all seemed false and contrived. He was just not naturally empathetic and open. She had become inured to his clumsy attempts at tenderness after he retired and now it was too late.

His body shook with sobs for a good half an hour.

9

Bobbette Grainger, paced up and down in her office. Her face was flushed and she was smarting at the interference of Dr Ziggefelde in the workings of the administration. Given the stringent constraints placed on her, it was difficult enough at the best of times. Everything from the records that were kept in order to track and catalogue the illegal process of removing parts from bodies and transporting them to collection points, to the legal work of the hospice, of which looking after people who were genuinely terminally ill, had to be meticulously controlled. The only difference was that some were really dying and the rest would be helped on their way, the date and time of death being commensurate with the need for the highest value put on the healthiest item in their body.

Dr Ziggefelde closed the office door behind him and stood, hands on his hips, in front of Grainger.

"I'm really not happy, Johannes, really not happy at all," she said, hardly able to stop her voice from trembling.

"Look, Bobbette, the girl was only trying to help and I can't see what you are worried about. She's not that bright, you know."

Grainger remained unconvinced. "Big bust more like, Johannes. For goodness sake, you could hardly keep your eyes off her bosom. I hope that *herself* doesn't get to know that."

Ziggefelde winced. "And you are not going to stir the pot, are you?"

Grainger shrugged her shoulders.

"Oh, for goodness sake, Johannes, we have to be really careful. Some of the letters that were taken out of envelopes were quite sensitive." She paused and added, "I still have an odd feeling about what she did."

"Well, all you can do is to watch her carefully. We've never had any problems like this before, so what makes you so sensitive?"

Grainger looked thoughtful and frowned.

"I'm a little concerned about Dr Beamish's suicide. He must have had records showing that he had dealings with the hospice, but the police haven't been here at all to question us. I wish that they had. Oh, heck, what the hell. I will keep my eyes open, but, Johannes, please don't make excuses for staff. It makes it difficult for me to assess what they are doing."

Dr Ziggefelde disguised his awkwardness. After trying, unsuccessfully, to make light of the situation he left the office and walked towards the reception area. The night receptionist, who worked up until nine p.m., greeted him. He waved courteously and walked past the desk. As he did so he glanced at the photocopier and something caught his eye.

He approached the machine and reached underneath, pulling out a piece of paper that protruded from the edge. It was a copy of an invoice for stationery. Intriguingly, it had page two on the bottom and the date was two days ago. He whirled around and half ran to Grainger's office. She was just packing up to leave.

"What's up?" she said, reaching for the light switch.

"This," he said, waving the paper. "When did you get a stationery invoice from, let's see, Frobishers of Norwich?"

Grainger went to her assistant's in-tray and grabbed a brown manila folder. Inside was all the mail that Dawn Clarke had arranged neatly. She leafed through the papers and found invoices from Frobisher's. "Here they are. Four pages, one, two, three and four." She stopped and looked up at Ziggefelde who was holding up a piece of paper marked page two.

"Page two, I believe, by the photocopier," he said ominously. I presume that you didn't copy this? If not, how many other items were copied and why?"

"Shit!" she said, and closed the door.

Jenny arrived for work the next day at the hospice and was greeted cordially by Grainger who gave her a few jobs to do. The atmosphere seemed normal and yesterday afternoon's tampering with the mail was not mentioned. She got stuck into the day's work, keeping her eyes and ears open, but this time dutifully putting unopened mail directly into mailboxes.

Jenny could see Dr Ziggefelde sitting in Grainger's office. The door was closed but the blinds to the office window open. She put her make-up mirror on the desk and angled it so that she could see what they were up to whilst facing the opposite way. It was not a wise move.

Back in the office, Grainger turned to Ziggefelde. "I can see a mirror on her desk, Johannes, and I bet she's watching us. Well, what d'you know?"

"Dear oh dear, what is going on?"

"I don't know, but I have some more bad news. Igor saw someone watching the hospice from the small copse, to the left of the building. He spotted him with our security night vision goggles he uses to regularly scan the area throughout the night."

Ziggefelde frowned and put his hand to his head. "Okay, let's try just one experiment to be absolutely certain."

He reached for a pen and began writing a memo. Then he addressed it to Artaxis Incorporated in the United States and wrote *confidential* on the envelope, leaving the envelope unsealed.

"Can you angle the security camera near the entrance away from the front door, to look in the reverse direction, in other words towards the reception desk?"

Grainger understood. "Yes, I can do it now," she said and turned to the control buttons on a panel to one side of her desk.

"Wait. Do it when I get into conversation with Dawn. I'm going to tell her to put it in a covering envelope and add that you and I are off to the conference room for at least a half an hour and don't want to be disturbed."

Grainger agreed and Ziggefelde strode purposefully out of the office and towards the reception desk. He saw the make-up mirror quickly covered with some papers.

"Hi, Dawn, look I have a big administration problem to sort out with Bobbette Grainger, but before we go to the conference room to discuss it, I need you to pop this white envelope marked *confidential* into the post for me? Sorry, I do need to be sure that it gets to the United States safely and quickly. You need to put it in a separate brown envelope, I've attached the address on a post-it note. Listen, I've gotta go quickly, so please don't disturb us in the conference room. Would you do that for me?"

He glanced up to the corner of the reception and saw the security camera slowly turning towards the desk.

"Yes, no problem, doctor. I can do that," she said cheerily.

Ziggefelde turned and purposefully strode off down the corridor, followed by Bobbette Grainger with some files under her arm.

Jenny waited a few minutes then looked at the envelope. It was too tempting and she gently parted the flap and pulled out the memorandum. The handwriting was scrawled and the text made little sense to her; something about consignments and priorities. Nevertheless, she made her mind up to photocopy the letter, then get it immediately into the post. She did this immediately and stuffed the copy into her handbag without folding it. Her heart was beating fast as she closed the bag, she had an odd feeling when Ziggefelde spoke to her earlier. He did not once look at her cleavage.

Back in the police operations room Jane and the team leafed through the papers that Jenny had delivered to them the previous day. It was an assortment of items from stationery and other invoices to 'thank you' letters from relatives. However, there were several interesting pieces of paper. Two doctors, from Ipswich and Nottingham, wrote in with recommendations for people to be admitted to the hospice; the common factor was leukaemia. But the most telling letter was from Artaxis Incorporated in the United States that appeared to give an encrypted receipt for research material and enclosed a cheque for fifty thousand pounds. Two letters from Egypt and Malaysia also gave receipts for research material and gave details of monies to follow. The Artaxis letter was a gem.

"This is really hot," said Jane.

Nicola could hardly contain herself, "There's something going on. Research material – what the hell is that?"

Farmer was less sensitive. "Bits. I bet you its bits. But how?"

"A network, they need a network, don't they?" said Gerry Winter.

"Steady boys, steady." Jane warmed to a good team, but knew that they needed to be kept focussed. "Let's just keep going over this information and plotting our chart. We need to relate all we know about Dr Beamish's patients, the Norwich Primary Care Trust Hospital and Rado Ilovic. The common factor was a leukaemia diagnosis, but keep looking for patterns."

She stood up and looked at them.

"Okay, here's an update on the international scene. This will not surprise you guys. The pattern of doctors' referrals to hospice-type institutions in various parts of Europe almost exactly fits what we seem to be uncovering here in the UK. It's all taking shape, isn't it?"

The rest of the time was spent making links to various facts and other data, checking and double-checking as they went along. Jane left them talking enthusiastically and went to her desk, put on her MP3 headphones and listened to James Galway.

Jenny took a call from Grainger and wondered why she was being summoned to her office. This had never happened before, Grainger usually talked to staff at their desks. She walked steadily to the door, knocked and went inside. Grainger's face was flushed and she looked a little odd. Then Dr Ziggefelde came into the office carrying a leather bag.

"Hello, Dawn. Nice to see you, sit down please. This won't take long."

"What won't take long?"

As she said that, Grainger quickly closed the blinds, then went around behind Jenny and pinned her arms behind the chair.

"What...?" Jenny blustered, then it quickly became obvious. Ziggefelde was coming towards her with a syringe. She struggled against Grainger's iron grip but couldn't move an inch. The needle pricked the skin of her right arm and she became dizzy and her head swirled - then she finally blacked out.

Within ten minutes, two men came to Grainger's office and bundled Jenny's unconscious body into a wicker linen basket. It was wheeled away to the rear of the building and loaded into a large green van that drove slowly out of the hospice grounds.

The evening receptionist took over the desk and was told that Dawn Clarke had taken a call on her mobile and rushed out of the hospice. It was explained that Grainger tried to contact the agency but there was no reply. If Dawn didn't turn up in the morning then the police would be called as a precaution.

When she returned to the office, Grainger shut the door and dialled a number on her mobile.

"Hello, yes, it's me. I checked and I was told that she should be held for the moment. We need to know what she's up to. What? Frankly, you animal, I don't care what you do with her. She's dead meat as soon as we've finished with her, so from the neck down she's yours."

Grainger clicked the mobile off and smiled malevolently. The inquisitive, busty receptionist would certainly be dealt with.

It was a starry night and the Maria Cresswell hospice was silhouetted against the sky, a cold mist forming around its base. Two security guards took it in turns to look through night vision goggles. It was as clear as could be. There was a figure watching the hospice through binoculars from the undergrowth nearby. Whatever the situation, they had clearance to eliminate the intruder.

Andy Crouch wriggled in the damp grass and tried to focus the binoculars on the rear offices of the hospice. Apart from seeing several patients in their rooms and the preparation of food for the evening meal, there appeared to be nothing suspicious going on. He did not even have a clue who the under-cover officer was and was beginning to regret being impetuous. He was getting fed up and turned to refocus his eyes, sore now after squinting through the small eyepieces on the binoculars. Then he saw two figures towering above him.

"Oh dear, it's a fair cop, as they say. I'll come clean..."

They weren't listening. There was a sharp crack and he felt something hit him in the middle of the chest. The bullet shattered the main artery in his body, venting blood into his throat. No pain, just complete shock and surprise, then a salty flooding taste in his mouth as he lost consciousness.

His body was lifted into a plastic bag and carried to a large green van. The men returned for the equipment and swept the area several times to find anything that had been missed. Once inside the van they searched his jacket and pulled out the homemade business card.

"It says Adam Critchley, freelance journalist. I'm gonna call 'erself later to see what to do next."

The second man grunted in agreement, but didn't really care. He just wanted to finish this job and have some fun with the new roommate back at their shack. This little escapade just got in the way.

They drove off to their base, one in the van and the other in the Crouch's car.

The shack was on the east side of the Broads in a conservation area, shielded by high bushes and reeds and populated by noisy small boats and lots of Canada Geese.

The vehicles skidded to a halt and they both got out. Crouch's body was left in the back of the van without a second thought. They had other things on their minds.

Jenny's body stiffened as the door to the shack burst open. One of her hands was handcuffed to an iron bed head and she was naked. She shivered with the cold and fear. During the time since she had regained consciousness in the shack, her tormentors had taunted her and removed her clothing. She protested loudly, but this only earned her a beating. Now they wanted more. Years of interrogation training in the army mirrored all such occasions and she was inured to nakedness and threats – the problem was, that was simulation in a constructed environment - this was real.

"Ello, darlin', it's your lover boys back to see you."

The uglier of the two men moved towards her leering and reached out for her. She rolled to one side earning a punch to the face.

"Tart, bloody tart," he screamed. "Not good enough for you, eh?"

"Hey, what's all this about?" said a new voice as the door to the shack opened. Through the buzzing in her head, Jenny recognised that it belonged to one of the travellers in the pub, a few nights before. If he recognised her, she was in even deeper trouble. He peered through the gloom towards her and she raised her arms in front of the top half of her face. It was the only thing she could do. He was transfixed. Then he walked slowly towards her. Her heart beat like crazy.

"Well, this one's a fine filly if ever I saw one. Any chance of letting me have her for a boy's bitch night at the barn?"

Jenny knew about 'bitch nights.' She remembered a brief from the Metropolitan Police on the subject. This was where the local druggies and long-in-the-tooth prostitutes were encouraged to perform for men at a so-called party, usually in a barn or warehouse. Doors were locked and performances of all kinds were expected on a makeshift stage, with the unluckiest being subjected to the attention of sometimes up to six men at a time from the audience. Some were paid a few quid, some were given drugs and those that objected were beaten for protesting. It was as low an event as it was possible on the scale of inhumanity.

For what seemed like an age he stood there with a hand on each of her knees looking at her. Then he got up and grunted.

"Mustn't get distracted. Things to do boys. As I say, save this one for the bitch night. I'll be back. See you both."

The men were busy swallowing beer by the bottle and they waved him away.

"I'd better phone 'erself. We need to get some guidance, bitch night or otherwise. Then we can settle down for the night." He cocked his head sideways towards Jenny. "I think she's gettin' anxious for our company."

They guffawed and he went to phone. After a few moments, he came back into the shack laughing.

"She ain't arf bright y'know. Really bright." He laughed again. "'Erself reckons they are both freelance investigative journalists. Okay, what we do is this. We take our friend in the van and his car to Cavendish Wood about ten miles east of here and dump him together with all his kit. Then we finish off Miss prim an' proper here using the shooter we used on the feller."

Jenny's head spun. The feller. What feller? What journalist and who was he?

The ugly man went on, "We make it seem as though she shot him, then turned the gun on herself. Cunning eh?"

The second man looked aghast. "Hang on. I've been waiting for 'er all afternoon. Let's go dump him first, then come back and have some fun. We'll take her later and finish the job. That way everyone wins, except poor old Liam, eh?"

It was no contest. He went over to Jenny and ran his hand up the inside of her thigh and grabbed her flesh. She screamed at him. Then to her relief he just laughed and left, evidently enjoying sowing the seed of fear.

After the door slammed, she lay on the damp mattress trying to keep her composure. It was the most frightening experience she had had in her life. Her heart raced. She fought against cloying despair that threatened to shut down her consciousness. *Think, think. Don't give up, think!*

Blood rushed to her brain, so fast she sat bolt upright. The wire that Jane had given her! It was in her underwear. It had diamond dust ground into it. *Where the hell was it?*

She trembled and looked around for her clothing. It had been thrown all over the place, some of it torn in the struggle. At first her throat thickened with nervousness and she was almost sick; she couldn't see her pants anywhere. Then relief gushed through her as she spotted them near a dirty heater in the corner. She reached out with her legs, but couldn't get hold of them.

Time and time again she stretched as far as her sinews allowed, but just couldn't reach the garment. In a last-ditch effort, she managed, with jerking movements, to jump the bed away from the wall gaining precious few inches. It took some time, but that was all that was needed. Eventually her right foot landed on top of her pants and she was able to scrape them slowly towards the bed.

She had to stop several times because she was physically and mentally exhausted, but fear drove her on. Slowly, she moved the garment across the last few inches of floor and up to the edge of the bed, and that allowed her to reach down with her left hand and grab it. Her hand was shaking, but she brought them up towards her shackled right hand then set about unpicking the cotton fixing on the waistband. That done, she unclipped the wire. It felt rough to the touch and that filled her with hope. The men had been away only twenty minutes. How she had laughed at Jane's inventiveness – now she wanted to buy her a crate of champagne.

Jenny threaded the wire behind a quarter inch metal bar on the bed-head, wrapped it tightly around her free hand and began to move it in a sawing motion as best she could, holding the other end with her tethered hand. At first her spirits fell when it slipped about the shiny metal not finding any purchase, but it began to dig in and slowly cut into the surface. The harder she worked, the deeper it cut and after about ten minutes, with the metal getting hot and her hands raw and bleeding, she had to stop. It was maddening, she was only a sliver of metal away from being loose.

She had to summon up more energy to finish the job and used a time-honoured technique to focus. Recalling how the men had touched her and what they were planning raised the anger inside her. With that thought in the front of her mind, she put her feet against the bed-head and pulled hard in a sawing motion, with all her might, at the same time screaming hard, "You bastards...argh!" It was the motivation she needed. The veins on her neck stood out with the strain and her face reddened. Quite suddenly, the metal bar snapped with a loud crack and she fell backwards against the mattress.

She was free.

Liam drove back to the shack. He was feeling cheerful having drunk three pints of cider and he ran over the prospect of the coming night's entertainment. It occurred to him that they would have to be careful. There was DNA to think of as well as other evidence. He would just have to be inventive. He drove slowly down the pot-holed road to the shack, careful of his Land Rover Defender's suspension.

As he turned in the yard his lights picked out the startled form of a woman wearing a black skirt and white blouse. She saw her look up then bolt into the trees. *Those bloody idiots!*

He accelerated to the spot where she had disappeared, stopped the vehicle, grabbed a torch and ran after her. She was easy to follow. Her white blouse picked up the light from his torch and his boots made it easy for him to slowly gain ground on her whereas her shoes only slowed her down. He shouted, but she was not stopping for anything. On and on they both ran dodging around trees and bushes.

The forest seemed to work against Jenny, tree branches reached out to her and blocked her path and roots tripped her as she stumbled through the undergrowth. Brambles ripped at her body and she flayed her arms against their embrace.

Liam gasped for air as he chased her, then he saw her heading for the lights of cars travelling along the nearby Horsey road. He realised this was what she was doing and tried to close the gap faster than was sensible and fell over a tree stump, crashing to the ground. Cursing loudly, he sprang to his feet again in seconds and resumed the chase.

Jenny was scared out of her wits, but had to make it to the roadway where she could see the lights of vehicles. At last, she reached it and fell out of the wood and onto the tarmac surface.

Neither she nor the oncoming lorry stood a chance. The driver's heart almost stopped with shock at the sight of a woman stumbling into the road and the look of horror in her face illuminated by the approaching lights. He registered every feature of her face and would never forget it.

Jenny was hit by the off-side of the lorry and thrown high in the air. She landed heavily and rolled over several times behind the vehicle. The driver of a car following hit his brakes and with a loud screaming and scraping of rubber, skidded to a halt. Its lights highlighted the crumpled heap only a few feet in front.

Liam looked on and smiled. The lorry saved him a job.

He made his way back to the shack. Once inside he looked at the bed and saw the cut and bent metal piece on the bed-head and the shambolic state of the room. He took out his mobile phone and dialled a number. Someone answered and he carefully explained that the receptionist had escaped and the circumstances of the accident.

"Yes, quite dead. Very sure, yes. You'd have to be a rubber ball to survive that. What now? Both of them? Okay. Yes, that's more than enough money. I don't like the clumsy bozos anyway, so it's no loss to me. I'll call you later."

He put the mobile into his pocket walked to the cabinet and helped himself to a large scotch, wiped his fingerprints off the bottle and waited.

Jane Kavanagh and DC Gerry Winter stood in the accident and emergency ward as the body of Jenny Willis lay amidst a mass of bloody bandages and tubes. Nicola Bradbury and Farmer had been sent to relieve the local police in the area and to look for clues. It hadn't been a popular move with the constabulary, but a call from the chief constable soon sorted that out.

Jane was on fire and thinking fast. She was icy cool.

"Gerry, get onto the local radio station, Anglia 105 or something like that, and tell them that a woman was killed tonight in strange circumstances involving a lorry. Then tell the local newspapers the same story. Tell them she was a lady called Dawn Clarke who worked as a receptionist at the Maria Cresswell Hospice. Then tell the hospice. They will only have a night receptionist on duty, but ask her to inform the hospice manager. That should establish a story-line for now and hopefully reduce suspicion."

Jane went to Jenny's side and ignored the admonishment of the nursing staff. Jenny was barely alive and was about to be transferred to the Intensive Care Unit. Jane touched her hand and whispered *good luck,* but there was no response. Her prospects for recovery didn't look good. But it was important to maintain mission focus and she walked to the senior doctor and asked to speak to her. At first the doctor was reluctant but was eventually persuaded and they moved to a quiet corner.

"I'll cut to the quick, Doctor," she showed her warrant card. "It is of immense importance that this woman is transferred to a ward under the name of Jenny Willis who suffered serious injuries in a factory accident. There will be reports that a woman was killed outright in a road accident and the name of that woman will be Dawn Clarke. Records must show that her body was transferred to the mortuary pending a post mortem. I will also need to put a disguised officer on duty twenty-four hours a day to guard Jenny Willis." She gazed back at the body. "Providing she lasts the course, that is."

The doctor made as if to object, but Jane silenced her. "This work has national clearance, Doctor. I understand your concern about the ethics, record keeping, and patient details and so on. Relieve yourself of every responsibility and put it all on my shoulders. This woman's work is going to bring some very bad people to justice. That's all I want to say. I have no time for anything else. You must of course keep this conversation a complete secret. Do you understand?"

The doctor shrugged. "Yes, I suppose so. I'll have to trust you. I will do my best." She turned and walked back to Jenny's bed and carried on treating her.

Jane looked the other way, her eyes moist. It took her back to her work in Bosnia when she involved an interpreter who was later kidnapped. She gathered up Jenny's belongings and put them into a plastic bag. A nurse handed her a piece of rough wire.

"You might like this. I'm not sure what the hell it is?"

Jane took it and held it up to the light. It was the wire from the underwear that she had given Jenny to use in an emergency. It was roughly worn and had obviously been used. It went into the bag with the clothing. Jenny's shoes were the last items to be put in the bag and they needed a separate carrier because of the mess on the soles. She waved a hand under her nose and turned to Gerry. "What a smell. What is it?"

"Unmistakable, my dear leader. It's goose shit. Horrible stuff. I went to York University to do my degree and the Dean and his cohorts thought it particularly jolly to populate the large lake in the university grounds with Canada Geese. This may have been a lovely wild-life theme, but the piles of goose droppings on the paths and grass were unbearable."

Jane crinkled her nose as she picked up the bag. She whispered, "Thanks Gerry. Stay here and be ever watchful. You know the score. You heard my brief to the doctor. If she steps out of line, give me a call as soon as you can. Be very clear that there has to be a record of death and a paper transfer to the mortuary. I'm not sure she has the will to do this job properly. It's vital. Make it happen, okay?"

"Yup, understood. Leave it to me."

Jane left the hospital with a heavy heart and tried desperately to keep her mind open and busy. If she thought about her lovely friend in a mangled heap she would fold.

The two thugs were incredulous when they entered the shack. The receptionist was gone and Liam sat there drinking their scotch.

"What...?"

"You couple of prize prats. How did you let the girl escape? And aren't you the lucky ones. She ran through the woods hotly pursued by yours truly, dashed out into the road and was squashed by a lorry full of vegetables. Can you believe that? So, have a bloody drink and think yourselves lucky."

He proffered the scotch bottle and the surprise and fear in their eyes turned to relief.

"Blimey, a close call that was," said the ugly man. "What now?"

Liam smiled broadly. "I called 'erself, and she did her usual problem-solving trick, she's quite a gal. Anyway, the plan is that you give me the gun and I drop it in the woods close to where she ran out into the road. It will look as though she was disturbed about killing her boyfriend, that journalist chap, Adam whatever his name is, and ran out into the road. Good plot, eh?"

Both men were relieved and grinned awkwardly. Without question they handed Liam the pistol and he checked the magazine. He turned to the men and stared at them, his eyes narrowing and his lips slightly pursed.

"Actually, that wasn't quite the plot, boys. The plot is that after killing her boyfriend, the journalist, in Cavendish Wood where they were having nooky in the back of the car, she was taken to a shack by two rough fellows and sexually abused, but somehow, she got the pistol from her captors and shot them both. Like this."

Before the tale registered on the faces of the men, Liam shot them both at point blank range. They slumped to the floor.

He now had to leave the pistol and an item of the girl's half way between the shack and the road, then double back to Cavendish Wood and leave another item of hers in the boy's car. He looked around and saw her handbag and a bra. They would do nicely.

Jane sat in the operations room back at the station in Cromer. Nicola Bradbury knew she was upset and gave her space. She put a mug of black coffee on her desk and helped to pull the few items of clothing out of the bag, placing them on a plastic covered table in front of her. There was no underwear. Jane commented again on the smell on the shoes.

Nicola laughed and said without thinking, "Oh, that'll be Horsey Mere. My mum used to take me there to go on the boats, but if we strayed into the nearby shoreline or woods, we always got our shoes covered in goose poo. It's disgusting."

Jane straightened. "God, you're the best." She picked up the telephone and asked to speak to the chief constable.

Nicola winced, it was late and he was renowned for his irascibility in normal working hours let alone approaching midnight. She watched as Jane moved to a quiet corner and spoke carefully, crafting her argument and outlining the possible outcome. She saw her smile as she put the telephone down.

"Well, that's that then. The chief constable is activating authority to call out the nearest police helicopter with night vision and heat imaging equipment. They will fly over the Horsey Mere area and see what they can find. They can direct Farmer who has already been sent there."

Nicola smiled at Jane's self-assurance and made mental notes for the future.

After examining the clothing, they repacked it in the plastic bag, putting it to one side. The question was: was Jenny's accident due to her undercover work at the hospice or something else? Jane's view was that it was unlikely to be 'something else'.

About an hour later, a call from the hospice manager Bobbette Grainger was patched through to the operations room and Jane got Nicola Bradbury to take the call, whilst listening on a party line.

"Hello, can I speak to the officer dealing with my missing receptionist, Miss Dawn Clarke?"

"Yes, DS Nicola Bradbury speaking and who are you, please?"

"Oh, I'm Bobbette Grainger. I'm the manager of the Maria Cresswell Hospice. Miss Clarke was working today. I looked up and saw her leaving in her car at high speed. It happened just after she took a call on her mobile. I overheard her say something like, 'Adam, I love you. Don't leave me. Let's talk…' or something like that. I've been so worried. She is a very steady young lady. Anyway, I then heard on the radio that a woman had been run over by a lorry. Is it her? Is she, well, is she okay?"

Nicola and Jane looked at each other – what an actress.

"Ms Grainger, thank you for calling, we do appreciate it. I am so sorry to tell you that Dawn Clarke died shortly after arriving at the hospital. She was in a pretty bad state and never regained consciousness. We are looking into the cause of the accident."

Jane thought she detected a relieved voice when Grainger said how shocked she was. Nicola was astute enough to follow it up.

"Yes, it is awful that no one is safe these days," she said.

"I've always said that," Grainger responded, "girls can get picked up these days so easily. It's just not safe."

"What makes you think she was picked up, Ms Grainger?"

Grainger stuttered. "Well, I didn't mean that she was picked up. I meant it figuratively speaking. As I say, she seemed to talk to some chap called Adam. Anyway, you're the police force, I leave it to you."

With that last remark, the call ended and Nicola turned to Jane. "She was making that up from known facts, guv. I'd swear to it, wouldn't you?"

"Yes, for sure, she was sounding us out," said Jane, smiling inwardly at the label, 'guv'.

It wasn't until two a.m. that the police helicopter could be mustered, but this was significantly quicker than it would have been in any other circumstance without Home Office clearance. It only took about thirty minutes for the heat-seeking equipment on the helicopter to locate the shack by the side of the lake. Farmer was called in from searching nearby and he quickly found the bodies of the two men who had imprisoned Jenny and a handbag. SOCO would deal with the situation.

Everyone worked throughout the night to gather information and log details as quickly as they could. They would meet at the shack at about mid-day, but agreed that if anyone slept in, they would be forgiven.

As expected, Nicola overslept. Jane arrived at the scene at mid-day and looked around the shack. What a horrible place it was. She shuddered to think of Jenny shackled to the bed. The place had been fingerprinted and photographed from every angle by the SOCO and the bodies of the two men were removed for examination. As Grainger had said, "...girls can get picked up these days so easily..." how convenient was that? Was she alluding to this place, trying to lead the police to a conclusion? Jane looked up and saw Ted walking down the path towards her. He had Farmer in tow.

"Look what I found," he said. "One very tired and hungry DC."

Before she could answer, he added, "And look what he found." He raised a plastic bag in his hand that contained a pistol and a bright coloured bra.

Jane regarded Farmer. "Well done, but you should've knocked off ages ago. You must be shattered. Don't drive. We'll take you back to Cromer."

They chatted for a while and then set off for the station to discuss the situation surrounding Jenny's undercover work and the next steps to take. On the way, Ted took a call. He frowned and turned to Jane.

"Well, what do you know? A man's body has been found in Cavendish Wood. He was shot in the chest. The only identification was a homemade card in his pocket identifying him as Adam Critchley, a freelance journalist. Surprise, surprise, he was not that person. One of the police officers called to the scene recognised him instantly. It was DC Andy Crouch. Now what the bloody hell was he up to?"

Farmer gulped and sucked in his breath. "Oh God."

They turned and stared at him.

"Is there anything you want to tell us, Farmer?" said Ted.

Farmer blurted out something about letting a few things slip during some drinks with Crouch, but he was sure that he hadn't said anything about the mission itself. Ted and Jane were unconvinced, but saw no reason to question him further when he was tired. He would need to explain himself later.

Ted and Jane left the scene and went for a coffee in Starbucks a few miles away. It was noisy with customers buying coffee take-outs and that made it ideal to discuss all sorts of issues without the danger of being overheard. A leather couch at the rear of the place was free and they took it.

Jane sat down beside Ted. He stirred a small sachet of brown sugar into his black coffee and relaxed. How strange life was at times. A month or so ago he was totally unfocussed. Now he was a different man in so many respects.

"Penny for the thoughts?"

"Oh, I was just thinking about ravishing the waitress, but frankly the coffee looks too inviting to let it go cold."

"Pah! Typical man. You lose your interest at the drop of a hat." She smiled at his silly humour whilst thinking of her father's advice that sometimes things said in jest are to be taken seriously. She continued. "While we are on the subject of ravishing, how is that lovely wife of yours?"

"Oh, she's doing really well." Ted looked at her. He knew he could tell her anything. "We had sex for the first time in a millennium the other day. It was so beautifully sublime we both cried afterwards. Can you believe that?"

Jane touched his hand. "Yes, I can. We all have the same emotions you know – even you, Mister smart-arsed Sanderson. Seriously, what is good, Ted, is that you are able to share your thoughts with me and I take that as a compliment. Wanna know something? I've watched you recently and you are such a good copper. You are a shade sharper than when I first met you and I believe it's down to your approach to Alison. It's made you more aware of the world around you. Do you mind me saying that?"

Ted huffed playfully. "No, of course not. And for what it's worth it's good to share things with you. You have a way about you, Kavanagh, let's just say that."

Over the next hour, they reviewed the current situation. DC Andy Crouch had been shot. They suspected that he was just trying to be clever. But where did it happen and why?

The bra in Crouch's car had to have been planted, there was no way Jenny would have removed it voluntarily. It was there to indicate that she was having sex and that Crouch was shot after that. It was a direct steer to the fact that she had been abducted and taken to the shack in Horsey Mere by the two men. Was she supposed to have shot the men, then run away in such a state that she ran directly into the path of a lorry?

"Ted, I think that's what they want, so let's give it to them," said Jane. "After all, we have to give the press false names and this way we protect identities whilst feeding the opposition the story they set up themselves."

Ted agreed without demur.

"Jane, I also think that with all this information to hand and the suspicion that they have killed three people and nearly a fourth, we can persuade the Home Secretary that it really is in the public interest to put a phone tap into the hospice."

Jane nodded in agreement. "That should be fun. I think that we should float the idea with the chief constable. He would love to argue that one through. Let's make him feel important!"

Ted laughed out loud. "Jane, he is bloody important and bloody powerful, and what's more he knows it, but yes, why not?"

Jane nodded in agreement and saw the funny side. She looked at her watch. It was time to discuss some pan-European progress on a direct link to MI6 back at the Ogden's bed and breakfast, and she was late.

Gerry Winters was patient and knew very well what had to be done. He spoke again to the doctor in charge of Jenny, using every ounce of charm and thanked her warmly for all that was being done to help his colleague. He told her how brave Jenny was and what good work she had always done in frightening and lonely circumstances. He The doctor looked sideways at Jenny's almost lifeless form.

However, the register of deaths had to be completed. The Home Office had given permission for this subterfuge. It also had to be followed through to the mortuary. This is where the doctor was most stubborn.

"Gerry, you're a nice bloke, but where do I find another body to go to the mortuary? It's all very well your boss saying do this and do that, but it isn't always possible."

"Look, I do understand, I really do. Let's just go and walk the course for a few minutes. To the mortuary I mean. Please?" His blue eyes flashed and he smiled persuasively at her.

"Oh, okay. Follow me, then." She led the way down the corridor her white coat swishing this way and that.

When they reached the mortuary, Gerry looked over her shoulder and noted the numbers she pressed on the security entry lock: 9 4 6 2. She took him inside and showed him the layout. On the wall was a simple white board with names alongside numbers. The numbers represented the storage units that moved in and out like filing cabinet drawers.

After a little bit of gentle persuasion, the doctor agreed to add a new name, Dawn Clarke, to the white board, against a vacant number - in this case fourteen. They went to the storage unit and pulled out the piece of paper in the holder at the front and on it she wrote: Dawn Clarke and reinserted it into the holder.

The doctor turned to Gerry. "That's as much as I can do, buster, a ticket on an empty drawer, okay?"

Gerry thanked her profusely and they left the mortuary. When they were almost back at the ICU, Gerry stretched and yawned.

"Well, it's gonna be a long night for sure and I deserve a sandwich and a coffee. I guess I will be seeing you around later?"

The doctor smiled at him, sensing a flirt and quite liking it.

"Yeah, a bit later. If you're lucky that is."

Gerry smiled back, the smile of a man who flirts as easily as breathing and headed towards the canteen. When he saw that the doctor was out of sight, he walked down an adjacent corridor and headed back to the mortuary. Once outside the main door he tapped in the security code and headed for the board. It was extremely unwise to try and fool the opposition with an empty box. He went to the board and changed the names around. Dawn Clarke became the name of the person in storage unit thirteen that housed the body of a Miss Arlene Jeffery, a young woman also killed in a car accident. He moved her name to unit fourteen, which was the empty unit and that of Dawn Clarke to thirteen, then went into the main storage area, located the correct units and exchanged the cards on them. He was about to go when he remembered his previous visits to mortuaries. He pulled open unit thirteen and the feet came into view first. On the big toe was a label and he untied it. In the desk under the message board, he found blank labels and quickly wrote the name Dawn Clarke on one of them, taking it back to the body and tying it on the big toe of the right foot.

He casually left the mortuary and strode back to the canteen.

At two a.m. a shadowy figure made its way down the main hospital corridor and past a nurse sorting X-rays and files at a brightly lit reception desk, she was tired and did not even look up. The figure reached the mortuary doors and after looking left and right, tapped in a four-figure code to the security lock. The door opened easily. Once inside it took only seconds to find the white board and the name Dawn Clarke. Storage unit thirteen was easily located with its label bearing the same name. The unit slid open almost soundlessly and two feet came into view, the label on the right foot confirmed the identity of the body. Before the drawer could be opened fully there was a commotion in the corridor and it was clear that security men were dealing with someone. The figure closed the drawer quietly and walked to the main door to peer out and see what the fuss was all about.

In the corner of the corridor a drunk stood urinating into a waste bin. The guards were remonstrating with him, but he just laughed at them. Whilst their backs were turned the figure moved quietly out of the mortuary and back down the corridor. At the entrance a young registrar looked up from her coffee waved and shouted.

"Hey, Mr Ilovic, what's this, burning the midnight oil to finish another research paper? You must really love your work more than your beauty sleep."

He stopped in his tracks, turned slowly, waved and walked out of the front doors.

10

China

Dragon Tattoo kept Chin Kwok entertained, but above all well informed. His knowledge of the workings of the Institute and its grisly side-line became clearer by the day, as he added more snippets of information. Chin got his most important tip of all. The bodies of executed criminals had been brought to the Institute as usual some days before and according to Dragon Tattoo, organs and tissue were ready to be shipped out to a cash buyer - a regular cash buyer.

Chin sat in his Volkswagen in a side street opposite the Institute, trying to keep his attention sharp lest he missed anything important. It was hot and dusty and the wind blew paper bags and litter around the street. He had to lower the window several times to brush off the dust so that he could see more clearly. Two children walked down the road from behind him, running a stick over the cars and they jumped when he sat up straight and shouted at them. They laughed out loud and ran away and an old man in traditional Chinese shapeless jacket and trousers looked up from a blue chair on a rickety veranda and smiled a toothless grin, jerking his head backwards as if to indicate the futility of chastising young people these days.

Suddenly, there was a loud bang and two large side doors were flung open just ahead of him. A small, white Toyota van, with what looked like air conditioning vents on top, moved out of the building. Chin nearly dropped his car keys as he located the ignition and switched it on. The engine burst into life and he lurched away in the direction of the speeding vehicle. Dragon Tattoo had dropped clues that his bosses in the warehouse were getting nervous and jumpy. He resolved to keep a good distance from the van. At first it drove slowly, turning right out of the site and past lines of school-children on a school trip. After about two kilometres the road widened and it accelerated away quickly.

Chin drove fast to catch up, then slowed to one hundred metres behind the van. They travelled out of the built-up area and into the countryside. Twenty minutes later it slowed and turned left following signs to Diqing Airport. Chin studied local maps and guide books and knew this to be a small aerodrome that operated just outside Kunmin. It was used primarily, by businessmen and small freight companies, but was being enlarged for larger commercial aircraft as well as some military planes. It had the poetically named district locale of, Shangri-La. The airport was a quaint conglomeration of new buildings and old rusted units. This confused mix made it ideal for covert operations, because there was no established security force. The van slowed and turned into the unmanned airport gates and drove towards a large old-style aircraft hangar in much need of renovation judging by its rusty corrugated iron sides and dirty windows. He followed keeping a good distance between the two vehicles. The van stopped outside and sounded its horn. A roller-fronted door was raised and it disappeared inside. The door dropped down and Chin parked about fifty metres away. He looked to the left and saw a medium sized twin-engine jet.

Chin left the car and cautiously walked around the warehouse. There were few windows, but where there were, no one was visible in the offices. He continued walking until he reached the back of the building and came to a larger window through which he saw some activity. He stopped quickly. Two western men, Americans judging by their height and dark glasses, were standing in front of several large boxes, signing papers. He bent to tie up his shoelaces whilst at the same time watching what was going on.

His heart almost stopped. One of the Chinese men looked out of the window and quickly motioned the others towards him. They stared at him. Should he run or talk his way out of trouble? The oppressive heat from the concrete roadway seemed to push at his chin and slightly dulled his senses. He missed seeing two men come out of a side door and walk towards him.

"Who are you? What are you doing here?" rasped an aggressive young man. His older companion kept his distance and appeared anxious and jumpy, looking to his left and right.

"Er, I came to complain. Yes, complain. The driver of a Toyota van pulled in front of me and nearly caused me to crash. He was crazy, very crazy. I have a right to complain," said Chin standing up straight and behaving in a very self-important manner.

"I see," said the younger man, "and where did this happen?"

"Oh, er, in a small village about a mile from here. A cyclist was involved too. But now I have told you, I suppose it is better for us to forget it. You just tell him to be more careful next time, eh?"

The younger of the two men smiled crookedly at him and he knew what was coming next.

"Oh, you can be sure your warning will be headed my friend. In fact, I was the driver of the Toyota, but I don't remember anything of the kind."

Chin's blood froze. He stared so hard at the young man approaching him that he failed to see his companion circle around behind him.

Then his head rang with a loud hissing sound and lights flashed before him as he sank to the ground.

The room stank of engine oil. Chin's head throbbed and his mouth was as dry as toast. He was aware that he was lying on a coil of ropes because the sharp woven edges dug into the fleshy part of his body. He could hear the sound of boxes being moved and men talking, or rather, shouting. Their accents were American. One was saying something like, "I don't want him to see us. We must not be recognised or identified."

As he tried to clear his mind and hear what was being said outside, he heard the sound of the metal door being unlocked. It opened and two men came in. He couldn't make them out at first, because his eyes were watery and they were framed in the light from the doorway. A light was switched on and he recognised them as the men who confronted him outside the warehouse. They stood looking at him. At last, one spoke.

"Who are you?"

Chin's mouth was sticky and he was scared. "I'm on holiday. I was in a near crash on the road and came to get an apology. I seem to have made a big mistake. But why all this? It was a simple mistake, I'm sorry."

"You lie," the younger man seemed angry. "But you will tell us everything."

Chin flushed with fear.

The young man's companion hauled Chin to his feet and pushed him towards a pillar and proceeded to tie him upright against the cold metal. A woman entered the room and Chin gasped. It was the petite, attractive lady he had spotted at the café back at Sang Yong, the one who seemed out of place and kept looking around. She approached him and smiled.

"Well, my friend, you get around. Your holiday seems to be very unusual. I have observed you watching the Institute from inside your Volkswagen. I also know that you have friends there_"

Chin interjected, "Oh, no, I have no..."

"_but you do," she said with a patronising laugh. Just then he heard a sound of something being dragged along the ground. Two men heaved a body into the room and left it at his feet. It was Dragon Tattoo - his face was a mass of bruises and there was blood oozing from his nose and mouth. He looked up at Chin and waved a hand as if in defiance.

"I will leave you both together," said the woman icily, "but when I return, I promise you, you will talk, loudly. Very loudly. You must make it easy on yourselves. This place is full of useful objects that we can use to help us get the information we want."

As she finished one of the men held up a blowtorch, the kind used to melt solder into metal joints. The blue flame roared out of its tubular opening, jagged and noisy. The man moved towards Chin and directed the torch to his left leg. The trouser material smouldered then burst into flames and he screamed with pain as the flames seared into his flesh.

The woman doused the burning material with a jug of water, whilst looking straight into his face. Without a word, they turned and left the room.

Perfect procedure, thought Chin. Threaten and cause some sharp hurt – something small and insignificant, yet very painful, he was then in no doubt as to the limitless possibilities open to them. Then leave him, a helpless victim, to contemplate his fate. His own thoughts would cause sufficient terror. He put his head back against the pillar.

Dragon Tattoo sat up, made a gurgling sound and spat out a mouthful of blood. It hit the floor with a splat. He waved dismissively at Chin and tried to smile again.

"Thirty minutes," he gasped and coughed again. Chin didn't understand, even when he kept repeating the same mantra. It was extraordinary, he even laughed, almost uncontrollably. "Thirty minutes..." he repeated through a mouthful of gunge.

Chin tightened his muscles against the unforgiving rope and thought to himself.

"Great. He's crazy, that's all I need!"

Fear dulls the senses. Chin raised his face and looked at the light bulb. The bare bright light burned a hole in his vision. He desperately wanted to hypnotise himself into a trance and drift away from this hellish situation, but he knew that was not the solution. Dragon Tattoo was still on the floor, resting on one arm. He was endlessly fiddling with a tooth that had been knocked loose. Finally, he yelled in triumph and raised his hand holding the offending bloody molar.

"You're quite mad," said Chin. This man seemed to be on another planet, not locked up with his life in the balance.

Dragon Tattoo still kept laughing. It annoyed Chin and made him even more anxious.

His stomach knotted as the door was opened and the woman and men entered the room. They stood in a line, menacingly regarding the hostages.

"It is time, Chin. Time to tell us who you are and what you are doing here," she drew closer to his face, "you will, Chin, you know you will."

Chin was too scared to talk or even try to make up some kind cover story. He had been trained in all sorts of interrogation techniques, but when you're in deep trouble, it all goes awry. The blow-torch was lit again, its noisy blue flame made a low hissing noise. He jumped with fright and was aware that he was shaking and urine was dripping down his leg. Telling them everything seemed a great idea and one that he was considering as a positive option, but he was aware that interrogators never believed the first words uttered by their victims. What a choice!

The woman stepped back and gestured to the man with the torch to proceed and he came closer, smiling and waving the flame towards Chin's face. Chin gave in and was about to tell him to stop, he would tell them everything he could conjure up to prevent the torture. Suddenly, there was a terrific commotion, men shouting and the unmistakable sound of stun grenades and shots being fired outside. The woman and her accomplices looked alarmed and ran from the room.

Dragon Tattoo shouted. "Ha! They come," and he laughed even louder. Chin looked down at him, "Wha'…?"

"You see, you see," and then, thankfully he stopped laughing and gave a loud sigh, "Republican Guard come - thirty minutes."

Giles G. Handon, an ex-USAF pilot with years of military and civil flying experience and his co-pilot Richard Brodski relaxed as their aircraft taxied down the small runway. When it reached the correct take-off speed, Handon pulled back on the control column and the jet engines roared as it climbed high into the sky. They were used to gunrunning, drug running and all sorts of skulduggery, but being caught by the Chinese People's Republican Guard was something they had not foreseen. This was a routine, regular run to pick up boxes, packed and refrigerated, for delivery to the USA via an airfield in Vietnam. They had done this run dozens of times before and had been told that all the consignments were arranged behind the scenes, but government sponsored. What the hell had gone wrong?

Handon looked up and spoke.

"Jeez, that was close. I was relieved just to do as I was told leave the packages and paperwork, as the Chinese officer directed, and get the hell out of the place. They just let us go - we were Goddamned lucky. If we'd been exposed, then our lives wouldn't have been worth a candle. The last guys to goof were never seen again."

His friend sat motionless as if in shock.

"I really thought that captain guy was gonna do for us. All that shit about us stealing the bodies of Chinese people. Hell, the way the soldiers laid into those Chinese guys, especially the girl, was grisly. Hell, I thought we were next. I really did."

Handon put his fingers to his lips. "Keep your voice down and let's just get back to Vietnam, then home, eh?"

Standing up Brodski reached for a bottle of mineral water and casually looked out of the window and froze. His face contorted and his eyes widened.

His gaze was fixed on two trails of smoke that were getting nearer and nearer to their aircraft.

He dropped the bottle.

Chin straightened his shirt and ran his hand down the dark material of the suit that the Chinese authorities had given him. He had been medically examined and questioned about his presence in China. Surprisingly, they had not approached Interpol and had given him a somewhat easy ride. The elaborately carved bench he was sitting on was comfortable and didn't look out of place in the enormous hallway of the Hall of the People's Republic of China, in Beijing. He looked at the exquisitely carved double doors in front of him and wondered what was to come next.

The doors opened and a diminutive young lady dressed in a tight red silk dress, beckoned him to follow her. He had entered an enormous room with a committee table made of marble on his right and pillars on each side of the room each holding a bright red banner with golden Chinese characters on them. In front of him in the middle of a large space was a dark mahogany desk. Behind it sat a severe-looking Chinese lady wearing dark rimmed spectacles. She spoke to him in Mandarin.

"Good morning. My name is Madam Lom and I am the Minister for External Relations for the People's Republic of China. So, you are," she referred to her papers, then looked up at him directly. "Chin Kwok. You have a British passport and you work for Interpol, or not, as the case may be. Most annoyingly to us, you are here illegally."

She paused and studied him as he answered nervously in the affirmative.

"And my guess is that your boss is called, Jane Kavanagh?"

Chin looked surprised. Now he was worried. Had he fallen out of the frying pan and into the fire? Madam Lom continued.

"Let me put you at ease. In the old days, people like you, that is to say those who grew up in Hong Kong, wedded to the west and its false values, would be treated harshly if you misbehaved. And make no mistake you have misbehaved. But times have changed and we want you to go home with a strong message. We will continue to take useful organs from executed prisoners. Indeed, we have no stifling politics in that respect or any other so we take organs from anyone who has died. These organs go to loyal Chinese people, Mr Kwok, remember that, Chinese people only."

Chin started to speak. "Yes, Madam Lom, I do understand, but it wasn't the Chinese people that I was spying on. It was..."

Madam Lom silenced him with a wave of her hand.

"We know what you were doing. Please don't interrupt or patronise me. How do you think your life was saved?"

She sat back in the chair and regarded him with a stare. A smile slowly crept across her face and she clicked her fingers to an aide in the corner. After a few seconds, Chin heard the sound of metal tipped boots crossing the marble floor. He turned around and spluttered, "Dragon Tattoo!"

"Captain Juang Chi of the People's Republican Army if you please, Chin," said Dragon Tattoo and he smiled broadly displaying the same awful teeth.

Madam Lom looked at Chin Kwok. "We have been watching the work of the Institute because our suspicions were aroused through various assertions in the western press. It took some time for someone to come and talk to us. Anyway, Captain Chi was our man on the inside. All we wanted was to be able to identify and apprehend the criminals who were organising transfer of human organs out of China. At first you got in the way, but I considered that letting you work alongside Captain Chi gave him some support, but more importantly, allowed you to categorically give first-hand evidence to anyone in the west who will listen, that the Republic of China does not engage in the illegal sale of body parts. You saw it all, Chin Kwok, and you will report it, in great detail, will you not?"

Chin understood the sense of what she had just said and simply nodded in agreement.

Madam Lom lifted an envelope from the table and addressed Chin again. "Mr Kwok, pay attention please. This envelope is going to be sent to Jane Kavanagh with my best wishes, it contains the consignment details and flight plan that the Americans had in their aircraft, together with some notebooks. It will provide her with all she needs to fulfil her mission. It is with the compliments of the Chinese Republic. No more needs to be said on this. No more suspicion. China will be left to do what it wants within its own borders. Do you understand, Chin?"

Chin nodded again. The thought of China doing what it wanted made him recall his conversations with Dagon Tattoo about the treatment of the Falun Gong.

"Now, Captain Chi, take our young friend and show him some hospitality. Then put him on a flight home."

She turned to Chin, for the last time. "Mr Chin Kwok, never ever set foot in this country without an invitation again. Do you understand?"

Chin muttered his thanks, stood up to go and allowed Dragon Tattoo, or Captain Chi as he now knew him, to lead him out of the office. He had to walk quickly as he tried to keep up with his friend's clicking heels marching ahead of him. As they exited the great building and descended the wide steps to the Beijing streets, he heard his friend laugh. "Aha, Chin, let's go somewhere I know very well. They serve really good rice wine."

Chin pretended to be absolutely delighted.

11

England

Ted stretched his long legs and settled back in his seat next to Jane. The BA flight to New York would be a long one. It all seemed surreal. He had not flown for years. In fact, he had not done anything interesting for so long that it felt like a major incident in his life – it gave him purpose. He needed time to regroup and take it all in: Beamish's suicide, Alison's depression and near suicide and now here he was with an Interpol agent who looked more like a film star. It had all happened so fast.

Jane looked at him. "What's up?".

"Oh, nothing really. Just thinking about events and, well, wanting to do more that's all."

"Ted, I've inveigled you onto this flight, relax," she whispered. "Let's talk more about this in New York. Meanwhile, as they say in the USA – enjoy!"

She handed him a manila folder full of briefing papers and he took the hint. That was just it. He wasn't in control, but for all that, he quite liked the fact that he was able to be creative and free to think and develop ideas, not at all like local Norfolk police work constrained by so many rules and paperwork. He read through the detailed contents again and made notes.

Artaxis Incorporated was a large organisation, controlling a consortium of companies based throughout the world. The business products were exclusively associated with medical research and all had a legitimate pedigree. They were paid handsomely for carrying out tests, researching the effect of drugs, gathering data and so on. Interestingly, a small element of their work also involved the transplantation of organs donated to them. This underpinned their work in developing effective immunosuppressant drugs and other medications, for which they had a fine reputation for quality. They had smaller associated companies in a number of countries, including Bulgaria, Romania, Germany, Turkey, India and Malaysia. Each one was autonomous in its operations, whilst receiving some funding from the parent company. The financial turnover of the whole conglomerate was billions of dollars.

However, it was the other papers in the pack that proved to be more interesting. Each of the Artaxis associate companies had further offshoots that provided funds to support the parent company. It was here that there had been several dubious practices exposed in the media. The incidents, were sometimes small and insignificant, but inevitably, when taken together, they caused an itch of suspicion that something was not quite right. There were accusations of stolen foetal tissue from abortion clinics, associate partner clinics that specialised in transplantations for people who paid money for organs and the now infamous case of Katrina Anatov in Bulgaria, which led to the investigation of a private clinic. Evidence was slowly emerging of direct links with Artaxis.

However, the trail was expertly covered, so much so that incontrovertible evidence was hard to come by. As usual, those caught offending would apologise and pay local authorities large sums of money to close cases, bribes were given and there was a hint of violence, but nothing could be proved because of the climate of fear that pervaded the more lucrative criminal actions. Some of the case studies were sickening.

A completely separate section in the paper file was dedicated to China's politics and high numbers of executions. China's aspirations to join the major powers on an equal footing, or even go one better than Russia, was dealt a major blow when the international press exposed the use of convicted prisoners as organ donors. The Chinese flatly refused to cooperate and it was difficult to make a rational assessment. Pressure on the Republic simply led to assertions that they did what they wanted with enemies of the state who lost all rights – and, clearly, their body parts.

He read the papers, paying attention to all the detail. He reflected that one day he had been investigating a suicide in the seaside town of Cromer in Norfolk and the next, he was looking at papers that concerned international crime.

America

Ted hardly felt the effect of jet lag at first, but as he and Jane got out of their yellow cab in the centre of New York and walked into the hotel, tiredness began to take over. They went to their rooms, unpacked and, after a steak dinner, which was actually breakfast, they took a break and slept soundly. Later they met in a quiet corner of the hotel bar. Jane put her hands directly onto the table palms down and looked straight at him.

"Ted, I need to be square with you. I like you. It's good to have you here, but you need to be very clear that this is my operation and I usually work alone. The deal is that we are travelling as friends under our real names. I am going to look different – no fancy stuff, just a change of hair, eye colouring and clothes, to look like Caroline Redbridge a freelance journalist with links to Friends of the Earth, Amnesty International and other such organisations. The real Caroline Redbridge has been responsible for a lot of critical journalism and is quite a crusader, so I expect to be as popular as a drunk at a christening party. Sadly, she is in a bad way in hospital in Coventry. Because of her penchant for privacy, her location is not reported at all in the main press. Even her associates at Amnesty don't know where she is."

She paused to sip a cool Martini and after eating the olive, continued. "I'll book into a separate hotel to this one, as Caroline Redbridge, then visit Artaxis who have an office on Fifty-Seventh Street. They know I am coming and I honestly don't know how this is going to pan out. My brief is to talk to them about the use of human organs in research and the possibility that some may be sold for a profit. I'll use some newspaper clippings and show my concern as a freelance journalist. Anyway, after my meeting with the executives I'll leave the hotel quickly, change somewhere, a bus station loo I suppose, then catch up with you and fly home. Before you ask, Interpol has arranged with the US authorities for airline records to show the 'Redbridge' flights in and out of the US." On this particular leg, this is an agreed joint Interpol and US operation.

Ted finished his Martini and grimaced. He was more at home with best bitter.

"That's a bit elaborate, isn't it?"

"Not at all. Doing this may just get Artaxis to do something silly, a recorded statement, email or text. At the moment they appear squeaky clean. We need all the evidence we can get, however small. They are clever bastards, but my experience is that it is the small seemingly insignificant things that start the cracks in the wall. They will photograph me for sure. They take no chances. I am told I look a little like Caroline. It's important that I am able to continue my work in the UK without being instantly recognised. That goes for you too. If you were photographed over here and then spotted and identified as a policeman in the UK, the alarm bells would ring loudly. So, stay away from me when I'm in Redbridge garb, Ted. I mean it. It's not elaborate at all. For your part, just meet with the FBI guys and get to know the plot and brief them with what you know about the, er, what shall we call it, the Cromer connection? So, I repeat, we can meet up before and after my meeting with the Artaxis executives, but not anywhere near there during my visit. That's about the size of it!"

Ted smiled. She was right. She was smart, very smart and he began to understand why she had been chosen for the mission.

After a few more Martinis, they returned to their rooms to sleep a little more and get their body clocks into New York time.

Robert R Karowitze Jnr, the president of Artaxis, sat sullenly at the head of a large polished redwood committee table, twirling his ballpoint pen in his right hand. His tanned features, below a shock of white hair, were taut and strained. In the corner behind him sat two men in grey suits, silent but not inconspicuous. He threw the pen onto the table and addressed three other men sitting across from him. His southern drawl sounded jagged in his agitation.

"Let me see, gentlemen, this here Caroline Redbridge, an investigative journalist, is asking questions about the sale of human organs." He paused to let the statement sink in. He picked up his pen and pointed at his audience. "Why? But I guess that whatever the reason, she's trouble. With recent blunders by some of our associates, we can do without this."

A younger man, swarthy and serious looking, pretended to review the notes in front of him and muttered supportively, "Yeah, boss, yeah," even though it was obvious to those present that the sense of it all eluded him.

Undaunted the young man lurched into an ingratiating tirade.

"Yeah, she sure is a lotta trouble, boss. Who does she work for? What's with this chick and what's her line, huh?" He flamboyantly removed his reading glasses and with a wave of his hand let them flop onto the papers in front of him, doubtless hoping this display would place him as supportive and a bit clever.

Karowitze was patient, but then one has to be with relatives. His nephew was a challenge. Family ties run deep in the south.

"Thanks, Hal. Now let's take the points we know already. Redbridge is a clever well-known journalist and able to get right inside a problem. There is a lot of evidence for that. She uncovered the failure of a big oil company in Africa to deal with local pollution in the sea around the oil wells. More than that, she only recently agitated for the cessation of harmful crop spraying in some godforsaken country in the east somewhere. This woman has a reputation for trouble."

Hal broke in again, "Yeah, boss. Just a trouble maker, a leftie pinko, yeah?"

This time he was completely ignored and a smartly dressed man called Ed Macabe, the head of internal security, looked up from his notes.

"Sir, I think we have a situation. There is no sign here that this woman will be placated if she is on to something and, frankly, some of our projects are now leaking like sieves. We thought we had dealt with the Bulgarian lady, but she escaped to the UK. In fact, her mother made it out too, to London, I think. That means only one thing. Law enforcement agencies are sniffing around, and that can only mean Interpol. We just need a period of time without mistakes or attention coming our way." He looked stern and shifted uneasily in his chair. "This lady poses a big threat, because, as I say, she doesn't give up. I don't like it, but we need to deal with her, boss."

Nodding, Hal sat back in his chair and on cue, drawled, "Yeah, boss, yeah. She's trouble."

Karowitze flashed him an angry gaze and he took the cue and said nothing further.

"Ed, you're right. We need a plan. I'm usually happy to ride storms, but we just seem to be having a whole damned sky full of 'em. We just can't take any more chances."

He turned to his nephew and smiled patronisingly. "Hal, why don't you go get some lunch, huh?"

Hal left the room without a word.

Ed Macabe leaned forward and kept his voice low. "I understand, sir. We need something kind of, well, accidental, if you know what I mean. I sketched something out. I know it looks complicated, but I'm sure it will work. It needs the special skills of your nephew, George."

Karowitze glanced at the notes and nodded.

George it was then.

Jane stood outside the large glass doors of the Artaxis building that was edged with stainless steel, its marble flooring catching the sunlight. Glancing at her reflection in a nearby window she approved of her business-like, but not corporate, ensemble. She looked entirely different. Her titian hair was now blonde and she had made her face up to look quite pale, and her eyes were now blue. She wore a tight beige skirt and matching jacket and underneath, a cream blouse. Practical suede shoes were the order of the day. Jane was the very model of a sensible person. A lone receptionist sat at a large desk and received her with a broad toothy smile.

To her surprise, a young man in a white suit came striding towards her and extended his hand. He was tall, broad shouldered and his hair was cut in an old-fashioned crew cut.

"Miss Redbridge, Caroline. Hello and welcome to Artaxis. My name is Gene Orson. Now if you will allow me, I will drive you to a reception, well, it's a kind of party we're holding outside town and that's where you will meet some interesting people who you will no doubt want to talk to. We can make suitable arrangements for that to happen a little later. Follow me, please, ma'am."

Jane agreed, albeit reluctantly, to accompany Gene Orson in his capacious white Cadillac to the soiree outside the city. This was unscheduled and unplanned. Ted would be unaware of her whereabouts and it was challenging.

The driver drove steadily along the five-lane highway and within the hour they arrived at a small airfield. Two small light aircraft were buzzing around noisily like angry wasps, with smoke trails showing their every move across the sky. Gene had been a good guide, describing places of interest and landmarks, but when they pulled into the car park his mood changed and he asked her to follow him to a large marquee. A party was in full swing and she heard a country and western group playing in the corner, where people were dancing and talking. The marquee was decorated with flowers and red, white and blue bunting.

To the left of the musicians was what looked like a VIP area and two men in dark suits and sunglasses stood at the entrance checking invitation cards. The group of people behind the white rope that circled the area, looked at her as she was guided towards them.

A short, rotund and ruddy-faced man, with white hair and a wide smile that stretched unbelievably from one ear to the other, stepped forward to greet her. He put out his hand, "Miss Redbridge, my name is Robert E Karowitze, Jnr and I'm the president of Artaxis. I'm so pleased to meet such a distinguished journalist."

Jane knew from his plastic expression that he was not really pleased at all. He turned to his right and waved to a tall thin man with a slightly hooked nose and bad taste in suits. "C'mon over here, Clem. Caroline, this is Clem Bainbridge, a US Republican Senator and vice president of Artaxis."

The man stepped forward and Caroline noticed his dull grey eyes and languid, expressionless face. "Pleased to meet you, ma'am," he said offering a limp hand in an almost disinterested way. "I hope you had a good trip."

After the niceties, Caroline accepted a drink and some buffet food and they passed the time of day. She was amused that even Americans discussed the weather. The party was to celebrate Artaxis's tenth birthday and everyone was in buoyant mood. The alcohol flowed and she was careful to keep leaving half full glasses and exchanging her drinks for sparkling water whenever she could.

Jane had been at the party for about an hour, when Karowitze half-turned to her and said abruptly, "Look Miss, er, Caroline, we understand that you are investigating the sad case of that woman, what's her name, the *prostitute*, Katrina Anatov in Bulgaria. Anyways, it seemed that just because that bunch of stupid people who ran that institute, who by the way are no longer associates of Artaxis's in any way at all, that you are homing in on us for some reason. Perhaps you can explain why?"

Jane looked either side of Karowitze and noticed the usual bunch of heavies suitably placed to deter the unwanted or intimidate selected visitors. She felt intimidated.

"Well, Robert, if I may call you that. It wasn't just the Bulgarian episode, unfortunate though that was. There have been a number of situations with offshoots of Artaxis worldwide where, frankly, it seems bizarre that a company like yours wouldn't know what was going on, due diligence and all that. I'm sure that Artaxis wouldn't want to be involved in any of the things that have been uncovered. You can't control everything worldwide after all. It may of course be a smear campaign by your competitors, but I would've expected to see much more of a proactive campaign from Artaxis to refute the claims. The fact is, sir, something's going on internationally. You must be feeling the pressure, if not personally, then on your share prices, which, if I have it right have dropped almost four per cent recently. I would be interested in your thoughts. Let me 'get to it' as you Americans say. Does Artaxis have any interest in trading body parts for cash?"

Jane noticed that Senator Carter looked down into his glass and several of the others shifted uneasily. Karowitze squinted at her.

"Now what in hell would we want to be involved in that kinda stuff for young lady? If we use human organs, they are legitimately donated and then used for important research, for which I may remind you, we are world renowned."

"I'll take that as a no then?"

"Caroline, you sure as hell can." He paused as if mentally summing her up, and continued to look straight at her. "Now, let's make sure you have some fun with us. This here's a big party and I'm mighty glad to be able to share it with you."

He turned abruptly and beckoned to a younger man in a flying suit. "Hey George, c'mon over here and meet an English woman."

He turned back to Jane. "This here's my nephew George. Used to be a US air force F15 fighter pilot. Say hello boy," he hit the man on the shoulder.

Jane instantly disliked the 'good ole boy' as soon as he shook her hand and smiled broadly and she was aware that he was doing his best to undress her with his eyes. It wasn't his lechery she disliked, just the way he didn't consider it necessary to hide it. They bantered for a while and good ole George kept talking about flying and how good he was. She made an excuse to go to the women's room. As soon as she was able, Jane stood behind a curtain and observed the group. It was clear that they were talking about her and George was being briefed. He laughed, raised his hands and let them smack the sides of his thighs. The others laughed too. They were quite obviously hatching something.

George stepped up to Jane when she returned to the group. "Hey gal, how about a spin? I like to treat my plane like my women, you know? Get inside 'em twice a day and take 'em to heaven and back!"

The gawping group of good ole boys, including Karowitze, guffawed and shuffled awkwardly. Jane blanched inside and maintained a steady disarming expression.

"Hey gal, that's the best offer you'll get stateside, let me tell you," Karowitze yelled and guffawed some more.

Jane had no choice but to go along with the offer. Conversation was becoming stilted and she needed some time to think. She found herself being led out of the building and towards a Piper Comanche light aircraft fifty yards away on a small apron. They climbed up and he strapped her in, then himself. He turned the key in the ignition and the engine spluttered noisily into life and they taxied down the short grass runway. It wasn't long before George proceeded to show off by looping the loop and swooping down on the crowd outside the marquee who all yelled and waved.

"Wooeeee, gal, ain't this just great? Some say flyin's better'n sex, but I ain't so sure 'bout that."

"Well," she replied testily, "some say that if you can do one well then you can't do the other, but I'm no expert."

George's smile turned to a sneer. He pulled back the control column and the aircraft began to climb high, then he levelled it out.

"Okay. Here it is gal. You know sumthin'? You got attitude. Pity really, because you are kinda cute. But orders is orders, ma'am. I'm kind of sorry 'bout this, but heigh ho, here we go."

He reached for the ignition key and switched off the engine. It was only then that she noticed that he wore a parachute and she didn't. He flung open the door, put his rear end outwards, blew her a kiss and stumbled rather than rolled out of the aircraft.

"Bye yo'all."

As he fell backwards, she noticed that he grabbed the key chain, but it stuck in the ignition and the chain was pulled out of his hand, the key fell to the floor with a 'plop' as it hit the rubber mat. Everything was silent except for the sound of the wind against the fuselage. Jane closed her eyes and adjusted to the danger.

The aircraft began to slow and would soon stall. Jane gritted her teeth. She had to maintain her composure and get the key before the aircraft spun out of control. It would throw her against the bulkhead and the G-force would prevent her from moving, let alone reaching the key. Unclipping her seat belt, she reached down into the pilot's seat-well, almost pitching herself headlong into the gap. Her hands moved frantically around the floor, searching for the key. As she searched in vain, she experienced weightlessness as the airframe began to hover in mid-air. In the last corner of the footwell she felt the smooth metal of the key and held it tight. There was little time left. The aircraft began to gradually fall. Jane moved quickly to the pilot seat, pulled the throttle back to halfway to avoid the engine flooding on restart, inserted and turned the key. After a few turns of the propeller the engine spluttered into life, but the aircraft was already now in a steep stall.

Her elation was tempered by the thumping of what felt like two pistons in her chest, as she tried desperately to recall the instructions given to her over a decade ago when she took her private pilot's licence whilst in the British army.

Think, you fool, think!

Her instructor had been an ex-RAF fighter pilot, qualified flying instructor, and he drummed into her the need to work strictly to standard operating procedures, SOPs he called them, so the brain simply took over in an emergency and reacted automatically. She recalled his voice: *SOP Jane, aircraft stalls and you work to rote, bish bash bosh, come on, woman, get on with it!* She marvelled at how he ate a chocolate bar as their training aircraft tumbled to the ground and she fought to control it. How she wished he was here right now.

Jane breathed deeply. The aircraft was dropping like a stone. She pushed the control column fully forward, kicked the rudder to port. It seemed like an eternity, but as the onrushing air hit the ailerons and tail rudder the aircraft slowly began to turn. As the ground hurtled towards her the airspeed increased over the ailerons, this gave the aircraft momentum and lift on which flight relies, but importantly control. The ground approached fast and at the last possible moment she pulled the control column towards her. To her relief the nose gradually lifted and the airframe moved upwards and away from the ground in a slow arc. She steered it gracefully to port and back up into the sky.

Turning her head, she saw the parachute and good ole George floating down to the airfield to her right. It was an opportunity that she couldn't resist. As soon as she was able, she steered the aircraft in a steep bank up and to starboard and circled until she could see the parachute in front of her. Then she aimed straight at it. Her fingers gripped the column. *George, I'm gonna scare the shit out of you boy!*

Jane aimed the aircraft straight at the hapless body of George as he dangled precariously on his parachute.

George's face creased with fear and he yelled, "Jesus Christ," and he waved and kicked his legs as he saw the aircraft coming towards him. His thoughts raced - it wasn't supposed to be like this. It should have been an engine failure, her stubborn refusal to wear a parachute. The crash would've been a very unfortunate situation. Now here he was almost voiding his bowels as the crazy bitch headed straight for him.

As the airframe passed immediately below George, he felt the urine in his bladder escape into his flying suit. The updraft of air pushed the parachute upwards and it made him swing crazily, veering towards electricity lines and he screamed with fear. Luckily for him, he missed the pylon but was swept some five hundred yards outside the main runway area towards a line of tall Redwood trees and the parachute caught at the highest point. He hung precariously from two branches that were beginning to bend sharply, his eyes were wide with fear. He was a very long way from the ground.

Jane turned the aircraft once more and flew past his rigid frightened form. He looked up and caught sight of her middle finger raised in salute. She gained height then turned back towards the runway, eventually landing a little too heavily and taxied to a halt just in front of the spectators.

Karowitze stood in front of Jane, his hands on his hips, looking menacingly at her.

"What the hell..." he spluttered.

Jane took stock of the situation quickly and decided to go for the 'little lady' approach. She knew that they wouldn't fall for that for too long.

"Robert, I'm so sorry. I hope George will be all right. I think he was fooling around a bit, he playfully said, 'I'm outa here.' I know that he was only joking of course. Then he, well, sort of fell against the door and bingo, it opened and out he went. It all happened so quickly."

Karowitze looked at Senator Bainbridge and they were lost for words.

"And where in the name o' heaven did you learn to fly?"

"Oh, when I was a teenager, I got my licence. It all comes back to you when you need it to. Quite amazing really."

"George didn't say anything at all? He just fell out?"

Jane realised that he was sounding her out to ascertain whether she held them culpable for the deed.

"Say anything? What do you mean, a loud, whoops, perhaps? Because that was all the poor man had time to utter. Where is he anyway?" she said disingenuously.

Karowitze pointed to a tree line in the distance and Jane saw a truck and ambulance heading towards it.

"Oh dear," she said, "I feel awfully faint. I think that I would rather like to go to the hotel and lie down. I'm sorry to spoil the party but that was quite an experience."

Karowitze hesitated at first, but said, "Sure, you must be quite shocked ma'am." He turned to his man. "Hey, Gene, yo'all take this lady back to the hotel now."

"Caroline, we can continue this conversation later this evening over dinner. You go back and rest now."

Karowitze's words were hollow and it was clear that he did not want her to go, but relented, happy for now at least, to believe her story. Besides, he clearly knew where the hotel was.

Jane looked over his shoulder and took in the scene before leaving with Gene. There were people who looked nothing like business people or scientists.

Gene sat in the back of the Cadillac with Jane as the driver drove back to the hotel. To her horror, she noticed a large black sedan follow them out of the aerodrome. This was not good. Jane needed to be absolutely free of these people in order to escape to Kennedy Airport in New York to get changed and make her way to Ted, her passport and home. Doubtless, it wouldn't be long before good ole George was rescued and would relate his version of events. That would surely seal her fate.

After about two miles along the highway, she saw a filling station.

"Gene, I'm really sorry, but I need a loo," she said.

"A what?"

"Sorry, I mean the bathroom, please, I'm desperate."

He yelled to the driver to pull in and the following sedan followed, parking behind them. Jane knew that about now they would be helping good old George out of the tree and Karowitze would be getting another story. Time was not on her side. She got out and went to the women's room. It was easy to scramble out of the disabled toilet window to the rear of the building, immediately behind it was a large patch of high grass and shrubs. There was the beginning of a path through it and she ran and placed her silk scarf at the entrance to it. Then she returned and made her way carefully to the front left of the building, peering around the corner. She would wait.

After ten minutes Gene got impatient and went inside. As he did so his mobile rang. All hell broke loose and she heard toilet doors being kicked in. He yelled and the two swarthy men who were sitting in the black sedan got out and ran to the building. She had to be quick. The driver of the Cadillac just sat there, head in his right hand, happy enough to let the world go by.

Jane bent low and moved over to the left side of the Cadillac. She reached the driver's door, stood up and said urgently, "Quick help me?"

The driver looked up, surprised. She reached through the window, grabbed his hair and brought his head down on the side of the door with a crack. It took only a few seconds to pull his bulk out from behind the wheel and get into the driver's seat.

The motor was running and she put the automatic into drive and gunned it out of the filling station. Gene and the two men ran out of the building, without hesitation one of them fired a gun. The bullet ricocheted off the side of the car. A Cadillac is a fast cart, but she knew that the lighter sedan would catch her eventually. The following car always has the advantage. Grand prix drivers know that, special agents know that and the approaching image in her rear-view mirror proved the point. All she could do was to try and outrun them.

For five or so miles she weaved this way and that, taking advantage of oncoming vehicles, sometimes overtaking in precarious places. But the traffic eventually thinned and the road became narrower and more dangerous as it rose higher into the mountains. The precipice edge was on the right side of the road and was unprotected by fencing or bollards. The drop was a hundred feet or more onto rocks.

Eventually, the sedan closed in on her. The men fired several shots and she could see in her mirror that Gene was remonstrating with them. Then they tried something else. Every now and then they came up behind her and shunted the Cadillac from behind. Because they had not thought it through, they hit the car on the left rear. This pushed right side closer to precipice, but Jane wrenched the steering wheel left so the car swerved towards the middle of the road and she was able to use the weight of the front to straighten out and continue.

She knew this wouldn't last and had to think quickly. Her security training came to mind, especially the use of handbrake turns. It was less effective in Belfast on tarmac roads with high kerbs and so on, but would be able to use the gravel to her advantage. There was nothing for it, she took a deep breath and put her foot hard on the accelerator; the engine responded readily.

As she approached a right-hand bend, she slowed the car appreciably and the sedan came up behind determined to push her over the edge with the same manoeuvre. Again, it hit the left side of the vehicle, but as it did so she put the engine in neutral, put her foot on the brake and yanked the handbrake, whilst at the same time turning the wheel sharply to the left. Without the expected object in front to take the hit, the sedan's forward movement propelled it faster to the right and the edge of the precipice. As Jane's Cadillac spun around 180 degrees its heavier front end hit the lighter sedan on the side. The sedan skidded to a halt ending up balanced half on the gravel and half over the precipice.

There was an eerie silence except for the hissing of steam from a cracked radiator and sound of the front wheels turning in the air. Jane jumped out and walked slowly towards it.

The men were petrified and clung to their seats. Gene sat in the front, white-faced and motionless. The man with the gun threw it out of the car window, waved in surrender and called out to her.

"Hey, stop bein' so stoopid, steady the car so we can get out," unbelievably adding, "we just wanna talk." He was swarthy and barrel-chested like so many other thugs she had encountered. These men reminded her of some of the Serbian hooligans she met in Bosnia – those who kidnapped her interpreter and brutalised young women and children without conscience. The hair on the back of her neck rose and she wrestled with her emotions.

Jane turned and walked away, but her thoughts raced madly and she slowed her pace, then stopped still. She had never, ever killed in the line of duty. Hurt in defence, sure, but never killed without reason. The voices of the men, now shouting insults and vile threats jarred in her ears. She took a deep breath and walked back to the car.

The facts of her situation were icily clear: they had tried to kill her twice. They would try again. They knew no mercy. Without hesitation, Jane put her foot against the rear fender of the car and gave it a push. It rocked violently, tilting further over the precipice, before finally sliding over the edge, the metal screeching as it scraped against the rough edge. The men screamed, "Stoopid bitch, don't do it," and more, but their voices were drowned out by the sound of the sedan as it slithered down the steep rocky slope. It bumped its way down, gathering speed before smashing into a large boulder and somersaulting. As it rolled the doors burst open and she saw the men's bodies flung outwards. The vehicle crashed into the ground and burst into flames.

Jane felt no regret whatever, just a steady calmness. The sun was bright, she smelled the sweet scent of desert shrubs - the threat against her life was gone.

She was relieved to be alive.

Ted Sanderson sat with an FBI agent called John Kowalski, a good-looking man of medium athletic build, with dark hair and a wicked sense of humour. He briefed his American colleague on the work they had undertaken in England and the evidence they had amassed so far. He opined that it would not be long before they would be able to put together a decent portfolio which, added to all the others, would be enough to bring charges against Artaxis.

Kowalski smiled. "Well, Ted, you guys have done a great job, really you have. Thank you. But I think Interpol and the FBI will need more than just a file or two to crack these guys. This business is bigger'n drugs, y'know what I mean?"

Ted sat back in his chair. "Yeah, Jane made that clear. But I thought nothing was bigger than that."

Kowalski leaned forward. "Ted, my friend, it's all about supply and demand. I promise you if horse-shit had the value that body parts do with demand as high because of the scarcity, then it would attract the same huge premium. Now then, consider how much you would pay for a kidney to save your wife's life? Given that as a start point, it really is simple economics." Kowalski continued. "Hold on to the fact that the world is full of everyday Joes, who, sadly, wouldn't be missed. Then factor in the value of one nice fresh cadaver with its tissue, spinal cord, corneas, kidneys, heart, liver, skin and bingo you've got yourself a lucrative income stream. Jeez man, there's no end to it."

Ted knew Kowalski was right. The popular view amongst liberals in the west that selling organs, although repellent, was vaguely acceptable if it meant a life could be saved, merely hid the possibility of a business opportunity on the most enormous scale. It was an opportunity that needed feeding and there was no shortage of entrepreneurial skill to do that.

Kowalski eased the mood.

"C'mon buddy, let me take you to a rib shack down the way and buy you an American burger, bigger than your limey mouth can cope with. While you're eating, I'll tell you about Jane."

Jane drove the battered Cadillac to her hotel and parked it at the far end of the car park. She held on to the steering wheel for a while and looked at her reflection in the rear-view mirror – she was surprised at how composed she looked. She locked the car and made for the rear door of the hotel. After making sure there was no one watching her room, she picked up her bag and left. It took her no more than a minute or two. On her way back to the car, she saw state troopers walking around the vehicle and talking into radios. It was time to change and she went back to the women's room, where she quickly washed out the blonde temporary hair dye, put on makeup and dressed in a different set of clothes - white ski pants, a light blue top that left a gap at her waist and sling-back shoes. She also wore plenty of bangles in her ears, around her neck and on her wrists. The discarded clothes were bundled up and after removing a ceiling square, she pushed them into the void, bringing the square neatly back into place. Her sunglasses were a little large and, as her mother would say, *common*, but they hid her eyes and suited the local style.

Holding a small American fashion purse, she left the women's room and walked out of a side door of the hotel towards a bus stop. It wasn't long before she was on a Greyhound bus to the airport, looking back at the hotel as more police vehicles arrived.

She hoped Ted wouldn't be late, lost or asleep.

Ted finished his burger and was left gasping for breath. "Blimey mate, that was a marathon – but delicious. Listen, I hope you don't mind me saying, but earlier on when you were talking about Jane, it sounded as though you knew her quite well."

Kowalski smiled and drank the last dregs of his Budweiser beer.

"Well spotted, my man. Yeah, we served in Bosnia together. I saved her life, fell in love with her, but she not with me. We remained really good friends though. So much so, that I worry about her, no more so than today."

"But why? She's just going to ask a few questions."

"Ted, let me level with you. She's actually going into the lion's den so that she can spook them into doing something stupid. It's much more dangerous than just asking a few questions. The other problem she has is that we have good reason to believe that the Mafia have infiltrated Artaxis. It's the big money angle, eh?"

Ted sucked his teeth. "The little minx."

"Perhaps, Ted. But I saw this chick take out three thugs in a street fight. She's no minx, Ted – a Tiger, yes, but not a minx!"

Kowalski looked straight at Ted.

"Jane has always done work she believes in and I know that she will crack this case for sure. She was seconded to Interpol a while back in order to interview a lady called Katrina Annatto, a leading witness against a rather seedy Bulgarian clinic based in Sofia. Katrina worked closely with Jane and later became a prime adviser and undercover worker for Interpol. Together they amassed significant information and case studies that will help to eradicate the evil trade in illegally obtained body parts. Frankly, buddy, on this one I don't mind admitting that we are all running to keep up with her."

Ted tightened his lips, "Yeah, that's Jane."

They spent the rest of the time exchanging stories and Ted learned more about her. Eventually he had to call it a day and they parted good friends, Kowalski back to his FBI machinations and Ted to meet Jane at Kennedy Airport.

He was now very anxious about her safety.

Jane made the journey from La Guardia to Kennedy Airport in no time at all. She was exhilarated by the action, and her heart was beating fast. She learned the hard lesson that it was crucial to return to her normal persona as quickly as possible, to compose herself, appearing ordinary and unsuspicious. It was important to keep the mind cool and alert. She walked briskly through the airport concourse, keeping he eyes open for Ted and anything that spelled danger. Ted was easily spotted. He was the only man wearing a sports jacket and tie – so English.

The airport tannoy was loud and the high-pitched announcer's voice grated on her already fraught nerves as it announced an incoming flight from San Francisco. To make it worse, it was competing with a large floor-cleaning unit that was being pushed along the concourse. As she strode up to Ted, she looked over the top of the cleaning machine and noticed several men in suits walking in a straight line abreast towards them. Ted looked up as she reached him and before he could speak, she grabbed and kissed him full on the lips, so tightly he could hardly breathe. His resistance softened. This girl could snog!

The men glanced at them, but passed by. After a minute or so Jane pulled away and looked about her. "All clear. I think those chaps were the bad guys." Assessing the effect that her kiss had had on Ted who was looking a bit dazed, she added chirpily, "Don't get any ideas feller. It was all in the line of duty!"

She turned and walked away and Ted searched his briefcase for her passport exclaiming loudly, "More bloody duty, that's what I say, more bloody duty!"

12

Romania

Gabrielle Todd, known to his friends as Toddy, sat in his seven-tonne white van just inside the Romanian border. He was listening to his favourite Bee Gees CD and munching a bacon sandwich, lovingly prepared by Sharon, the co-proprietor of the Truckers' Café just inside the seaport of Harwich on the east Suffolk coast. Michelin star it was not, but then that's not what the average trucker or delivery van driver wants. Home cooked English food and a good laugh cheered the spirits in advance of a long drive, and it was also a chance to flirt with her. Every driver who succumbed to her vibrant humour and personal attention, vowed to come back to the café as he came in and out of the country. Toddy liked the Dutch and German food served in efficient and clean motorway service stations, but Romanian roadside cuisine didn't inspire his taste buds one little bit.

It was Sharon who had come to his rescue and packed him a large box of bacon sandwiches. The brown bread and salty butter provided the perfect accompaniment and his mouth watered at the thought of them. He had slept a little in his cab and used some of the hot water in his flask to wash and brush up. Toddy was of the old school and had high standards of personal hygiene and dress. His friends teased him about it but he would never let these standards drop.

The journey from the Maria Cresswell Hospice en route to the Ceausescu Institute of Health just outside Bucharest had gone very well so far. He preferred to travel off-peak, in order to miss the rush hour traffic in the countries he transited through. His life had been made immeasurably easier over the decades since border controls had been lifted under the Schengen Agreement within the EU, then eased into eastern bloc countries.

Toddy was glad of the courier work offered by the hospice. Delivering sensitive medical equipment that had to be kept at a constant temperature meant that he had to equip the van with an efficient cooling system, but it had proved to be a good business venture, with frequent trips to Romania. It helped that his overheads were low and the work was always cash-in-hand. He was a pensioner, living in a mobile home and yet he retained all the skills and knowledge needed to do many other one-off driving jobs. Life couldn't be better. He didn't really need the money, but the work kept him busy and he enjoyed it. A donation to a Romanian children's home gave him a feeling of satisfaction.

The stars shone brightly above the forest canopy as he got out of his van and breathed the cool night air. He stretched several times, forcing every joint in his body to extend beyond the hunched and compressed configuration caused by the last two-hour driving stretch. The cold air filled his chest and rejuvenated him.

Then something hit his head, which filled with white noise. He lost consciousness and fell to the ground.

The Romanian police were better than Toddy had expected. They sat at his bedside in a local clinic and questioned him several times about his cargo, what he had seen on his journey and what he remembered of the incident. He was very upset and described a bang on the head and white lights and remembered nothing more. His van had been burnt out. It was now no more than a charred smouldering heap of metal. His wallet had been stolen but it was impossible to work out what else was missing due to the destruction of the van.

The police sympathised and said it was due to itinerant criminal classes moving through the country towards Western Europe. One policeman ruefully commented that it was good for Romania that they were leaving the country and this earned him a glare from his superior officer.

Toddy was declared fit enough to travel and given hotel accommodation by the British Embassy to tide him over for a few days until he could sort out insurance details and talk to the owners of the consignment. He was not looking forward to this. Failure had never been on his agenda and he didn't like it one little bit.

England

Mike Hancox dialled a special number and waited as it connected. Jane Kavanagh answered.

"Jane K."

"Ah, Jane, my dear girl. News for you. The intercept worked and our people executed it to perfection. I should ask them to write the next script for East Enders," he reached for a large glass of scotch.

"Oh, good. So, what have we got?"

"Right then," he replied, his throat glowing with the taste of Talisker single malt. "The boys mugged the poor old van driver on his way from the Maria Cresswell Hospice to The Ceausescu Institute, or whatever it's called. They made it look like a case of theft and yob spree by stealing the driver's wallet and trashing the vehicle. That was of course intentional so that the body parts that we knew were being transported could be removed and placed in our own vehicle. To avoid possible suspicion, we replaced the parts with bits from an abattoir. The bill of lading was interesting though. They claimed to have been transporting sensitive medical equipment."

"Mike, that's great news. Is the driver okay?"

"Oh yes, he's all right. Just a tap on the bonce, that's all. We called our embassy to ensure that he got gold-plated treatment. He's an innocent party when all said and done."

"Now the exciting part starts," said Jane, voice hardly betraying the excitement she felt. "How soon can we retrieve the DNA?"

"Steady on, my girl, that's going to be done as soon as the intelligence van arrives back from Romania. But it will be done, that's for sure. We'll get a set of DNA codes. Our next hope is that the experts will match just one DNA sample, that's all, with someone who has recently passed through the Maria Cresswell Hospice."

Hancox paused and took another mouthful of whisky, letting it slide gently down his throat. He took a drag of his Gauloises cigarette and felt the nicotine overpower the alcohol buzz. He loved the feeling of being close to a result and was amused at the title of his preferred nicotine, it was a French cigarette and the name meant, 'Gaul Woman' - Jane was certainly all of that.

"That's what we are waiting for, old girl," he said after a few seconds, "without that information we are, frankly, pissing into the wind."

"You'll get it, Mike, I promise you that."

Hancox knew that Jane would harry the technicians, morning and night. He smiled again and thought, *The Gaul Woman rides out...!*

Jane made small talk for a while and they both rejoiced in that familiar feeling that secret service agents have when the chase hots up. She wished him well and promised to call him as early as possible. The call had been taken in the guesthouse on a secure phone. When she finished, Margaret Ogden put her head around the door and said softly, "Cup of tea?"

It was four a.m. Although she was tired, Jane just wanted to get on with the job.

"Yes, wonderful. Just what I need to keep me alert at this time of day."

"Ah, I remember those days well," replied Margaret. "Go into the conservatory, I put the heating on just in case. The tea will only take a few minutes."

Jane tightened her towelling bathrobe around her naked body and slid her feet into her slippers.

They now had a chance of unequivocally identifying the link between the hospice and the Romanian Institute, where medical tourism flourished. There would be denials from the Institute and they would lament the lack of proper recording as to where various organs came from, in contravention of European rules. They would agree to update their systems in the future, of course, and that would be the end of their involvement. Ethics vary in depth and weight, depending on which country is involved. The farther east you go the less emphasis is placed on such bureaucracy or the niceties of behaviour. Jane pondered that it was probably only the fact that so many western European aid agencies were now very closely involved in the terrible scandal of thousands of children languishing in so-called 'residential homes' throughout the country that they were safe from 'body part' butchery.

She made her way into the conservatory after collecting a buff-coloured file from her cabinet. She opened it and sat in a large wicker chair that she had almost claimed as her own. Margaret left the tea on a side table without saying a word. She knew better than to deflect a colleague who was deep in thought.

Jane absentmindedly raised the cup to her lips and sipped the hot Earl Grey tea as she flicked through the papers. She put the file down, grabbed a pencil and writing pad and began to sketch the situation in the form of a rich picture of events. The answer came quickly.

The next day, Jane spent two hours with DC Farmer Hovens. He recited from his notes. "Mr Mason, eighty-two years old, Florence Barnaby sadly only forty-five years old, and finally, Hermione Radcliffe sixty-eight years old. Only Mrs Radcliffe was local. The others came from, let's see, Birmingham and Milton Keynes." He paused and turned over the pages of his notepad. "Those are the latest registrations of deaths from the Maria Cresswell Hospice, guv."

"Farmer, that's brilliant," she said. "Now tell Ted Sanderson and DS Bradbury what's needed and I'll call them quite soon. Tell them everything I explained to you earlier and keep it very secret and I mean, *very*." She paused and added, "Emphasise that we must get a DNA sample from one of the recently deceased and that the Radcliffe relative is the quickest route. Can you do that please?"

Farmer accepted the important task readily. He often felt that he was just the messenger boy, but this involved being trusted to brief key players. He desperately wanted to be part of the solution – it would make the job so much richer.

Jane left the office and he set about making the important calls.

It was about ten a.m. and he was unable to contact either of his senior officers who were involved in a meeting with the chief constable. Time weighed heavily on him and he considered the strong possibility of independently taking action to secure the DNA.

Why not? he thought. It was a simple enough task. He gathered up his notes, put them into his briefcase and headed to the motor pool to secure a police vehicle for an hour or two.

A rambling old farmhouse constructed of grey stone and with a slate roof was home to Jeremy Radcliffe. It was the sort of building that made the minds of property developers buzz with excitement at the prospect of exclusive renovation to its former glory. However, this was a little above Radcliffe's means as the fading paintwork, crumbling plaster and rusting iron railings showed. Despite its plainness, made worse by windows that were too small for the symmetry of the building, it had an odd sort of solid character.

Radcliffe heard the old-fashioned bell ring and sat up straight in his winged leather chair. The fire crackled and he was reluctant to move. His heart had been broken and there was nothing of interest left to him now. He missed Hermione so much. Whoever it was could simply push off. To his immense annoyance, the ringing of the bell had that insistent nature to it, not the simple *one press and then depart* sort of ring that the local vicar or some other do-gooder would use. It rang for the third time and he shot out of his chair in high dudgeon, striding purposefully down the hallway, his metal studded boots clicking on the wooden floor.

"What do you want?" He almost shouted as he pulled open the front door and confronted the fresh-faced young DC Hovens.

"Oh, sir, good morning. I am Detective Constable Hovens and I wonder if I might ask you a few questions?"

"Questions? What about? The frequency of which travellers steal from my buildings, or perhaps the continuous trespass by the local yobs across my garden area as they transit home from the pub vomiting the contents of their stomachs as they go? Perhaps you are going to arrest someone. That, I will listen to. But then, your lot never did anything in the past so, pray tell me why I should listen to you now?"

Farmer regarded Radcliffe with awe. He had never met such a man so eloquently bitter.

"No, sir, nothing like that I'm afraid," Farmer narrowed his eyebrows and continued, "I wonder if I may ask you for a sample of your late wife's DNA, anything will do, sir, a hairbrush would be more than enough?"

Radcliffe glowered at him for a few moments and for a while said nothing.

"Come in," he said and opened the door wide.

The smell of lavender polish and moth balls pervaded the air and the old pine floor boards creaked as he made his way down the dimly lit corridor, passing unpolished brass candlesticks and dark oil paintings hanging on the fabric covered walls. They entered a large lounge at the back of the property. He was ushered to sit down in front of the fire. Radcliffe remained standing with his foot on a large brass footrest in the hearth.

"So, detective constable, what exactly is it you want and why?"

The phrase, *think things through,* is useful, and wise advice. Now, was just that kind of moment, but this was definitely not what Hovens did.

"Right sir, well, I'm not at liberty to reveal the reasons for our investigations, but it shouldn't be of great concern to you. We just want to follow various lines of enquiry," his voice trailed off a little.

Radcliffe was no fool. In his past life as a senior civil servant he had controlled the young and inexperienced and even those who moved on and were into high power politics, and he could spot dissembling when he saw it. He stared at Farmer who in turn felt his body literally wriggle with discomfort.

"So, will a hairbrush suit you? Hair samples are deemed to contain lots of DNA." Radcliffe's face was riven with suspicion.

"That will do nicely, sir. Thank you." Farmer was greatly relieved and inadvertently telegraphed the fact to Radcliffe.

"How about some tea?" said Radcliffe, looking out of the window at DC Hovens' car parked at the side of the house next to his Land Rover Defender. Before Farmer could refuse, he added, "I insist. I cannot have you coming all this way and not offer some kind of hospitality."

Radcliffe left Farmer by the fireside and went into the kitchen. Something was wrong. What would the police be doing with Hermione's DNA? He had seen her laid out, serene and calm with that deathly pale look that even the most accomplished undertakers couldn't disguise. For what reason was this being done?

"I won't be a minute," he said loudly, and clattered the cups around so they made lots of noise. The he filled the kettle and put it on the Aga stove, closing the flap on the top that provided a whistle when the water was boiling. He quickly ducked out of the back door and made his way to the policeman's car.

The car door was not locked and he opened it and peered inside. A briefcase lay on the passenger seat. He got in and opened it. It contained several writing pads, all of which had doodle and writing over them, a map, mobile phone and some pens.

"Ah yes, doodles," he thought to himself. He recalled the times he stalked his Whitehall office at night, back in his days as a senior civil servant. He would idly look at papers on the desks of subordinates reflecting on their doodling. Some wrote ideas, others simply sketched or made some cryptic notes that belied their irritation.

'Radcliffe's a bastard' had been a fairly popular scribble in his day. He was not an easy man to work with and no one ever crossed him; not that it bothered him.

He flicked through the A4 notepad from back to front, eyes almost popping at the rambling notes that jumped out at him. His senses screamed at what he saw.

Van – Romania. Travelled from hospice. Body bits – DNA test. Tell DS asap. Get evidence quickly!

There were lots of scribbles showing times of a meeting that day, a couple of telephone numbers and a sketch of a van elaborately drawn as if done during a conversation – then it had been scribbled over.

Bits, *he thought,* what bits?

Then it occurred to him. DNA identification was needed because a van carrying human bits and pieces had been apprehended in Romania en route from the Maria Cresswell Hospice. It was obvious. Hermione had died and they removed pieces of her for research or something else. His head suddenly hurt and he felt dizzy with anger and frustration.

Radcliffe walked unsteadily back to the kitchen and tried to continue, but it was impossible to behave normally as rage rose in him. Then anger simply overwhelmed him and he clenched a cup tightly in his hand and when it refused to be crushed, he threw it at the wall. It smashed loudly.

"Everything all right, sir?" said DC Hovens.

Radcliffe felt tears welling in his eyes. Could nobody in this bloody world be trusted. His subordinates had reported him to a minister for blowing a whistle on illegal government activities and now his wife's body had been violated. He composed himself as best he could.

"Everything's fine," he shouted and realised what he would do next.

After five minutes the kettle began to boil and the whistle let out a slow whine, moving up the scale to a shrill screech. DC Hovens thought that something was wrong and went to the kitchen. The kettle was by now rattling noisily as the steam forcing its way out of the spout. There was no one there. He was confused, but didn't notice that that there was a space above the range where a shotgun used to be. When he ran outside to the courtyard, he saw that Radcliffe's Land Rover Defender was nowhere to be seen.

The tension in the air at The Maria Cresswell Hospice was electric and there was an eerie silence. The receptionist had fainted and office staff in the vicinity scattered for cover and called the police. Radcliffe stood in front of Bobbette Grainger. She was petrified and her legs shook violently. He held the shotgun level to her stomach, his bloodshot rheumy eyes glaring angrily at her.

"Now, why don't you just explain to me what's been going on with my wife's body?" He spoke very slowly and deliberately.

"I don't know what you are talking about..." She stopped when he raised the gun closer to her face. Her eyes were transfixed on the double-barrelled muzzle.

"Don't give me that. I spent years working with people who lied for a profession and I don't need to explain to you how it is I know when someone is lying. Now then, if you value your looks or even your life, tell me all about it." He cocked the gun and

Grainger gave a helpless and reactive, "Oh...!" Her legs shook and she had to hold on to a nearby desk for support.

"She died, sir, and, oh dear. You know that. Someone in need, er, a great need, had to have a kidney, you see. We would've asked, but you were so distressed. I was sure that you wouldn't object and it didn't seem right to, well er, that is, oh dear. Don't kill me, please don't kill me!" She pleaded incoherently and tears cascaded down her cheeks.

Radcliffe's face contorted and he began to shout at her, asking more questions. She fell to her knees and sobbed forgiveness. A police car skidded to a halt on the gravel outside the hospice and Det Supt Ted Sanderson got out and ran into the foyer.

He stopped in the doorway and shouted, "Mr Radcliffe, don't do anything stupid. Please think before you act, sir. Please."

Radcliffe slowly lowered the shotgun and half turned towards Ted Sanderson. Just then an armed police unit drove up and scrambled out of the van shouting, "Armed police, put down the gun."

Radcliffe smiled sardonically. "Quite like the cinema, isn't it?"

He swiftly turned the shotgun around and put the muzzle in the direction of his mouth.

"Oh, for God's sake, I just don't care anymore," he said, his tear-stained face sweating and contorted.

The blast of the shotgun cartridges blew the side of his head apart and blood, bone and grey brain matter splattered Grainger and the reception desk.

She didn't stop screaming for a full five minutes.

Ted Sanderson was commended for his bravery, but chided for disobeying standing orders regarding attending a scene of crime in advance of an armed squad of police officers. He made sure that DC Hovens' feet did not touch the ground and he was immediately transferred from special duties to another police authority.

Ted took his disciplining with good grace. He felt terribly sorry for Radcliffe, but had little sympathy for Grainger. She suffered a complete breakdown, which was fortunate because in her state of mind, she was unwittingly revealing clues. Police psychologists trained in gentle interrogation technique worked on her and carefully drew out every detail. She was a pitiful sight now, broken completely by the terrible events at the Hospice.

A day later, he stood in the special briefing room and looked at the display boards. The phone rang - it was Jane.

"Hi, it's me. How are you?"

"Well, I've had better times. Watching a man's skull disintegrate before my very eyes is not so nice. But knowing that the Grainger woman is singing her heart out is comforting. My only worry is this has alerted others who may be implicated in the hospice."

"Be that as it may," said Jane, "but the reason for my call is to tell you that we have the evidence, Ted. We bloody well have it, bang on. The hair from Hermione Radcliffe's brushes revealed that the DNA on organs and body tissue in the van are a direct and indisputable match. We have the link, Ted. Now you can seal the hospice and make some arrests."

Ted was overjoyed and wasted no time at all. Within hours, police surrounded the hospice and its staff were separated and interviewed. The patients were transferred to other hospices in the area and a team of doctors and nurses was drafted in to re-examine them and ensure their safety and care.

Sadly, the key consultants and support doctors were long gone.

Mike Hancox spluttered down the phone to Jane. "Bloody local police, block-headed fools, and we were doing so well. Damn and blast them, the doctors have escaped. Never mind, we have the proven links and there is still a blazing light on the horizon even if we will find it difficult to catch those responsible in Norfolk. I just want to give you an early heads-up that matters are reaching a final crunch, Jane. It's bloody good news. Soon after the hospice debacle, we traced calls made from someone in the hospice to the States, to Artaxis to be precise, and those are being decoded now. In addition, our friends in the Romanian police sealed the Ceausescu Institute very quickly and they are getting to work on the staff and doctors alike. Their methods are, shall we say, a little more precise than ours, thank goodness."

Jane was taken aback. "Good grief, the Romanian police, I don't believe it?"

"Yes, that's right. After years of being the whipping boy for all sorts of human rights abuses, they decided to put matters right. This whole situation seems to have offended their sensibilities more than we thought it would and has given them a chance to look good. Mind you, we did offer them the opportunity and to their credit they took it. It also helps their case for greater working relationships within the European Union. Telephone traffic from the hospice increased and was duly intercepted. I can tell you there was some interesting stuff in those messages."

He breathed deeply and added, "I do believe that our friends in Artaxis are in melt-down, my girl. It's just a matter of time. Well done indeed."

Jane thought she could feel his smile radiating down the telephone, but thought him a little critical of the local police. As she put the phone down, her thoughts went to Jenny Ellis recovering in a rehabilitation centre. Now they had the evidence and people to interrogate on both sides of the channel it was time to focus on the chase.

This was not going to be at all easy.

13

Jane Kavanagh looked up from her papers when Ted entered their shared office. The evidence from Chin Kwok, with the added detail from the Chinese authorities, was explosive. Artaxis had been named as the organisation that chartered aircraft to collect human organs from a local airport and transport them via Vietnam to the United States where they would be sold at premium prices to those who could afford to buy them. The precision and detail were flawless. She passed the information up the line with enormous satisfaction. She wanted to fly out to Beijing and thank Madame Lom in person, but knew that wouldn't be acceptable.

Ted sat down at his desk, which was alongside Jane's, and noticed she had a satisfied look on her face. "Good news?"

"Ted, it couldn't be better at this stage of the game. The China link has been broken and, more importantly, there was no political dimension to spoil the result. To quote Confucius, *we live in interesting times!* They've worked miracles in tracing the route for human organs from executed prisoners, through the couriers and right to Artaxis's door."

"Great stuff. And here I was hoping to raise your morale by good news from the UK side..." he broke off and playfully looked at the ceiling, "but it's small beer, I suppose."

"What? Ted, what have you got, you bastard, don't tease!"

"Okay, here goes. DS Nicola Bradbury, our very own star of the CID, complete with a degree in agriculture and dress-making..."

Jane broke in, throwing a plastic coffee cup at him. "Get on with it, man!"

Ted laughed and continued, "Okay, quick and simple then. We've got a GP who contributed to the Maria Cresswell scenario, to confess. Right, got to go now..." and he made to leave the office.

Jane laughed loudly and stuck her foot out to stop him. "Right then, yes, I give in. Take your time, at least I know it's worth it now. Proceed, please and I will not interrupt."

Ted cleared his throat, smiled and continued. "Seriously, Jane, it's good news, as good as yours that is. Nicola and her team painstakingly traced five GPs in East Anglia who have taken their patients through the renegade Royal Norwich Hospital consultant Rado Ilovic and The Maria Cresswell Hospice route. Investigation revealed that they all had problems, marital, money and maybe just plain arrogance at the world around them. They nailed two GPs who were the weakest candidates, which was a good move because the remaining three were as tough as nails. Two of them had almost been barred from practicing medicine and were not pleasant at all. One of the weakest links, in Lowestoft, was very close to cracking when the so-called professional CID investigating officer suddenly tried the 'crash and bash' technique. There were clear indications of high income and large cash withdrawals, but no evidence of luxury. The officer was sure that he was on to a winner. At the end of the interview, he confronted her with this, intimated that it was for drugs and grabbed the doctor's arm and pushed her sleeve up past her wrist to her elbow, revealing tale-tale scars."

Jane looked skyward and muttered, "Prick!"

"I agree, Anyway, he confidently challenged her to deny she had a drug habit and said that a long period of incarceration was on the cards for her, reminding her that in prison she would face agonising 'cold turkey', as well as attracting a lot of interest from some rather butch residents of HM Prison Holloway. She was petrified. The defence lawyer furiously intervened and there was a shouting match. Unfortunately, contrived or not, after being left alone to reflect with her lawyer, the candidate was conveniently diagnosed with a complete mental breakdown under duress. The investigator had to legally back off."

"It's difficult, I know. Sometimes surprise aggressive tactics work but more often they don't," said Jane reflectively. "But there is still evidence, right?"

"In her case, we face a delay in her interrogation, because she is allowed thirty days to recover and be interviewed again when in a less stressed frame of mind. But..." he raised his eyebrows, "with the second candidate, the moral really is 'slow is pro'. This time it was gender reversal. A newly promoted female CID investigator in Norwich sat with a male GP, in his thirties I believe, and gently took him through the misery of this obscene trade. She opted not to openly question him at all on his involvement. Rather, she outlined as much heart-breaking evidence as she could, laying all sad aspects of victims lives as thickly as possible: people killed for their organs, false diagnoses leading to death rather than simple organ donation, broken families, torture and intimidation, dirty money, and loads more. Pure non-violent communication. It was a bleedin' masterpiece. He didn't so much crack, as enter a phase of intellectual atonement. We can hardly get enough pens to keep the recording going."

Jane leaned back in chair, straightened her skirt and breathed out slowly. "Fucking marvellous, Ted. This calls for an early stack from work. We can't do any more today that's for sure. Can I hear the clink of glasses in the Rose and Crown?"

It was a long lunch.

Mike Hancox, sat at his Georgian desk in Whitehall and looked out of his window at the hustle and bustle of London. He raised a glass of single malt whisky. "To you, Jane, my feisty, *'Gaul Woman'*. You are simply the best!"

His phone rang, jerking him back to ground. It was his FBI colleague in the United States, Clem Rosenburgh.

"Clem, you son of a gun, what news?"

"I'll be brief, Mike. Things are going real well buddy. After gaining access to the Artaxis headquarters and removing hardware and files. We confronted the key players with the irrefutable evidence from China and expected further evidence from the UK and the rest of Europe. As expected, a long queue of plea-bargainers formed. That's something we do here that you don't in the UK."

Mike spluttered, "More's the pity!"

"The house of cards tumbled and the FBI had to draft in extra resources to deal with the investigation. Mike, the network was damned enormous and we were surprised that some well-known medical institutions, research laboratories and hospitals came under suspicion, such was the need for capital returns in these areas. One well-known senator went to ground but was eventually apprehended at the Mexican border. The Senate and Congress were alerted and both Republicans and Democrats agreed to set up a joint committee with links to the UN, to oversee the situation and sort out the mess. We Americans do what we're good at. We get on and clear up the mess!"

They chatted amiably, as successful people do when they have scored a victory and cleared some of the protocol and briefing processes. Then broke off, agreeing to catch up with each other at the upcoming international security seminar in Washington DC.

Mike put down his glass after swallowing the last drop of whisky. Then he frowned. He knew quite well that when wrongdoing is perpetrated on such an enormous scale as this, it has many tentacles. It attracts evil people.

It wasn't over.

14

Dr Johannes Ziggefelde sat dejectedly in front of two men. They were in a wine bar in Ipswich, that was situated in the popular area of the docks, previously home to old storage sheds and poor housing and now very much up market. It was one of those places that masqueraded as a living room, except the books were screwed to the wall. He cradled his glass of wine in his hands, rolling it between his palms as if warming it.

"This is a disaster. We must close down quickly and make a run for it."

Guido, the larger of the two men, with a distinctly Mediterranean appearance, shook his head. "No, definitely not. The hospice is broken, finito! But the network is strong and so long as no leads are uncovered it can be patched together in a different form and we can find another central purchaser. Artaxis Incorporated is going to crash soon. Those American fools will then take the Fifth Amendment, turn to God to gain sympathy or get into plea-bargaining. Whilst they do this we must regroup. This business is too good to throw away. Besides, your leader is brilliant and together we will continue to make lots of money. Keep the faith, Johannes."

The other man laughed, slapped Johannes on the shoulder and went to get more wine. Johannes was not placated.

"It's all right for you and our so-called British leader to talk, but the heat is rising and I am in the firing line. Sometimes I think she is possessed by the devil himself the way she makes decisions. Besides, we have the attention of a local policeman who is well respected and clever. He is getting closer and closer. I cannot go back to the hospital. It all happened so suddenly."

"I understand," said Guido, reaching for the full glass of red wine put in front of him by his companion, "but your illustrious leader has a plan to slow the investigation down and buy us all time. Now, let's see, where did you say the superintendent's wife is?"

He smiled and raised his glass to Ziggefelde who at first looked bemused, then smiled in return as he fully understood the innuendo.

The receptionist at the rehabilitation centre looked at the passes being proffered: a policeman and a doctor. They appeared to be in order, but just to be sure she decided that it was best to call her manager.

The manager came to the reception office quickly and looked at the passes and then led the visitors to a private room. He closed the door. "Hello, I'm the centre manager, Ian Ferguson. What can I do for you?"

As they sat down, the policeman spoke. "Mr Ferguson. I'm sorry to bother you, we have a very serious situation. You have a patient, a Mrs Alison Sanderson?"

"Yes, we do, but ..."

"Look, this is important. Her life may be at risk, because her husband is involved in a high-profile police investigation involving dangerous European criminals. We have some information that leads us to believe that she is in danger of being kidnapped." He narrowed his gaze at Ferguson and looked serious. "We have to get her away from here to a safe house without delay. It's for her own good."

Ian Ferguson had never experienced a situation like this before. "Well, if you put it like that. She is much, much better, I must say, and..."

The policeman cut him short. "Mr Ferguson, we need to act now, quickly. There is no time to waste. Trust me, she is in great danger..."

He handed him a protective custody order indicating that it had been raised in the Norwich police station and suitably stamped and authorised by the chief constable.

The doctor looked straight at the manager. "It's really for the best. We're aware of her condition and I want to reassure you that she will receive high quality medical treatment and counselling. But as my colleague says, we do need to act quickly."

Ian Ferguson was comfortable with the identity and story spun him by the visitors and made administrative arrangements for Alison Sanderson's transfer to protective custody. He escorted the policeman and doctor to her room where she lay on her bed asleep. They quietly woke her up. She was drowsy, but despite this objected strongly to being moved, because she was due to leave the rehabilitation centre within a few weeks. After some persuasion from the doctor and the manager, she reluctantly packed her belongings.

Alison turned to the policeman. "I'll just give my husband a quick call to let him know that I'm okay."

As she reached for her mobile the policeman picked it up. "Why not wait until we get to the safe-house, Mrs Sanderson?"

She was surprised because his demeanour had taken a slightly sterner style. Alison stared at him for a second, before her old self kicked in. "Thank you, but no. I want to call him, now. Please give me my phone," she held out her hand and the policeman looked straight at her.

"If you wish," he said, glancing at the doctor. As he handed her the mobile telephone his hand went into his raincoat pocket and closed around the butt of a pistol.

Alison dialled her husband and after a few moments, cursed. "Bloody voicemail. Stupid man never leaves it on when he should do," and left a message describing the situation, telling him to call her as soon as he could.

The policeman's fingers uncurled from the pistol and he half-smiled. "Yes, I know. Typical. Blokes and mobile phones eh? I'm just the same."

Alison was unamused and irritated. She was just getting things sorted in her mind, even Dr Strangelove was happy with her progress. What was all this fuss about? She made her way through the door and down the corridor with the others following her, carrying her bags and signing papers as they went.

As the car drove away, Alison was uncomfortable that she was squashed in between the policeman and the lady doctor, despite the spare seat in the front. To cap it all, the driver was useless, displaying none of the talents that she knew most police drivers had after passing the rigorous police driving courses. Her eyes settled on his blue shirted shoulder and to the dark blue epaulet. She became alarmed. It did not have the standard chrome personal police number on it. His hair was none too tidy either. As her thoughts formed, she began to feel confused and edgy.

Her heart beat faster and she felt a panic attack coming on and struggled to control herself. She turned sharply towards the policeman on her left.

The man noticed her edginess, grimaced and reached behind her, grabbing her arms and pinning them to her side.

"What are you doing?" she said, now frightened and confused.

Then she felt a sharp prick in her left arm, her head became fuzzy and her ears rang. Everything started to go hazy and she blacked out.

As Alison began to lose consciousness, she knew that she was being kidnapped. The very people who posed as her protectors were her abductors. That thought was with her as she later awoke, her mouth dry, her tongue swollen. She took in her surroundings. As she moved, the bedsprings creaked. Her limbs ached, she felt sweaty and her heart palpitated.

Sitting up and she looked around the dimly lit room that was now her prison. It smelled woody, like a shack or a lodge. The interior walls were made up of thin horizontal planks painted light green. A dull light shone from a fitting in the ceiling, its cracked shade throwing a shadow on the linoleum floor. As the ringing in her ears began to clear she heard the sea and the screech of gulls. She was not tied up and concluded that the door must be locked or securely guarded.

Breathing deeply, she put her feet on the floor and stood up unsteadily. Her eyes were accustomed to the dimness now and she could see a small wooden bedside locker, a chest of drawers with one drawer missing, a small Formica-topped table and four chairs. On the left of the room, there was a second door that was half open and she could just make out a small toilet and washbasin. There was a strong smell of disinfectant.

Alison tried to remain calm, but her mind was in turmoil. It had all happened so quickly. Why was she here? She guessed that it had something to do with Ted's work, but not knowing what it was all about added to her anxiety. It was frighteningly painful.

She felt giddy and slightly disembodied, and sat back onto the bed. Despite her anxiety she was trying hard to think clearly; she had always prided herself on her ability to do that, before her breakdown that is.

I'm jolly well going to do that now! I will, I will...

Looking at her watch, she realised that she had not taken her mid-afternoon or early evening sedatives. It surprised her that even under all this terrible pressure and fear, she didn't seem to need them.

Stress and exhaustion pushed Alison into a deep sleep. When she awoke again, it was darker which made the room look even more menacing. The door burst open and the man who had posed as a policeman, accompanied by an aide and the doctor, walked into the room \ and switched the light on. The light pierced her eyes and as she tried to focus, she was roughly hauled out of the bed and across the room towards the table, and pushed into a chair. The glare of the light prevented her from seeing clearly and her heart beat hard against the side of her rib cage. She maintained her composure by breathing deeply and slowly.

"Good morning, Alison. Yes, it's morning, three a.m. to be precise. I'm so sorry to wake you. But then we never sleep in the criminal world," said the man. His accent was unmistakably Irish. The other man laughed, showing a line of misshapen blackened teeth.

"Alison, your clever husband, the man I call *the white crusader,*" he laughed mockingly, "is making things very difficult for us, so we need you to write a note. In it you will ask him to recognise that your life is in danger and to slow down the investigation into the Maria Cresswell Hospice, for at least one week. That's not so long now, is it? Can you do that for me, please?"

Alison sat up straight and glared at him. "Go to hell."

The man smiled menacingly, then slowly leaned back in his chair, holding his hands out on either side of him.

"I'm sorry you can't see reason and I suppose there is no other option." He sat forward and brought his hand around in an arc and hit Alison flat on the right side of her face. The blow was so hard she almost lost consciousness and her head filled with lights and white noise. Tears welled in her eyes so that she couldn't see properly.

"Write the letter, Alison. I don't have time to be nice to you, but you must realise that I am not very nice anyway. So, do it. You know it makes sense. No one will judge you. But if you should still refuse, you will have to face at least twenty-four hours of attention from two of our bodyguards. One is from Kosovo and the other is Serbian. Both are wanted for rape in their own country and I can tell you, Alison, it will not be pleasant. If you are no use to me, then I will wash my hands of you. Simple as that."

He grabbed her hair with his left hand and she felt the sting of it and yelped. He dragged her off her seat to the window and forced her face against the cold glass, flattening her nose against it. Sitting outside under a garden heater two heavy-bodied men with dark complexions looked up and smiled. One licked his lips and the other grabbed his crotch with his left hand and blew her a kiss. They were the worst specimens of manhood Alison had ever seen and she felt sick. To make matters worse the man held her hair tight and with his right hand pulled the band of her trousers up very tight so the centre seam cut into her. She whimpered with discomfort and fear, catching her breath as tears filled her eyes.

"And you never know your luck. Alison. When they've finished, I might find time to get to know you myself."

He let go and she staggered back to the table. The doctor caught her and eased her into the chair, waving the men away. They left the shack and she cradled Alison's head in her chest, stroking it gently.

"Alison, these men are really very cruel," she said, feigning apology, "I have to employ such types, but that is the nature of our business. Just write the letter, I promise you that your action will harm no one. This is about our escape plan. Nothing else. I've written the script here. All you have to do is to copy it out. Make it easy on yourself and you will find your way back to your loving husband when all this is over, in one piece, unharmed. I give you my word on that."

She handed Alison a biro pen and some sheets of cream writing paper.

Alison took the pen and her stomach tightened as she was faced with the fact that it was the only way to avoid the awful treatment promised her should she refuse. Unsteadily, she wrote the letter they wanted and then signed it. She felt empty and humiliated at having to do something that she didn't want to do. When she finished, the woman lifted Alison's left hand and deftly removed her wedding ring. Alison let the pen drop to the table and, unnoticed, reached down and wiped her right hand against the sole of her shoe. Then she rubbed it against the underside of the writing paper leaving grubby stains behind. The woman picked up the letter, read it, and nodded to her, before finally slipping the wedding ring into the envelope and inserting the folded letter. She left the room without comment or a backward look.

Alison stood up and walked unsteadily to the bed, falling onto it with a heavy thump. The door closed and there was the sound of a key turning in the lock. Loud footsteps thumped along a wooden boardwalk. Ignoring the food and drink left for her, she buried her head in the greasy stained pillow and was overcome by fear, frustration and helplessness – she sobbed.

When she awoke, her head thumping from the kidnapper's blows, she sat up and put her legs over the side of the bed. The springs complained loudly and she stopped, letting the room forget the noise. She wanted no more attention.

How ironic, she thought. Just as she was beginning to conquer her demons this happens. She now felt as helpless as a toy in a doll's house, her newfound confidence dashed by brutality.

Out of the corner of her eye she saw a large beetle scurrying left and right, trying to find a way out of the room. She sympathised. Then she got up, followed the insect and when it stopped, picked it up carefully between her finger and thumb. There was a slight gap in the window frame and she inserted it inside. It scurried through to the outside world.

How ridiculous was that - was she hoping that fate would acknowledge this, balancing the equation in her favour?

The shock and pain of the last twelve hours made her focus. Her mental state had been taken to the edge and now, on the way up, it was subjected to more stress and it was finely balanced; half of her wanted oblivion and the other half wanted to survive. Slowly, the old Alison began to emerge victorious: Ted, the man she loved with all her heart would be so worried, so for him she would survive, come hell or high water, she would bloody well survive!

Ted stared in silence at the note that lay on the dining table at his house. He had held it close to his heaving chest soon after opening and reading it. The time that elapsed between the Alison's kidnap and the receipt of the letter had been terrifying. The note was blunt and to the point:

Dearest darling Ted,

I love you and need to appeal to you to save my life, which is in great danger. People you are interested in have kidnapped me. They are intent on ensuring that they have time to get away from the UK. Their request is simple. They want you to slow the investigation down for at least a week so that they can make the necessary arrangements. My safety is guaranteed if you accede to their wishes. If you don't, they threaten to rape and torture me, and then dismember my body. In the name of our love, darling, please do as they ask so that we can be together again. I beg you.

All my love,
Alison.

Despite the pain in his heart, Ted knew that he had to take the letter to the police station. There was no other way. He knew all too well that the kidnappers could do as they wished and that Alison's safety was not guaranteed. He carefully placed it in a cellophane envelope.

Jane stood in the operations room with her arms folded across her chest. She knew what he was going through and knew she couldn't help. Nevertheless, certain facts had to be dealt with and quickly. She broke the silence. "Ted, we all appreciate your bringing this letter in, but you need to square things with yourself and us. Are you able to stay in control and act rationally when the woman you love in such mortal danger?"

Ted straightened himself, put his hands on his hips and looked at the ceiling. He was silent for a short while. He was treading a nervy tightrope.

"Jane, you have a right to ask that. I would in your shoes. But nothing is going to get in the way of us catching these bastards and I mean nothing. So, let's start doing some police work, eh?"

DC Winter blurted, "Well done, boss!" The rest of the team concurred and showed their concern by closing in on the table and looking directly at Ted.

Jane put her hand on his shoulder and said, "Well then, we all agree, so what's next?"

Ted felt his chest tighten, but took a deep breath and forced himself to speak.

"Okay. Fact: we know they want to escape the UK but we don't know how. Fact: they are in hiding somewhere with Alison and it must be within a fifty-mile radius of here. Her letter was postmarked Norwich. Fact: we must give them the impression that I have slowed the investigation down. Perhaps they, or others involved, will make a move that we can spot and home in on them."

The team agreed. Jane stroked her chin. "Yes, a press release. Something saying that those arrested at The Maria Cresswell Hospice are being questioned and no one else is being suspected at the present time, so we have ceased further investigations."

Nicola Bradbury added, "Perhaps we can focus on the weak GP and release the other two stronger suspects with an apology that comes straight from you, guv. That would filter back to the kidnappers."

"Thanks, Nicola" said Ted, "that's not a bad tactic, but I think that we can add to that - a subtle approach. We have to make the criminals believe that the investigation has slowed. This will play to our favour."

The team craned forward and Jane let him hold the floor. "I see two strands of action. First, misinform and mislead the criminals into believing that the whole thing was now just a tidying up exercise. That means constructing a credible press release saying just that. We did it with Jenny Ellis's situation, it can work again. The other, is to work hard to try and find clues as to Alison's whereabouts and the possible escape route for the criminals."

DS Bradbury concurred. "Got that, guv. I'm on it."

The team dispersed after Nicola allocated tasks and the letter was passed to the forensic department for analysis, to look for clues: saliva, fingerprints or something else. Ted busied himself to keep his mind off the awful situation that Alison was in.

It wasn't easy.

Ted led the questioning of the hospice staff starting with Bobbette Grainger. She was aware of her rights and that the psychologist's reports could not be used in evidence against her. Her legal representative arrived and after the tape recorder was switched on, she was cautioned. Ted settled back to ask questions, with DC Gerry Winters taking notes. He opened the interview.

"Ms Grainger, or can I call you, Bobbette?"

"You may not," she snapped, and her face contorted with rage, "What the hell am I doing here? I'm a bloody victim, you know? A crazy relative blows his head off and I end up in here, locked up and treated like a criminal. I was questioned, illegally I might add, without a lawyer present and was in a state of confusion and terror. Nothing I said can be relied upon. I'm sure you are aware of that."

Then she smirked and Ted did his best not to lose control. He desperately wanted to shake her by the throat.

"Ms Grainger, I am sorry you see it that way. Tell me what you know about a company called Artaxis Incorporated?"

"Nothing at all. I've never heard of them."

"No? Despite the fact that you have some invoices and payments to and from the company?" He paused. "But, let's move on. We are keen to know more about doctor Johannes Ziggefelde and let's see," Ted referred to his file, "a consultant called Rado Ilovic. Listen carefully. We have enough tapped telephone conversations and other evidence to put you behind bars for the rest of your life."

Grainger started to speak but Ted raised a hand. "No, don't speak, just bloody well listen. You have helped to run one of many units associated with a parent company called Artaxis Incorporated, which successfully harvests body parts for sale around the world. Oh, and we know that, like the others, you don't care to wait for donors to actually die of natural causes."

He paused for breath having forced the words directly at Grainger, by leaning towards her and staring straight into her eyes.

Grainger gathered her wits and tried to smile, but her nervousness made it look crooked and pathetic. She determinedly persisted.

"Circumstantial evidence, Superintendent, purely circumstantial. As of now, I refuse to answer any more of your stupid accusations. I maintain my position of innocence."

Grainger's solicitor scribbled on his notepad and gave Ted and DC Gerry Winters a shrug of the shoulders as if to say, *that's her legal position.*

Ted sat back in his chair and held a pencil between his fingers. "Okay then, have it your way. No doubt you know that by pleading guilty and giving us useful evidence, we can try to get your sentence reduced. It's all about facing the inevitable, you see. I think we have a trump card." He got up and walked slowly to the door, and opened it.

Grainger started to speak. "No bloody wa...," she stopped mid-sentence. Her eyes widened, her chin dropped open and the colour drained from her face.

Through the door Grainger saw the unmistakable figure of Jenny Ellis.

The next morning having spent the night writing press releases and carefully sifting and endlessly rereading evidence, from interviews, the team emerged from breakfast in the canteen and went to the operations room. Ted stood in the doorway and tried to look cheerful.

"Good morning, thanks for all your work last night. But before we begin the briefing, let's thank an important member of this investigation."

From around the door came Jenny Ellis. She limped slightly and her face showed some bruises now mainly healed, but her grin was still in place. Her presence livened everyone up.

Jane was overjoyed and hugged Jenny as they all patted her on the shoulder. Jane had been concerned about Jenny's recovery and knew that she had responded to treatment, but it was news to the team and a great fillip for them all.

She saw Ted standing to one side and went over to him. "And the next bit of good news will be getting Alison back. I promise I won't sleep, Ted, until we find her alive and well. Trust me."

Ted looked at her and then at the ground, holding back the water in his eyes. Then he composed himself and touched her arm lightly, before addressing the team.

"Right then, let's let secret agent Ellis get back to her champagne and caviar at the hospital. She's done us proud over the last day or so. Let's go. Let's get some work done."

The team wished Jenny well and finally settled down to discuss the results of their work. Nicola Bradbury and Gerry Winter told Ted that they had spent most of the night going through all of Beamish's belongings.

"Guv, I was convinced that we just needed to go through all the records and receipts again and again." Gerry groaned theatrically. Nicola continued. "We checked receipts and records, then looked at the bank transactions. What a bunch of fools they were at the bank. You remember they had strict procedures about handling large amounts of cash, to prevent money laundering? Well, it was all about local trust in their GP that went too far, so he was able to make all sorts of payments in cash. Anyway, you'll also recall the large payments he made to charities. We all thought him a jolly good chap, dishonest perhaps, but nevertheless a good chap. However, Farmer and I noticed that one charity in particular had a very unusual payment."

Gerry took over. His excitement was palpable. "Yeah. All the payments were round figures of five hundred pounds or a few thousand pounds, to Cancer Research or Alzheimer's Research. But there was a single payment to the Royal National Lifeboat Institution for an odd figure of seven thousand five hundred and forty-five pounds. It was quite a while ago."

Ted blurted, "He bought something!"

Nicola Bradbury responded, "Yes, Guv, he did. He bought a boat, a large powerful rigid inflatable boat, a RIB. It's capable of carrying six people and working in rough water, with a speed of up to 10 knots. It was being sold by the RNLI to make way for some updated boats. And before you ask, yes, we have been on to the RNLI and they confirm that the RIB they sold Beamish was in good order, capable of a sea journey and what's more we know where it is moored: at the small east coast port of Wells by the Sea. She beamed with enthusiasm and pride as she met questions with answers, and her responses led to suggested plots, as they tried to link the port with the possible kidnappers' hideout. These finally produced a section of the Norfolk countryside, stretching out from the Cromer to Lowestoft coastline towards Norwich.

It was late in the afternoon, when Jane came running into the operations room waving a piece of paper. She addressed the team, but looked straight at Ted.

"Guess what? Your Alison is a bright cookie, Ted, and must have listened to your police antics and tricks. On the back of the writing paper were clear finger marks. The smears contained a mix of salt water, a few grains of grey sand and small traces of diesel oil and, wait for it, blue fluid, the kind you put in portaloos on boats."

"Boss," said PC Gerry Winters, "I'm convinced that Alison's near the Broads or a marina, and close to the sea, but I would guess, judging by the grey sand, it is with easy access to areas at or near Wells by the Sea."

Ted hurriedly pulled the map towards him. "Gerry, you may bloody well be right son, you may be right. The clues are getting us closer." He looked up at Jane and winked, "Thanks, buddy."

They were now approaching the end of the fourth day since receiving Alison's letter and the week asked for by the kidnappers was halfway over. They must now be almost ready to move. The tension in the team room was immense as everyone ached to find just enough evidence to enable them to get out of the office and into the field.

The next day, Ted was agitated and had to admit privately to Jane that he just wanted to get out and scour the triangular area between the Broads and the coast. The coast was the most likely geographical area to search. It had been a busy night and they had argued back and forth before agreeing a potential grid.

Jane was sympathetic. "Ted, you've got to hold it together. Your call to arms for as many police to go under cover in civilian clothes to saturate the area to search for Alison is a good one. But to make it work you've got to brief them to search specific areas in a grid formation, against key criteria. When each grid is clear they move to the next one. Got it? You can do this, Ted."

Jane's military background was useful. Ted understood and took the maps and grids from Jane, turned to her and said, "You're good at this. Better than me. Thanks."

Jane waved him away. "Begone man, the fish in my ponds are many and this pond is a small one. Besides, for you it's personal. Go find Alison."

In the isolated holiday shack on the edge of the Broads, Alison sat disconsolately on the edge of her bed. She was briefed in no uncertain terms that if she wanted to stay alive and not endanger any innocent members of the public, she was to do exactly as she was told. If not, the female member of the group would shoot her through the side using a silenced pistol held under a folded waterproof jacket. There would be no second chances. She was told to wear very dark sunglasses.

Liam, her tormentor, led her to a scruffy estate car and she was put in the back with a man to guard her. He sat in the front of the vehicle and his bodyguard was driving. That was some relief at least. Jane was spared his touch, his smell and the sight of his dirty teeth whenever he pushed his face into hers. The skin on her scalp was still sore from where he had pulled her to the window a couple of nights ago. Hatred and loathing bubbled inside her, but she was helpless.

The air was heavy and dark grey clouds were beginning to crowd out the pink sunset. Spots of rain whipped against the car windows. There were few people around, mostly locals on their way to the shops, hunched under umbrellas or hooded overcoats. The wet pavement reflected the streetlights. Alison felt blind in the dark glasses, even though the sun was rising, and the lack of vision made her feel sick as the car weaved through the streets and she was unable to get her bearings.

After about half an hour the car slowed and turned sharp left, travelling along a slightly rutted road. Alison could make out the unmistakable sound of rigging banging against metal masts. They parked and she was ushered out. She desperately wanted to run for her life, but knew she couldn't. There were too many people guarding her. It was windy, wet and still quite dark, and unlikely that anyone would be around to hear her anyway. She was roughly guided along a slatted wooden walkway and they finally stopped. Were they going on a boat? Why was she here and where would they leave her? Her mind whirled, partly out of fright and partly confusion. It was terrifying to be absolutely powerless.

There was an unmistakable sound of tarpaulins being removed from something, then heard powerful engines being started. The woman's voice said something about the lack of comfort and a cocktail bar. The men laughed and Liam said it was to enable a quick getaway not to be a 'gin palace'. Once on board the boat, Alison immediately felt the swell of the sea and her legs wobbled and she fell over. The woman shouted angrily at her to get up and the second man pushed her into a seat. He leaned towards her and she smelled his foul breath on her face. He secured her hands behind her back with cable ties and put them a bar at the rear of her seat.

"Now listen carefully, Alison, you will need to hang on to this seat very hard. This is a fast boat and it's going to be a rough and bumpy ride over some very high seas. The forecast is bad, but we cannot wait any longer. Do you fully understand me?"

Alison mumbled an affirmative. No sooner had she done so than she felt the boat move through the water thudding into rolling waves. Her fingers strained at her hand-hold.

The sea state was decidedly rough.

Ted stood in a small holiday lodge looking at a partly made bed in one of the bedrooms. He put his hand onto the grubby duvet that must have been used by Alison over the last few nights and felt his heart race. If only they had picked this grid area instead of another. They had almost finished, three areas remained and, as bad luck would have it, this grid area came last. Ted had opted for the two areas close to the Broads rather than those to the north near Cromer. But this was the place, for sure, for certain; his Alison had been here and cleverly left a lipstick under the pillow - he was too late. He punched the wall in frustration, then pulled himself together and reached for his radio to call the unit that was watching the marina at Wells by the Sea.

"Bluebird Six, this is Bluebird One, over"

"Bluebird one - Six here, read you clearly, over."

"Six, this is One, any sign of a woman under any kind of escort?"

"No, sir, no sign, and the ex-RNLI inflatable Beamish bought has been located and is under observation, but there's no one around."

"Damn, we found where Alison was held, but they are long gone. Hang on then, we'll be down with you soon. Call up if there is any sign of life at all - over."

"Okay, sir, will do. Out."

Ted and the other team members arrived at the small harbour in Wells by the Sea and he told his driver to detach from the rest and tour the area slowly. It was a small, quaint place and he was sure that large groups of strangers would arouse suspicion. He waved to Bluebird Six as he drove past them and deliberately followed directions to the marina dock where the Beamish's inflatable was moored. He stopped a short distance away and watched it rise and fall in the water. It was unwise to be in this spot, where he could be seen by the criminals but something was wrong - terribly wrong. It was very dirty. The tarpaulin had come loose and was flapping around in the wind, the plastic windshield that arced around the front of the boat was also smeared with bird droppings, which would have given little visibility even on a good day. Then his jaw dropped. One of the engines had come loose in the storm and hung away from the back of the boat by about twelve inches. Behind it, where clean metal should have been, was a large patch of rusty metal, where the bulkhead had given way to the weight of the engine and the constant movement of the water. This boat could never have gone to sea on a calm day, or any day for that matter.

He scrambled out of the Land Rover and ran through the wind and rain to the edge of the mooring. The boat was in a terrible state. It might have been in fair condition when it was purchased from the RNLI, but if boats are not maintained they quickly corrode and become unseaworthy. He ran back to the vehicle and grabbed the radio, switching it on.

"All Bluebird units, the inflatable at Wells by the Sea is definitely not the one we're after – it's a wreck. Speak to me guys." His heart was beating hard and he was beginning to feel helpless. He had to think. Just then the radio crackled.

"Bluebird One this is base. Over."

"Base this is Bluebird One – what have you got?"

"Just thought you'd like to know that when you left the cabin, that the undercover operatives on the ground questioned several local people and three of them identified a grey Volvo Estate as being parked at the shack. One contact said that it left at about seven o'clock this morning. They must have passed us on the road. Sorry, Guv."

"Base, okay, it's not your fault. Thanks for that. Call all marinas in the triangle and call out the duty managers if necessary. We have to throw caution to the wind. Tell them to get outside right now and look for a grey Volvo Estate. They mustn't do anything, just call us immediately."

Base acknowledged the instructions and Ted held the handset tight. *God, please keep Alison safe!*

Jane drove up to his vehicle, her Jaguar skidding to a halt. She wound down the window.

Ted shouted through the wind at her.

"What the hell are you doing here?"

"Just trying to keep up with things," she said. "Ted, I've been listening to the radio messages. They're not that far ahead of you and my guess is that they're using the bad weather and dodgy sea state at the moment to get away from UK territorial waters. You're closer than they could have imagined. Don't give up."

"So, what now?" said Ted putting his hands to his head to wipe away the rain.

Jane looked along the quayside.

"That...that's what," and Ted followed her pointing finger. To the right of the marina there in all its glory, lights and all, was a large inflatable powerboat operated by the Royal National Lifeboat Institute.

"We commandeer the boat, crew and get out there and search for the enemy – that's what!" Without waiting she headed for the mooring.

Ted hesitated for a second then his spirits rose and he found himself running after Jane. They both shouted to the two crewmen who were struggling to tether the boat to the quayside in the rough sea. It would be a difficult piece of persuasion and time was not on their side. Ted knew that for once he would let Jane do the business and he hoped like hell that she succeeded.

Jane got straight to the point, explaining that this was international police business and that a woman's life was also at stake. She made it clear that one bullet across their bows and they would turn around. They needed a fast boat - a very fast boat. This was their only chance.

The crewmen, bemused at first, responded enthusiastically. "How about this then," said the volunteer crewman brightly. "It's a Humber 10 metre sports pro, twin engines..."

Ted broke in. "Look feller, you're the best, the boat's the best, but let's just go now!"

The crewman responded cheerfully to Ted's irritation, realising the gravity of the situation and immediately began dealing with the mooring ropes. He looked over his shoulder as he worked. "Sorry, of course I understand. Get in the boat, let's go."

They jumped in and secured the seat belts in the upright seats. Their hopes rose, as they looked at the sleek white shape of its long nose slightly upturned, elegant and yet aggressive in appearance. The engines burst into life and they felt their backs pushed into the seats as it roared away, cutting rather than bouncing through the incoming waves. White foam gushed behind them as they pushed forward and into open water.

Large waves pushed them up into the air and Jane felt the deck forcing itself against her. For a moment she was weightless as the craft fell back into a small trough and water sprayed over her. Her lips tasted salty and her stomach was sore from straining to hold on to the safety line as they headed out to the open sea.

On the other inflatable some distance away, Alison gripped the seat with her legs and hung on to a bar with her handcuffed hands for all she was worth. White spray showered her as the boat lurched up and down and waves battered the prow. She wanted to be sick but it was so rough she couldn't manoeuvre herself into the right position. It was comical, almost unreal and very frightening. Her hands were tied behind her back and she was very scared. The boat was only going at half speed because the waves were large and frequently splashed over the side. She not under cover and was soaking wet and shivered with the cold.

Her captors leaned forward and into the windscreen, trying their best to avoid the spray and peer through its greasy rain-splattered surface. The woman was on the radio and talking wildly to someone, when she suddenly stopped and pointed behind them towards the coast.

Alison followed the direction of their gaze and saw a large brightly lit boat powering through the water towards them.

The crewman shouted to Ted above the sound of the wind and waves. "I think we have your prey, sir!" He smiled broadly, "It is a smaller Humber, in which case we have a good chance of catching it."

The chase continued for twenty minutes, but to Ted it seemed like a lifetime. They needed to stop the other inflatable before it left the UK's twelve-mile territorial limit outside which they had no jurisdiction. Despite the state of the sea, their superior speed closed the gap, and the crew urgently looked to Ted and Jane for direction as to the next move.

Ted's gaze was transfixed on the boat ahead. "I can see her, it's Alison," he shouted, pointing his finger. He was elated but his face reflected his fear for Alison.

He held the restraining strops tightly and noticed how much better poised Jane was. He squinted through the squall as the crewman did his best to steer the same course as the other boat, but was only able to see which direction it was going when they were on the downward side of the waves. The white crested waves rose and fell relentlessly. A few wrong turns would cost them time.

The sky grew darker and the peaks and troughs of the waves became deeper. The lead crewman shouted, "It's getting' pretty perky and approaching force 7." His colleague looked up and grunted agreement.

A massive grey rain-cloud then engulfed them, white lines of rain falling hard, hitting their faces and getting into their eyes, making the chase more difficult. It was almost unbearable.

To Ted's relief the rain only lasted five minutes and after the cloud passed visibility improved enabling them to turn their craft on to a straight course to pursue the criminals. Alison's fate was in his hands. His life flashed before him and he yearned for a chance to make everything all right for her. He regretted not being more in control when she suffered frequent bouts of debilitating depression. In this situation, where life was in the balance and time is short, thoughts race, leading to unnecessary self-recriminations and regret.

Ted was jerked out of his thoughts by the crewman. "I think we're catching it, sir," he yelled as he increased the throttle.

Jane took hold of a leather safety strap and pulled herself level with the second crewman, and shouted into his ear. "Don't go up behind them. They may be armed we can't be sure. Even if they take a shot it will be devilish difficult to hit anything in this swell. Move wide and around in front of them, I can see that their craft is smaller and the windscreen wraps around the boat, preventing them from taking a shot at us. We need to push them off course and back towards the coast."

The crewmen looked at each other, nodded their approval and took a wide arc to starboard before turning sharply to port and in front of the other craft, which was forced to take avoidance action. As they crossed its path, it slowed then resumed its straight course again throttling away hard. They repeatedly drove the kidnappers off course and although they were slowing it down and doubtless making them use valuable fuel, it persisted in trying to get away from the UK mainland.

Ted hung on like crazy and from time to time he could just see Alison crouched close to the back of the boat where she had been thrown by the yawing of the craft. He felt helpless and it hurt like hell. His gaze moved from the two men to another passenger, a woman, who seemed to be giving directions. She turned to one side and he recognised her instantly: it was Dr Patricia Lenahan, Doctor Beamish's general practice partner. His mind raced and he realised that Beamish must have been totally under her control which would account for the high number of patients directed to the bogus consultant in the general hospital and then to The Maria Cresswell Hospice.

He gripped the wire handrail and gritted his teeth, staring intently at her. The boats drew closer and as they arced in front again his eyes met Lenahan's - they were getting the best of them. His attention was broken by the far-off sound of a larger and faster craft belonging to the coastguard that was approaching, the powerful white beam from its searchlights homing in on them both, slicing through the choppy waters.

Lenahan cynically waved and moved towards Alison. She hauled her off the seat and dragged her by the hair towards the stern. At first, a wave made them fall over, but she got to her feet, then casually pushed the struggling Alison over the edge of the boat and into the foaming water.

Ted's heart missed a beat as he watched helplessly as Alison slide over the side and into the foaming water. Lenahan waved, pointed to the helpless thrashing body in the water and the boat moved away at speed.

Ted screamed, "You bitch." He turned to Jane. "Stop the boat, stop it I say, go back for Alison."

Alison tried to keep her head high but her mouth filled with water and she spat it out, feverishly trying to stop it clogging her throat. The shock of the cold water brought her into survival mode. She was a good swimmer but now had to deal with the fact that she could only use her legs because her hands were tied behind her. Her lifeguard training came in useful and she did her best to balance on her back using her legs in breaststroke fashion to steady her weight. Her head was barely inches from the surface and she desperately tried not to swallow water, which surged over her with every swell of the waves.

Jane saw Alison's body drifting in the swell and then jerked her head back towards the front as the other craft accelerated away. Then, to everyone's astonishment, she grabbed a lifebuoy and thrust it hard into Ted's grasp.

"Save Alison," she screamed through the wind. Then she grabbed a life-buoy and twisted the beacon light on the top to make it flash, looping the cord around Ted's head in one move. Without hesitating, she used all her weight to push him overboard.

At first, in his surprise and shock, he lost control of the lifebuoy as the sea engulfed him. He spat and gasped for air as he reached the surface, thankfully the cord around his neck remained connected and he pulled it quickly towards him as he swam towards Alison who was now struggling for her life. The searchlights on the approaching coastguard vessel picked out the white of her face and hands. Her movements were slowing, numbed by the cold water and Ted heard her spluttered cries for help. He had to be quick.

Jane turned to the stunned crewmen, pointing to the coastguard craft and said strongly, "Sorry boys, mission first. Don't worry. They'll both be picked up in a few moments. Now come on, let's get back to the chase."

The crewman understood and followed her positive direction. They were angry at the action of the woman on the boat they were chasing and wanted to see her caught.

Despite the loss of Alison's weight, it was obvious to Liam that their craft was still not fast enough. He was furious and screamed at his companion to maintain speed and get clear of the chasing boat. However, they were losing ground and it was clear that they needed to shift some of the gear to make the boat lighter.

Lenahan shouted above the sound of the wind and waves, "I'll take the wheel you two keep shifting stuff, start with that spare raft and that box over there," she pointed her hand to the stern. In between the swell of the waves, they threw overboard all the heavy items that were not strapped down, this had a good effect, but not good enough.

As they bent to give the last heavy box a final push, Liam turned and froze as he saw Lenahan pointing a pistol at them both.

"Sorry boys, time to lose even more surplus weight," she said, and pulled the pistol trigger several times in quick succession. Enough of the bullets found their target and the men spun backward and into the water along with the heavy box.

Now appreciably lighter, they moved forwards much faster and maintained distance. Lenahan somehow managed to keep control whilst loading another clip to her pistol, and fired six shots over her shoulder.

This changed the situation and Jane's crewman pulled back on the throttle. It was now becoming too risky and they were almost at the limit of UK jurisdiction.

"Don't give up. We've got to get her."

Jane urged them on as she looked back and saw the coastguard boat circling Ted and Alison, then returned her gaze to her target ahead. She just needed one more push and shouted, "Come on, chase them, we're nearly there."

The lead crewman at first hesitated, then swore and punched the wheel. He turned to her and shouted, "You're bloody mad, woman!" But he was angry, very angry. He had seen the hostage thrown overboard and the murder of two men and his anger overcame the politics of it all. He pushed the throttle hard and made a very fast wide arc to the port side of the other boat. When he was far enough away, he turned tightly, opened the throttle and came at it head on.

Lenahan tried to fire shots over the top of the windshield, but it was hopeless as the waves bumped her up and down and the bullets missed wildly.

As they approached at high speed, Jane heard the crewman shout, "Hold on tight." Seconds later, he throttled back as they met the target head on and the heavier weight lifted them over the smaller craft leaving them straddling it.

Jane wasted no time and leapt off the port side, throwing herself at the prostrate Lenahan, who was struggling to her feet. Alarmingly, she still had hold of the pistol, but Jane managed to stretch her arms out straight, catching the pistol-hand just as the gun discharged. They rolled and wrestled, with neither gaining an advantage. Eventually when they were half-standing, the pitching of the crafts tipped them both into the sea.

Jane gasped for air and to her horror realised that her adversary was not a good swimmer. She was panicking and grabbed Jane like a limpet and it was like being wrapped in barbed wire. Moving her right hand up towards Lenahan's face she forced her fingers into her eyes and she briefly let go. Jane quickly freed herself, moving around behind her to void her grasping arms. To her relief the bright searchlights of the coastguard vessel lit up the water around them both. Now, Lenahan was weakening and Jane saw her chance to get her into a life-saving position. Holding Lenahan's head up with her left hand under her chin, she slowly kicked in a downward motion keeping them both afloat. Just in time, as her limbs ached at the effort, strong arms reached down and brought them both into the coastguard vessel.

Jane's lungs were raw with heavy breathing and racked with salt water. Once she started coughing, she couldn't stop. She heard the sound of Lenahan being sick.

Back at the port of Wells by the Sea, both boats pulled into the safety of the harbour and moored in the lessening swell. The bodies of the two men had been located and hauled on to the coastguard vessel. The police removed them and placed them into body bags before putting them into a waiting ambulance. Dr Lenahan was under guard and had to be stretchered into another ambulance. Jane, wrapped in a blanket, climbed the ladder and walked away towards an unmarked police vehicle where DS Nicola Bradbury and PC Gerry Winter stood.

The sky was lighter and the rain had passed, and the sound of the screeching gulls as they swooped over the marina made everything seem quite normal and calm.

Ted was already on the quayside nearby and was wrapping another dry blanket around Alison. He held her tightly as if trying to stop he wind from blowing her away. He looked over his should and whirled on Jane as she passed.

"What the bloody hell do you..."

She stopped and faced him directly.

"Stop it, Ted. It was my call. You saved Alison and I got my target. I did what I had to do. That's it. Sorry. Okay?"

Ted looked at the ground, clenched his hands, then turned and hugged Alison tightly. "I know who she is," he said. "The woman. It's Dr Patricia Lenahan, the other partner from Dr Beamish's general practice."

Jane put her hand to her head. "Jesus Christ, it all falls into place."

15

Jane slept more soundly than she had for some time. Her body ached where she had pulled muscles during the conflict a few days ago, but mentally she was feeling immensely satisfied – it made the body aches more worthwhile. All the pieces in the jig-saw were now in place and all that was needed was for the powers-that-be to put them together. She limped to the safe house breakfast room. On a single table laid out for her, was a large brown envelope leaning against a milk jug. She sat down and carefully removed the contents.

It was from Mike Hancox. He enclosed transcripts of various interviews on a CD. Jane grabbed a banana and glass of orange juice and went back to her room. She put the CD into her laptop and listened to it. The interview with the hospice manager was interesting, Grainger had nowhere to go after being confronted by Jenny Willis and gave hours of information. Doctor Lenahan was more restrained and gave nothing away.

The CD included a recording of Katrina Anatov, who spoke with passion and great clarity to the European parliament. She outlined her personal situation, leaving out no detail and went on to describe the horrors that beset her. She paid tribute to the support that she had received from the British Embassy who cared for and protected her before handing her over to MI6 and Interpol investigators in London. Her eloquence won over a sceptical audience and the large auditorium was absolutely silent, before finally erupting into spontaneous applause.

Alarmingly, a separate Interpol briefing paper outlined evidence so far detailing the network of bogus private clinics with links to Artaxis that stretched from Budapest to Lisbon. The commodities traded ranged from bone and sinew to, cornea and aborted foetuses and their umbilical cords, and even more lucrative items such as lungs, livers and kidneys and, of course, hearts. Sometimes more was earned for research items than organ transplant deals, such was the hunger of pharmaceutical and other medical institutions for laboratory material.

Email support was received from all parts of the globe in response to an Interpol bulletin, as civilised governments pledged to rid the world of this ghoulish trade. It emerged that hardly any country was safe from the seductive profits that transplant surgery or the cash that research institutions offered. The important thing now was that the networks were going to be starved of money and support as nations supported the investigation findings and pledged to do more.

In a covering note, Hancox told Jane that the standing ovation Katrina received would give her enormous confidence to replicate her plea to the United Nations assembly. He went on to say Artaxis Incorporated crumbled fast when the FBI raided their headquarters. Plea-bargaining in the USA always seemed to produce good results and once the house of cards began to tumble, many who were anxious to prove that they were not associated with the evil business became state witnesses to save their skins.

At the end of the report, Hancox told her there was a small white envelope in the package. Jane found it and noticed that there was some Chinese writing on one side, as well as her name. She opened it, a fragrant smell of magnolia tickled her nose and she drew out a postcard with a picture of Peking on one side and a message written on the other.

Jane,
I promised to send you a postcard when we had sorted out our bad people. Here it is.
Good luck with your quest. China has no need for this type of thing. It is emerging as a major industrial and technological power and we want to show the West that we are capable of sorting out such criminal actions. Besides, our own loyal people need organ donations and we will continue to provide for them in whatever way we see fit.
With best wishes,
Madam Lom,
Chinese People's Party

P.S. Chin Kwok is safe and well and flies to you today.

Jane remembered the promise. Madam Lom had style. There was no denying that. She was also glad that Chin was safe and was returning home.

As Jane contemplated this, she recognised a voice from the radio that was tuned to a local BBC station. It was Ted, on the news. Leaning forward, she turned up the sound just as he ended by paying tribute to the Norfolk police for the high standard of policing and promised that Norfolk could consider themselves well protected from crime in all its forms. He sounded confident and upbeat. She hoped that Alison would fully recover and that both their lives would change for the better.

Jane sighed heavily and tied the Interpol file with blue fabric cords and pushed it towards the back of the desk. It would go by secure courier to Hancox in London. She felt good that it was a successful end to a mission that she felt so strongly about. It had been a very long haul. She sat back and let some of the memorable incidents cross her mind: the inscrutable Madame Lom, the bravery of Katrina and the cheerful teamwork with the Norfolk Constabulary. She winced when she considered that she would, at some time, have to return to the constabulary to pick up her stuff and confront Ted Sanderson.

Jane sipped her orange juice and peeled her banana. She regarded a separate A4 brown envelope that had arrived in the post that morning and knew what it contained. She opened it slowly with a paper knife and read the contents. The briefing note described her next mission in detail, with diagrams, background information and a few photographs. She gazed out of the window to the countryside beyond, bathed in a warm yellow glow as the sun went down.

Well now, this one is going to be a challenge!

Ted fingered the letter in his hand several times, picking it up and putting it down, flapping it against his free hand, before resolutely putting it into his inside pocket. He would deliver it to the station today after a very special lunch with Alison, at their favourite pub in Norwich. He would tell her how much he loved her and how proud he was of her, then outline plans he had for their future. It had to be a joint project that they both had to agree to. The bottom line was that he was retiring from the police force. The chief constable tried to work his magic with Ted, offering him promotion and new duties, but Ted steadfastly refused. The letter in his pocket confirmed his resignation. Running a bookshop and café would be an exciting challenge and pay well enough for them both.

He looked up as Alison entered the room. She was lovely in a blue print dress that allowed a slight bulge at the front. They both had a lot to thank the rehabilitation centre for.

Scotland

Josie Welshman sat with several other young people around a small table in a seedy bar on Union Street in Glasgow. It was warm and they had been well fed. It was a better place than a cold doorway in a wet street. There was even the promise of drugs, a spliff or perhaps some cocaine. The man who was helping them seemed genuine enough and when he was out of the room, they laughed at his gullibility. They would take him for all they could, then move back to the streets – none of them cared much for the squeaky-clean accommodation provided by the local authority. It was all disinfectant and boredom.

Two scruffy boys drank beer and flicked bits of pizza at each other. Unnoticed, Josie got up and sauntered slowly through a door at the rear of the bar, into a dimly lit room that smelled of cannabis.

"Okay, I got them here, so just give me the cash and I'll go," Josie said to a man sitting in an armchair talking on a mobile phone. He finished his call and looked up.

"You've done very well, Josie, very well," he said with a slight Germanic accent. He stood up and grabbed a bottle of spirit and a glass from a bar. "Have a quick drink on the house and I will get your cash."

He offered a large glass of scotch.

"Cheers beers," she said, grinning, and downed it in one gulp. Almost at once she felt drowsy and she started to black out.

The man led her to a chair. Within minutes she was asleep. He checked her eyelids, then went to the door, opened it and looked at the group of young people, who lay in various positions on chairs and the floor. They were also all sound asleep.

He dialled then spoke loudly into his mobile phone, there was no need to whisper. "Hello, yes, no problems. It always works. Yes, none of them will be missed. I am sure they are all long term homeless. I will bring them to the clinic. Vidor will help me load them, but it will take some time. Of course, I will be ready to operate, I am not yet that old, my friend. Just have the money ready. Bye."

He put the phone into his pocket.

Vidor entered the room and nodded to him. He looked down at the sleeping body of Josie Welshman. She was attractive, but above all very fit and healthy. He saw only a carcass that housed individual valuable organs, each with a price tag attached.

The End

Printed in Great Britain
by Amazon